The Fortress

T. A. Styles

TRANSCENDENCE PRESS

The Fortress

ISBN: 979-8-9879684-0-6 (Trade Paperback)

ISBN: 979-8-9879684-1-3 (eBook)

For children. Mine and everyone's.

Contents

1. One 1
2. Two 8
3. Three 13
4. Four 21
5. Five 41
6. Six 47
7. Seven 58
8. Eight 71
9. Nine 82
10. Ten 88
11. Eleven 92
12. Twelve 102
13. Thirteen 121
14. Fourteen 129
15. Fifteen 144
16. Sixteen 151
17. Seventeen 160

18. Eighteen 172
19. Nineteen 195
20. Twenty 206
21. Twenty-One 213
22. Twenty-Two 221
23. Twenty-Three 237
24. Twenty-Four 251
25. Twenty-Five 261
26. Twenty-Six 269
27. Twenty-Seven 275
28. Twenty-Eight 282
29. Twenty-Nine 291
30. Thirty 297
About the Author 300

One

Make a child safe. Save a life.

This was Sim's new motto since reluctantly opening his doors to the little girl, Elizabeth, who was wandering along the street in front of his house in the days of his greatest despair.

She had arrived either as part of God's plan to torture him for the rest of his days or to facilitate his penance. Two weeks earlier he had shot to death his wife, Amanda, and his young daughter, Sara, and though Amanda was near death from the viral disease that had killed most of the rest of the world, Sara wasn't sick at all. She might have lived. She might have grown to be a bold and beautiful leader in this new world, but he never gave her the chance. He robbed her of her life.

It was Amanda's suggestion that they all should die together, and Sara had begged to go with her mother. Sim woefully carried out this plan almost to the end, but when it came time to turn the gun on himself, he couldn't do it.

In the following days, he hoped to starve or die out of pure anguish. He had heard of people who died from a broken heart and wondered, why not him?

Then Elizabeth showed up. He saw her through the curtains and opened the doors.

Make a child safe. Save a life.

In many ways, having Elizabeth in the house was like having Sara returned to him. In other ways, it was a minute-to-minute reminder of what he had done.

Over the weeks that followed, and because of this little girl. Sim cleaned himself up and went on supply runs with Elizabeth, many times carrying her on his back, as they traveled near and far seeking out food, batteries, weapons, first aid, medications, seedlings, soil, and a great many other things.

They dragged beds and mattresses from nearby homes to fill the rooms of this enormous place, and also took time to scrub and disinfect everything like new.

There are probably other children out there just like you. We can save them. They don't have to die.

Elizabeth loved to run up and down the stairs and play hide-and-seek, always forcing Sim to be the seeker.

Sim started seeds in the basement and planted fruit-bearing trees in the backyard while also building an arsenal of weapons that were kept locked in that same basement's storage closet.

Elizabeth helped him clean and make the beds, and he taught her how to use small arms to protect herself and the home.

There was only one time when Sim grew angry with Elizabeth and that was when she explored Sara's former bedroom on the third floor. Sim looked all over for Elizabeth and found her on Sara's bed. He took her by the arm and pulled her down.

"Ouch!" she cried, pulling away. "That hurt."

"I'm sorry," Sim said. "But I told you not to come in here."

"Well, it's just like any other room, except there's a lot of purple."

Sim was seeing the room for the first time since before Amanda and Sara died. "She liked purple. It was one of her favorite colors."

Elizabeth looked around. "It's pretty. But the ceilings are too low. At my house, I had a small room like this, but it was a toy room. Maybe we should get lots of toys and put them in here."

Sim smiled. Maybe it was time to make a change. Regardless, he knew he would still see Sara's face in every one of his dreams. Sometimes her expressions were angry, other times she was smiling, and sometimes she was crying. There would never be a day in his life when he wouldn't have to fight to forget what he had done.

Keep a child safe. Save a life.

The home didn't see too many visitors. Most of them walked right on by while Sim and Elizabeth watched from the windows. But, one time, an older man caught sight of them as they were on the front steps enjoying the glorious sunlight of a spring day.

"Oh, goodness," the man said. "It almost looks like normal times here."

Sim withdrew a gun and held it at bay. He tucked Elizabeth behind him.

"No worries," the man said. "The name is Walter. Walter Lancaster. You all live here?"

"What do you want?" Sim asked.

"Just passing on by," Walter said. "Maybe you wouldn't mind me staying for a couple of days and letting me offer my company. It would feel...normal for a change."

The man seemed harmless. He was portly, not seemingly agile, balding, and his breathing was labored.

"You look like my Grandpa Fred," Elizabeth said. "Can he stay, Sim?"

Sim looked from Elizabeth to the man, and back to Elizabeth. "Well...I don't know...I...We aren't really used to company."

"I won't bother you more than a couple of days," Walter said.

Sim smiled and relented. He didn't trust adults anymore. They were all desperate. Seekers. Takers. It was survival of the fittest in every world, but more now than ever. All they needed to do was invite the wrong person into their home, and their happy existence would end. Maybe in the blink of an eye.

Isn't that what I want? What happiness, anyway? What I am doing is obligatory. That's all. It's not my *existence that's at stake in this house. It's Elizabeth's.*

Walter ended up staying a few weeks before Sim insisted that he leave. He was no danger, but his presence was counterproductive to what he was trying to teach Elizabeth.

Just let me have another plate. The girl too. You practically starve her.

Can't she go on a walk with me? It's a beautiful day. You never let her do anything fun. It's just work, work, work.

You're teaching her to use a gun? A little girl? Is that smart?

Why do you make Beth get up so early? There's more time than ever to sleep now.

After he started calling Elizabeth "Beth," it was the last straw. Walter had gotten too comfortable and had become a hinderance.

"I guess I'll head back to the heights, then," Walter said as he descended the fortress steps.

"The heights?" Sim said. "As in Grizzland Heights?"

"Yes," Walter said. "There's a guy named Charlie not too far from here running the place. It's just getting off the ground. Things are a little topsy turvy up there, so I thought I'd look around a bit more. People need organization. Security. He could learn a thing or two from you guys, that's for sure."

Sim found Walter's statement ironic, given how the man rebuked many of their daily practices and routines.

"Is his full name Charlie Brewer?" Sim asked.

The man shrugged. "I don't have a last name. He's a tall black fella with long hair and a bit of a hardened face."

Sim laughed to himself.

"When you get there, tell him Mr. Ford says hello, and that I'll be up to see him."

"You know Charlie?" Walter asked.

"He was a student of mine in normal times," Sim said. "I'm happy to hear he made it."

Sim and Elizabeth watched Walter from the porch as he strolled off with a wink and a nod.

Elizabeth took Sim's hand. "I'll miss him, but he kind of smelled. Why didn't he ever take a bath?"

"I don't know, Liz," Sim said. "But at least we know he has a place to go. We'll have to visit as well and catch up with Charlie."

That night Sim tucked Elizabeth into bed, and she was staring at him for an extra-long time.

Sim noticed this and asked simply, "What?"

"Are we going to look for more kids, like you said?" she asked.

Make a child safe. Save a life.

"Yes," Sim said. "I just...wanted to make sure we had enough supplies. That we were ready."

"You've been saying that for a long time," Elizabeth said. "What if those kids out there are scared and lost like I was? They're waiting."

Sim smiled guiltily and thought of Sara. He closed his eyes and heard in his mind that fateful gunshot.

Pop!

He opened his eyes again. "I'm scared, Elizabeth. I guess I was a good man...but I don't deserve children. I don't deserve *you*."

"But we *need* you."

Sim smiled, suddenly feeling more important than he had a right to.

"And this place has so much room!" she exclaimed with a glowing smile. "It's bigger than Magic Kingdom."

"It's our fortress, indeed."

"Is that what we'll call it?" she asked. "Not a kingdom?"

"A kingdom sounds a lot bigger than what we have here. What we have here is just a small part of a kingdom. Maybe from here we can *build* a kingdom. Anyway, there is an expression I remember from all the reading I used to do."

"I like to read too," Elizabeth said. "Next time we go out we have to find more books for the library."

"Will do," Sim said. He placed a hand over Elizabeth's heart. "The saying was 'prepare your heart as a fortress, for there is no other.'"

Elizabeth crinkled her nose and pulled back her head. "What does that mean?"

"It means, your heart should be stronger than any house. So, this house can sure enough be our fortress, but there is also a fortress inside of you. And from there, a kingdom can rise."

Elizabeth's eyes widened.

"Tomorrow, since you did such a wonderful job deciding if Walter should stay or be told to go, we are going to paint your hand, and place our first handprint on a mural that will hang right above the fireplace."

Elizabeth smiled.

"And this will be the test for the other children to take. I forsee a day when the mural has lots and lots of prints. And I want to thank you for that."

"Why?" Elizabeth asked.

"Because I think you saved me when you showed up here," Sim said. "You might have saved a lot of people."

"Because I'm a fortress?"

"That's right," Sim said. Then he placed a kiss on her forehead and said goodnight.

The next day, Sim laid out a white sheet across the floor. Using some orange craft paint, Elizabeth placed her hand print in the middle. Then they strung up their new mural over the fireplace. As they admired their work, Sim turned to Elizabeth and puffed out his chest.

"Okay then," Sim said.

"Okay what?" Elizabeth said, puffing out her own chest.

"Let's go find you some brothers and sisters," Sim said.

Elizabeth smiled and the two left the fortress that day, hand in hand.

Two

We are the fortress, and the fortress is us.

Three years later...

"I don't want to," Baby said, her eyes tearing up.

Sim looked at her, sympathetic, but knew *she* had to vet the man, perhaps even kill him. As a rite of passage, each orphan had to vet a trespasser by first formulating an assessment of their intent and either inviting them to be processed to their sister community, the heights, or else get rid of them if they proved hostile. That was Sim's rule of the house and so that is the way it was. It was dangerous, but Sim felt it was a necessary part of their training and growth in the new world.

"I know, Baby, but it's your time," Sim said. "We will be close by watching."

He didn't choose the name Baby for this little girl of nine. *She* chose it. *My brother always teased me when I cried.* She was not allowed to change it even though she twice asked over the years. This was another of Sim's rules.

"What if he's dangerous and I can't hurt him?" she said.

Sim withheld his true emotions. "Then you could die if we don't get to you quickly enough. I won't be able to save you from everything in this world."

He found Baby when she was six, milling about in trash cans, trying to find scraps of food. *I have a place where you'll be safe. Will you join me?*

She went with him, though even at six she was unsure. What other choices did she have? Three years later, it was her turn to see how well Sim's training had paid off.

"You've been working with these knives for six months now, Baby," Sim said, peering into her green eyes. "If you need to use them, it'll be all but instinct that guides you." Sim handed Baby two Ka-Bar knives, presenting them to her handles out. She took one in each hand and regarded the long black blades with noticeable tension.

Sim redirected her. "Remember," he said. "Letter X. Show me quick."

Baby held firmly onto each knife. She licked her dry lips as she slowly crossed her arms in letter X fashion then swiftly uncrossed them with the blades out. Sim smiled, though he was nervous for her.

"That's good, Baby," he offered. She turned around and ambled out the front door of the fortress as if it were a normal day and she was headed off to await the school bus. Sim quickly closed the door behind her and retreated to the nearest window where he unlatched the wooden shutter and peered through the glass that lay behind it.

While Sim waited at the window, Leo approached from behind. Leo was ten and loved Baby as much as he loved Sim. "It's rough," he uttered while placing a hand on Sim's shoulder.

Sim did not turn around. "Yes, it is," he muttered. "But you made it through just fine."

"My guy was an old fart who wanted to share a bag of popcorn," Leo said. "Did you really think I would have to kill him? He's sitting pretty at the heights now probably living better than he ever did. This guy out there could be a real threat."

"You got lucky, Leo," Sim said. "He could have been as dangerous as anyone. Young or old, if someone finds a gun and thinks they're John Wayne...it can be all over in a second."

"Who's John Wayne?" Leo asked.

"Never mind," Sim said.

Baby felt weird inside. Tingly. Her heart was pounding as she approached this man who paused about fifty yards from the house when he saw Baby coming closer. *Move slowly. Look vulnerable.* Baby had asked Sim what that meant.

Like you need help. It'll disarm him.

Baby proceeded with caution, adding a fake limp to her walk. The notion was hers, but it slowed the encounter, which increased her anxiety. She pushed the blonde locks from her eyes and took in some deep breaths because that is what Sim told her to do when she was having a panic attack. *Breathe, Baby.*

It is what he told them all when they felt scared.

She stopped a few feet away from this dirty and disheveled man. Everyone seemed to be scruffy and unkempt in these days, except the kids of the fortress; Sim said that even in times like these, one must maintain their standards. What did that mean? *We don't have dentists, but we can still brush. We can keep clean, too. We can keep our clothing nice. We can do our hair still. We can maintain. We will.* And that's the way it was. Ever since JZ came to the fortress, anyway, and put the bug in his ear.

Baby could not tell if the stranger was friendly or mean. She hoped nice. Then her job would be easy and it would be all over quickly. She had the knives tucked away in each side pocket of her blue jeans just in case. The man's face was round and had lots of hair on it. Scrubby hair. Like it needed shampoo and a rinse. He had a short neck, which made her wary.

"Aren't you a pretty girl," the man said with a half-smile. "Do you live here?"

Baby maintained her poker face as she stuffed her hands into her pockets.

"Don't be afraid," he said. "I'm not going to hurt you."

The man said this, but Baby could see that he was reaching for a knife from a brown sheath that was hanging from his left side.

I guess this won't be an easy one. Me or him.

"What color are your eyes?" Baby mumbled.

The man leaned in, curious, as he slowly withdrew his knife. "What was that?" he asked.

"I want to see your eyes up close," she said, timidly.

"Why, sure," the man indulged. "My eyes are brown, but I always wished they were blue."

He kneeled, coming face-to-face with Baby, each peering into the other's eyes.

As he thrust his knife upward, releasing it fully from its sheath, Baby reacted with two quick motions, first crossing her arms, to yank the tactical knives from her pockets and then uncrossing them with a vicious, whooshing, snap. *Letter X.* The man dropped his own knife and put both hands to his neck as spurts of blood burst where Baby's knives had opened the carotid arteries on either side. Baby felt the warm blood splatter across her face, staining her blonde hair, and she screamed.

Before the man fell to the ground, Baby heard Sim arrive behind her. She knew the sounds of his boots on the ground and the noise his long coat made as it flapped in the wind.

Though well behind, some of the others had followed Sim out.

"Baby!" Leo yelled.

"Baby!" Big Will said, a brown retriever barking at his side. *Gigi.*

She knew all of their voices and to hear them at that moment was quite lovely, but she was in shock over her first vetting and kill and could scarcely move.

Sim ignored the man slumped on the ground and placed one hand on each of Baby's delicate shoulders. He looked her up and down and took the knives from her hands. "You're okay," he said. "Thank God."

"Oh, Baby," Leo whined. "I thought he hurt you."

"He almost did," Baby said. "He had a knife and was going to kill me!"

Baby saw Big Will, eight years old, watching them from the side, his hand resting on top of Gigi's head. He wasn't as physical with people as he was with his dog, but could hardly be while holding his weapon, an AK-47, which was almost as big as him. Though she could see the relief in his eyes in finding her safe.

"You did it, Baby," Sim said, pulling her bloodied body close to him. She felt his warmth.

Baby cried in his arms but felt proud. She would get her handprint on the flag now.

Three

SIM, BIG WILL, LEO, and Baby entered the fortress as JZ, thirteen, and Flip, twelve, were rushing down the master staircase.

"Good job, Baby," JZ said, a sharpened throwing axe buried into the waistband of her pants.

"Yeah, really," said Flip. "I thought you would chicken out," he laughed as he squawked his arms like a chicken. "Bawk-bawk-bawk."

The pair passed by Sim who said nothing as they left to retrieve the body of the fallen stranger. It was their duty to clean up messes of this nature. They would dig a hole on the outskirts of the property in the area known to the orphans as Restland, and promptly place the body into it before filling it back in.

"Can we put my handprint on the flag now, Sim?"

Ace then appeared from the living room with the flag in hand. Its normal place was hanging over the fireplace mantle, but he had taken it down in preparation for adding Baby's handprint. There were currently thirteen prints on the banner and Baby's handprint would make fourteen. And though there were fourteen people living in the house, a pair of them, Yamil and Miracle, were currently too young and not quite ready for the initiation. The extra two were the prints of orphans who had died along the way.

Elizabeth, Sim's first orphan, died from an infection before any of the others met her. The other, Tak, was murdered when he sneaked out of the fortress to get water from the creek in the days before the well had been dug. He should have waited for Ace to accompany him, but he wanted to prove he could get the water on his own. It was his last mistake. They found his body at the edge of the creek, laden with three bullet wounds and the shocked expression his face wore in death.

Sim later tracked down the man responsible and cut off his head with a machete. He put it on a pike at the edge of the fortress property and roared after doing so. The other orphans watched his anguish from the window. That was a year ago.

Ace, seventeen years of age and Sim's second orphan, discovered at fourteen, spread the flag out on the living room floor. On the tapestry were the colorfully painted handprints of all the orphans encircling the words: *The fortress is us*. In normal times, one might find such a tapestry design in a school or a club house, but in these times, it was so much more.

"What color do you want, Baby?" Sim asked.

Baby, the blood on her face and in her hair now dried, replied, "I think purple. It was my mom's favorite color."

"Perfect," Sim smiled.

Ace opened the bottle of purple paint and dabbed the end of a thick bristled paint brush with it. He then coated the inside of Baby's right hand in a series of swipes using the brush.

Baby giggled. "That tickles." She pressed it gently upon the flag and Sim put his large hand over hers to add more pressure. He held it there for several seconds as he teared up, her little hand buried beneath his own.

"Sara's favorite color was purple too," he said. "You remind me so much of her, Baby."

Sara was Sim's daughter, Baby recalled. He had once told them Sara and her mother were the first to be buried in *Usland*, the property cemetery for loved ones, but he rarely spoke of either of them.

"Was she good with knives?" Baby asked.

"It was a different time then," Sim replied. "She was silly and loved horses."

Ace smiled hearing him recall his daughter, remembering when he met Sim.

Ace was "Cody" before he got to choose his own name at the fortress. When everyone started to die, he was fourteen. He watched as his mother, father, sister, and brother deteriorated, one right after the other until they were each gone. He stayed at his house crying and hopeless among their rotting corpses for days until he ran out of food. Though despairing, he did not wish to die.

The larger world disappeared within two months from the start of the outbreak, and all that remained in the wake of this world event were the people who lived through it. In normal times, he would watch movies and shows with his father featuring the apocalypse, and they would enjoy them as fantasy, all the while eating popcorn and laughing. Then, one day, it was real.

When he dared leave his house, he remembered how deafeningly quiet everything was. The stillness of the world was haunting. He brought his father's .22 caliber revolver with him, understanding even at his age that without society, people were more dangerous.

The only two people he saw that day were a neighbor and Sim. The neighbor was his former little league coach when he he'd been on the Johnson's Hardware team at the age of eight. The man was nice, but competitive, and Cody was never a strong athlete, so they didn't get along that well.

Like Cody, Coach was wandering the streets aimlessly, as if looking for a lost dog. Though it was *he* who looked lost. Bewildered. His eyes were dark shadows beneath the brim of his baseball cap. Cody did not fear the man, but he was reluctant to strike up a conversation with him. In normal times, people rarely regarded one another in passing, so it made sense to Cody that this etiquette be retained.

When Coach saw Cody, it didn't register right away and the man passed right by him without a word, so Cody thought he was home free. But then the man stopped abruptly two paces beyond where they had passed one another.

"Cody?" Coach said.

Cody stopped and turned around to greet him.

"You survived," Coach said, looking the boy up and down as if trying to ascertain if he was perhaps only an illusion. "What about your family?"

"They died," Cody whispered, the words full of pain.

"Everyone did," Coach said removing his cap to reveal a sweaty mop of hair.

"Well, we're still here," Cody corrected, drawing the man's perplexed gaze.

"True enough," he said. "But be careful. People are doing crazy things now."

Like in those movies. "Why?" Cody asked.

"I guess because they can," Coach said. He then spied the gun in Cody's waistband. "Keep that thing close to you and don't be afraid to use it."

Cody didn't know if he was afraid to use it. Or had the instinct to use it. His father had brought him to the gun range several times to shoot, so he knew how to hold the gun and fire it at a paper target. But at a person?

"And check out the store down the road...there's still a lot left, but who knows how long it'll be before others come for it. Get everything you can now."

Coach turned to leave, but Cody called after him.

"Where are *you* going?" he asked, wondering why the man would leave a child to his own devices under these circumstances.

"Nowhere," he shrugged. "Anywhere. It's all the same place now."

Lost.

Cody nodded and the two parted ways. He might have asked Coach if he could join him, but he didn't particularly like the idea of wandering the earth in a daze alongside Coach. Surely there had to be other options.

He made his way to the convenience store as Coach advised, and that is where he met Sim. The man was a strange sight. He was primly and properly dressed, as if he had just come from a dinner date. He had on a long dark coat, blue jeans, and a pair of dress shoes. Gray. His face was a bit scruffy, an appearance he didn't think much about until he would meet JZ.

"You alone?" Sim asked.

"No," Cody said.

Sim smiled. "I'm sorry about your family."

Cody crooked his head. "I told you—"

"You're lying," Sim said. "But most people wouldn't know or wouldn't care. They see you alone and vulnerable even with that gun. A desperate man with nothing to lose will overpower you. He'll take everything you have, then he will kill you. Even before the days of the virus, so many lacked respect for human dignity or humanity, in general. As you can imagine, it is much worse now."

"Getgone" is what the virus was nicknamed when it first appeared.

If you get it, you're gone.

Cody wanted to cry, but he did not. "Why?"

"Because—"

"They can," Cody finished the answer to his own question.

Sim nodded. "I'm Sim, by the way. And I see you. I'm not one of those people. I would never harm you. I want to keep you safe."

Make a child safe. Save a life.

Cody yanked the revolver from his waistband and pointed it at Sim. "How can I be so sure?"

Sim nodded. "Listen—"

Cody pulled the trigger and following a short pop, a bullet cut into Sim's shoulder. The impact threw Sim back onto a waist-high cooler. His eyes widened. Clearly, Sim did not expect this from the boy. He held up his hands. "Wait!"

Cody stepped closer and pointed the gun at Sim's head. There was a time when Sim would have wanted him to pull that trigger again, but not anymore.

"I'm a father and a teacher," Sim yelled. "Or, at least I was. I want to help."

"Yeah, and Coach was a coach and the random guy who wants to kill us was a mailman. What we were doesn't mean shit anymore." Cody's face hardened as he sneered at Sim.

"Yes, it does," Sim said, still holding up his arm in a defensive position. "That's the point." He winced in pain as he raised himself off the cooler.

Cody lowered the gun with reservation while taking slow steps backward to retain his distance from the man.

"I don't know if that was completely necessary," Sim said, clutching his shoulder wound.

"I'm sorry," Cody said looking downward in shame. "I just saw my old coach and he told me to watch out for crazy people."

"Is that what I am?" Sim said.

The boy offered no reply.

Sim shook his head. "It doesn't matter. You did exactly what you should have. At least now, even if I was dangerous, I'm subdued." He then prodded his shoulder wound while Cody looked on, perhaps not sure how to proceed. Sim glanced up at him after completing his self-examination. "Clean shot, though. No bones broken, from what I can tell."

"That's not your real name," Cody pointed out, ignoring Sim's self-assessment.

Sim lowered his eyebrows. "No. You're right. In my former life I was kind of a know-it-all. I had all the information you needed on anything. Or so I tried to make it seem. My colleagues started calling me 'Sim'. Short for SIM card."

Cody knew exactly what a SIM card was, but such luxuries as smart phones were a thing of the past.

"You said you were a teacher?" Cody asked.

Sim nodded. "Among other things. Sixth grade for ten years. If you remember being a student, as I do all too well, being a teacher gives you a whole different perspective. When my daughter died, I nearly gave up. But then a little girl showed up on my doorstep and inspired me to do something else instead. Sadly, she passed last week. It wasn't supposed to be that way."

Sim's eyes grew glassy as he retreated in thought.

First Sara, then Elizabeth. Who next?

"What?" Cody asked.

"She...we, both thought to invite more children to be part of what we started," Sim said. "A home for kids who needed a safety net."

"And how do you know there are any children left?" Cody asked.

Sim shrugged. "If there is you, then there are others," Sim said. "I'm going to find them and bring them home...to this place."

"Home?"

"Follow me, if you will," Sim said. "And remember this..." Sim said. "You are the fortress, and the fortress is you."

Cody followed Sim, though he couldn't explain why. Perhaps it was his instincts telling him that Sim was for real. Or maybe he left with him because he had nobody left and no place else to go. At any rate, he followed him, ten steps behind the whole way, his gun at the ready, until he was confident the man was not leading him to his death.

In the end, he was glad he followed because he discovered Sim's truth that day: the fortress, which Sim had already established, fortified, and stocked. And Cody was the first orphan in the next era. He was given thirty days to pick a new name, because in the new world, Sim said you could have any name you chose; but after it was chosen, you could not change it again while you lived at the fortress. And you could not reveal that selection for thirty days. Then it was done.

Cody chose Ace.

Four

JZ GRABBED THE DEAD man's arms while Flip grabbed his legs and the two dragged the corpse across the field that was at the west corner of the fortress compound.

"I can't believe she actually had to kill someone," Flip said. "And she hardly batted an eyelash."

"She's tougher than she looks," JZ said. "She just hides it. She likes being Sim's baby."

"Is that why she named herself that?" Flip asked.

"She was too little to choose her name," JZ said. "Just like you. What kind of name is 'Flip' anyway?"

"I was a gymnast before," he said. And that he was. Since he was three. He was as thin as a rail and as flexible as a rubber band. He often performed for his fellow orphans and Sim even made him a pommel horse to continue his practice. Sim could make anything, as he made himself out to be a master of all trades.

"Still," JZ said, "he should either choose our names himself or wait until we are teenagers or something like that. Kids can't choose their own names, or you end up with a collection of names like half the orphans in the house."

"Some of us have our regular names," Flip said. "Like you, Teddy, and Leo."

"Sim never gave Leo a choice," JZ said, dropping the corpse's arms to take a break. "Because he liked the name. If he hadn't, Leo would have some corny name now too."

Sim discovered Leo in his room about three miles from the fortress, not too long after he met Ace. His parents were rotted corpses lying in their bed and the family dog was in between them, also dead, which was strange because the virus didn't impact dogs, in general. When Sim entered the little boy's baseball-themed room, he was dirty and frail and playing with...Legos. Sim saw that he had been working on a structure, which he continued even after Sim entered.

"Tell me about what you have made," Sim said, kneeling beside the boy who barely acknowledged Sim's presence.

"It's a space station," the boy said. "Mommy said we were going to get sick, and I thought maybe we could be safe in space. I thought I could build a rocket ship to take us away."

Sim smiled. "That was a special thought, young man."

"Mommy and Daddy said we would go to heaven together," he said.

"You know what, Lego man," Sim said. "You were chosen to stay here instead. Like me. To remember your parents' love and to give it to others in the world." Sim cupped the boy's face in his hand. "You are a fortress."

"'Lego man' is not my name, silly," Leo said, as he turned away from him and went back to playing. "Legos are toys."

"Tell me then, what *is* your name?" Sim asked.

"Leo," the boy said.

Sim laughed. "Close enough."

Leo stared at him with big eyes, the size of dollar coins. "I like you," he said.

"Then you'll come with me," Sim said. "To our new home."

"A fortress?" Leo asked. "I can make a fortress out of Legos."

"With you and the others, yes," Sim said, releasing the boy's chin from his gentle grip. "But without you, just a house."

"Can I bring my Legos?" the boy asked.

"Of course," Sim said. "You can bring from here whatever you like."

"Yaay! I'll bring my guns, too!" Leo sprang to his feet and ran to the other side of his room to where his dresser stood.

Guns?

Leo opened one of the drawers and peered back at Sim with a toothless grin. "I have a lot of them."

Sim, curious, walked the short distance over to the dresser and smiled when he saw the boy's collection of Nerf guns. Small ones. Large ones. A zillion blue foam bullets with orange tips.

"Well, that is quite the collection," Sim said.

Leo smiled. Sim and the boy toted the large bin of Legos and all the Nerf guns back to the fortress and Sim later used those Nerf guns to teach the orphans how to shoot. They had massive wars in and around the fortress to practice those skills and these war games would teach them more about engaging in fight than any other methodology that Sim could deploy. Sim would later deem it fate that Leo had all those Nerf guns on hand.

But that was Leo. Full of surprises.

"We're almost there," Flip complained, ignoring the history lesson. "If we're not back soon, Ace has to come out and check on us and I don't want him to come out and check on us."

"Why not?" JZ said, stars in her eyes.

"Because he thinks we need him for every little thing," Flip said. "*You're* just going slow so he *has* to come out because you have a crush on him."

"Don't be a dummy," JZ said. "We're going to see him when we get back anyway. Besides, we're like brothers and sisters, all of us. Of course, I don't look at him that way."

Flip laughed. "You're so full of it." He swooped down to grab the corpse's legs again. "Now let's get this done."

The pair dragged the rigid corpse the rest of the way to the burial ground, which was nestled at the border of the compound defined by an old wire fence. The fence was there before the end of things. It had grown weathered, but they did their best repairing it as needed.

"Now the hard part," Flip said. He grabbed the shovel that lay beside a tree. They kept it there so they didn't have to worry about dragging it back and forth. Flip shoved the pointed end of the shovel into the ground to start the hole. When he got tired, he would switch out with JZ. They marked time in weird ways since the clocks stopped.

JZ stood over the grave with her hands buried into each side of her waist, watching Flip's progress, when he was suddenly attacked. The man sprung out of nowhere like a wild animal and tackled him to the ground. Flip's shovel rocketed from his hands and landed several feet away. The man regained his stance quickly and held Flip's small body in his grasp. JZ instinctively drew out her axe and positioned it to throw.

"Put it down," came a voice from behind her. She heard the clicking of a gun's hammer and swallowed hard. She lowered her hands but did not drop the axe.

The other man holding Flip had a knife to his exposed throat. JZ turned around and side-stepped so that her back was to the fortress. The man turned with her so that he was now facing the imposing three-story brick home.

"Don't move another step," the man with the gun said, his eyes piercing. His body was firm and healthy. "Put down the fucking axe."

"What do you want?" she asked, keeping the axe firmly placed in her hand. "Because if you want to kill me then do it now because it's the only way I'm letting go of this axe."

The man turned to his partner who was holding Flip at knifepoint. "Slit his throat."

As he said this, Flip raised his leg and brought it down hard, driving his heel into one of his captor's feet. The man shrieked as the sound of a single bullet zinged through the air. JZ watched as the face of the man holding the gun exploded like a popped zit. She spun around and wielded the axe above her head with both hands. She tossed it with purpose, and it landed between the other man's eyes as Flip scurried away. Within a minute of the encounter, both intruders were dead.

JZ turned to the house and gave a thumbs up signal. Their sniper, Shark, was only fifteen, but he knew how to get the job done. He spent many hours per day guarding the property with his rifle in hand. He must not have spotted them coming, but he sure enough saw them once they arrived.

"Fuck," Flip said. "Now we have three bodies to bury."

"You know Sim doesn't like it when we curse," JZ said.

"Sim has too many rules," Flip said. "He's a control freak."

"Whatever, wild child," JZ said. "We're going in and getting more help with this. I am not gonna be out here all day long with you burying dead bodies."

"It's been almost a month without anyone bothering us and now three in one day," Flip said.

"When it rains, it storms," she said. Sim used this phrase often whenever they encountered problems.

As they conversed, Shark yelled to them from the top of the fortress.

"Run!"

JZ and Flip regarded each other with curious eyes after hearing Shark's frantic cry. They immediately took off sprinting with large strides over the field, past the gardens and fruit trees, onto the side porch and through the door that led into the kitchen. Sim closed the door behind them.

"What's wrong?" JZ asked, panting heavily, and bending over with her hands on her knees."

"There are more," Sim said. "Take your positions right away and stand by."

"How many?" Flip asked.

"Go!" Sim said.

JZ stayed put, as the kitchen was her domain, while Flip dashed to the second floor to cover one of the east-facing windows. At the foot of the window, Misty had gathered a multitude of glass bottles stuffed with beige rags cut from a sheet that billowed over each rim. She had the plastic lighter protruding from her right-side pocket.

"How many?" Flip asked.

"On *our* side?" Misty asked, "Look for yourself."

Flip glanced out the window and saw five marauders stealthily approaching across the field. The fortress had never faced an attack of this nature.

"What the hell is going on?" Flip remarked.

"Yeah," Misty said. "It's a good thing they all didn't advance at once when you guys were out there, or you and JZ would have been sitting ducks. It reminds me of this time when a hive of bees attacked me after I tried swatting one in the group. I got stung eight times. Can you imagine?"

Misty, the storyteller, was eleven. She was likewise tall, agile, and gifted with a quick wit.

"What the hell is happening?" Flip asked, ignoring her tale. "This isn't right."

"Focus, Flip," she yelled. "I'm sure Sim will have an explanation later. He always does. But for now, we have to kill them...all."

"Easy for you to say," Flip said. "You're not the one charged with digging holes."

Misty smiled.

Flip wondered about the rest of the perimeter. How many of these people were there actually? "Why the hell isn't Shark taking any of them out?"

Just then, a shot rifled out from above. Misty turned to Flip with an accusatory glance. "You were saying?"

Flip saw a man fall flat on his face and offered an arm pump. "He got 'em!"

"Looks like a dozen or so!" Sim yelled up the stairs. His voice was large and encompassing; thank goodness, as it was all they had to rely on since the walkies went dead. "Five on the east, four on the west, two in the front, and one in the back! I want firebombs on the east and west from the second floor and we'll advance from the first in thirty seconds."

They had planned for it, and now it was reality. Misty grabbed one of the alcohol cocktails as the five on their side advanced. Flip grabbed two revolvers that were sitting on a nightstand beside his window.

"Save your ammo," Misty said. "They'll take care of this on the first floor after I light them up."

"Then at least let me throw one," Flip pleaded as he put his revolvers back on the stand.

"Here you go, whiner," she said.

Each lifted their respective window and then Misty lit the alcohol-soaked rag that was hanging out of Flip's bottle. It ignited with raw fury.

"Jesus," Flip said, arching away from the flame. "We'll burn the house down."

"Just don't drop it until you have it out the window," Misty said. She then lit her own and the two tossed them at the same time out their respective windows. Flip's firebomb landed on one of the marauders and exploded into a fiery ball. The man's screams echoed throughout the yard as he tried running away, his body in flames. That's when Shark finished the job with a single shot. Misty's firebomb landed at the feet of two others and as the bottle exploded into flames before them, they backed away and shielded their eyes. Shark took shots at them as well, but neither hit their mark.

As the five marauders approached from the east side, Sim scurried to the west side of the house where King was waiting alongside a set of two exposed windows off the dining room. He was holding a large hunting knife in one hand and a .38 special in the other. King was fifteen and no-nonsense. He was a runaway before things ended and so that meant he was an orphan before he was an orphan.

"How many?" Sim asked.

"Four," King said in a bass voice that betrayed his age. "Coming down the hill and using the trees for cover."

Sim had often talked about clearing the hill, but never followed through. The tree-studded hill was a natural resource, and from it they got wood and animals for food. Yet, Sim knew the west side was an Achilles heel in these situations.

"Thank you," Sim said. "Be ready. I have two approaching from the street." He ambled around the dining room table and into the kitchen. "JZ, how many?"

"I only see one," she said, propped up on a counter and peering out the window above the kitchen sink. That's when the first of Shark's shots sounded.

Sim ran to the master stairwell and shouted. "Looks like a dozen or so! Five on the east! Four on the west! Two in the front and one in the back! I want firebombs on the east and west from the second floor and we'll advance on the first in thirty seconds."

He ran back to the living room where Ace was standing alongside the fireplace, his back to the wall and a small caliber gun clutched to his chest. "They're getting closer."

Baby, still bloodied from her earlier encounter held a knife in each hand and waited with Big Will and Gigi on either side of the double-door entryway.

"Wait for the fire from the second floor," Sim said.

"Sky has the little ones in the play room," Ace said.

"Then everything is set," Sim concluded. "Just like we trained." Sim, though bothered, felt an air of pride.

"I never thought we would actually see the day, though," Ace said.

"If I didn't think the day could come, I wouldn't have prepared you," Sim said. He turned to Baby and Big Will. "You handle the two out front, Will."

Big Will nodded. "You open the door when you hear the firebombs, Baby," Big Will said. "Are they armed?"

"Looks like only close-contact weapons," Ace said. "I don't see any guns. And the only shots I've heard have come from Shark."

"It's hard to tell when they are ducking through the trees," King chimed in.

"It doesn't matter," Sim said. "Just fire at anything that gets close. They're sitting ducks."

"Don't they know that already?" Ace asked.

"There's more going on here, Ace," Sim said. "We can speculate later."

Just then, two firebombs crashed outside of Ace's window. Screams filled the air. Two firebombs then crashed outside King's window, courtesy of Teddy on the second floor, west. Ace whirled around and pulled open his window and started firing, as did King.

Baby thrust open the heavy entryway doors and dove out of the way as two marauders climbed the front steps. Big Will, his little body packed with power, opened fire with his AK-47 and sprayed the two men with bullets before they had a chance to retreat. Gigi stood at the open doorway barking ferociously at the mayhem. The intruders' bodies recoiled like rag dolls and tumbled to the broken sidewalk at the foot of the stairs. Big Will stepped back and Baby closed the doors and locked them with the deadbolt. She acknowledged Big Will with shrug.

"That was easy," she said.

Gunfire echoed from the fortress on the east and west sides as King and Ace went to work shooting down the men that had tried to flank them. In the meantime, Sim ran to the basement and exited the fortress below ground level into a pit that made for a convenient bunker. One only needed to climb the small stony slope to access the field. He had with him his wooden spear and he was ready to use it.

He caught sight of a man who had evaded the hail of bullets that Ace was firing from the window. He dug his way up the small slope and pummeled the man with his body. The intruder was shocked to see Sim and had little time to react. The two tumbled to the ground. Sim was the first to recover and impaled the man with his spear through his middle back as he attempted to claw his way back to a standing position. The mortally wounded assailant screamed in agony as Sim withdrew the spear and thrust it again into his dying body.

When the job was done, he scouted the area. The four others that were advancing on that side were lying lifeless in various areas of the open field. The fire from the gasoline bombs danced with the light wind.

Sim retreated through the metal door and shut it behind him. That's when he heard JZ's screams.

JZ spied the man advancing on the backside of the house, but lost track of him quickly, after Sim asked for her count. It was daylight, but the small window above the kitchen sink offered a limited view. She stretched her neck to either side then jumped down. There was another window on the right side of the counter, but she didn't see anything from there either.

"Shit," she whispered. She didn't want to call out for anyone because she knew with the sounds of the firebombs and gunfire that everyone was engaged. Plus, she wanted to handle the situation on her own. It was her job to defend the backside, after all.

She ran to another window off the kitchen, but it faced the east side of the house, not the back, and though she saw the mayhem ensuing on that side she did not see the man she'd had eyes on before the firebombs started.

She moved to the right-side door, which led to the sprawling, yet weathered, porch deck. The door used to be glass, but Sim converted it to wood with a small square of plexiglass in the middle so they could see out. It offered a view of the west side of the house and tree-filled lot as well as a portion of the backside of the house.

She glared through it and saw fire on the west side, heard men screaming, and bullets popping, but saw nobody else. It was possible this intruder had advanced to the flanks with the others, and this is what she had hoped.

She opened the door slowly after taking the axe from her waistband and took two steps back. As the door creaked on its brass hinges, she waited expectantly for someone to make an appearance through the opening so she could dispatch him with her axe. When nobody came, she stepped forward with caution, and as she crossed the threshold of the door to the porch, someone grabbed her by the neck and threw her to the ground. Her body hit the deck with a thud and her axe flew from her grip. As she tried to recover, the man advanced upon her with a knife. JZ was set to defend herself when Ace barreled out the door, throwing himself into the intruder. The two flipped over a patio couch and crashed into a glass table on the other side of it. JZ screamed.

She jumped to her feet and ran to Ace's aid as he scuffled on the floor with the man who still had his knife firmly gripped in his hands. He was on top of Ace and had managed one swift downward thrust. The knife pierced Ace's upper right-side chest and he howled. JZ ran for her axe that lay nearby and grabbed it. She jumped upon the intruder's back and started hacking away fiercely at his back and neck. The man jumped up as blood sprayed from numerous wounds. JZ flew backward and came to rest on the couch as Sim appeared at the door with his spear. He circled the couch deftly and plunged the spear into the man's chest and removed it in one quick motion. The man fell backward and landed on top of Ace, who let out a short groan.

Sim regarded them both and then ran to the edge of the porch to secure the west side of the fortress. He heard no sound and detected no movement other than that of a raven cawing from a telephone wire.

A single sniper shot from the roof alerted them that they weren't in the clear.

"Inside," Sim said. "We're all downstairs tonight. Have Sky look at that wound. It needs to be cleaned thoroughly and a round of antibiotic started right away."

Sim thought of Elizabeth. She had sustained a nasty wound from a rusty nail that was protruding from the porch deck and never told him. She thought a simple band aid would do it. By the time Sim became aware of her injury, it was too late.

Ace scuffled to his feet and stepped over his attacker's body as he trudged through the shattered glass of the patio table. He inspected his shallow wound, which spilled a generous amount of blood, despite the superficiality of it. From the couch, JZ looked upon him with sympathy, her body stained red as well, but with blood that was not her own.

"Thanks," Ace said as he offered a hand to her. She accepted his gesture and he pulled her up from the couch with his left hand in a single motion.

JZ scoffed as she glanced down at the corpse of the man who had attacked her. "That'll teach you."

"If death was the lesson, then he sure enough learned it well," Ace quipped.

Sky sat the little ones close to her in the corner of the third-floor room on the west side. It was a smaller room with lower ceilings. Sky was the mother of the group. She also taught the daily lessons in English and math to all the children. At fifteen, she knew she loved children and wanted nothing more than to protect them. The little ones. Yamil and Miracle. Yamil was six, only three when he was discovered. His mother had been alive when Sim crossed paths with them. She was fighting death to tend to the boy's needs. She rejoiced when Sim swore his oath to her that he would protect him and she died that same day, perhaps allowing herself the luxury of escaping her pain knowing that Yamil would be saved.

Miracle was the last orphan found when Sim wondered if there were any orphans left in the world. He was four at the time, and so he had survived for eighteen months prior to his discovery, and nobody could figure out how. He was discovered in a house that, based on the pictures on the wall, was not his own, and so he had wandered there from wherever he came. He was naked, his hair wild, his body caked with dirt, dry urine, and feces, but he was not feral. He was smart for his age and could speak and understand when spoken to.

Sky sought out the fortress on her own. She was the only orphan not discovered by Sim. Unlike the usual stranger, she did not ignore the "no trespassing" signs. She waited on the edge of the fortress's front boundary, a street, and screamed for entry.

"I know you have children in there!" she yelled. Her voice echoed crisply through the corridor created by the fortress and the hollow homes on the other side of the street. "Let me in!"

Shark watched her intently through his binoculars from the rooftop as she waved her hands wildly. The others watched from their windows. Ace warned Sim it could be a trap. Sim did not discount this, but rarely followed through with advice from the orphans.

He opened the double doors but stood behind them. She took this as an invitation to advance. So, she did. She proceeded up the concrete steps to the doorway, but Sim blocked her entry with his tall, lean body. King and Ace stood behind him expectantly.

"I guess I should thank you for not killing me," she said to him.

She was pretty. Brown hair and brown eyes. Well kept, in clothing that looked as if she had just purchased from a local department store.

"How do you know we have children here?" Sim asked to the point.

"I've been watching you," she said. "I followed you when you picked up a boy the other day. Plus, I heard stories from my uncle. I'm smart, you know. I can teach and take care of them."

Sim thought of Leo and this girl having eyes on him without him knowing. He usually had a keen sense when someone was watching. You had to in this world. "What is your name?"

"Alyssa," she said sweetly.

"Where are you from?" he asked.

"Saratoga," she said.

"That's thirty miles from here," Sim pointed out.

"It's not been easy," she said. "I can't do this forever."

"You don't look like you've had it too hard," King remarked.

Alyssa tossed her hair back. "Well, we can't walk around looking a mess, can we?"

"How old are you?" Sim asked, ignoring the banter.

"Nearly thirteen," she said proudly, stiffening her posture.

"Are you alone?" Sim asked. "And don't lie to me."

She ignored him in favor of sneaking glances inside at the other orphans. "How many people actually live here?"

"Answer the question," Ace said.

"I'm alone," she replied. "Since my parents. My uncle made it. He's the one who showed me a map to this place, but we ran across some bad men on horses in Malta and while I hid in the bushes—"

"It's okay," Sim said, holding up a hand. He wanted to spare her the pain of her memories.

"You're bleeding," King said, noticing the crotch of her faded denim jeans.

Alyssa's cheeks reddened. "So much for not looking a mess. I'm tired, and need to clean up," she said.

Make a child safe. Save a life.

"You can stay with us," Sim said. "Be part of our home. Because that is what this is...our home. But the people in it...we are the fortress."

Alyssa nodded. JZ stepped in front of her. "And so is this place."

"Take her to her room," Sim instructed JZ. "She'll bunk with you and Misty." He then redirected back to Sky. "We'll discuss your role here in greater detail tomorrow, but for now, note that you have thirty days to pick your fortress name. Change it or keep it the same. It's up to you. But you won't reveal your choice until thirty days from now and you can't change it again while you are with us." He grabbed her arm. "And this is most important to understand...You'll have to defend this place alongside us if you stay. You'll have chores and you will learn how we survive here. It's not always pretty, but we're a unit."

Alyssa nodded. "Thank you."

Once she established herself as the house mother, teacher, and nurse based on her instincts, abilities, and desires, she would be less so designated to be on the front lines of combat. Yet in order to earn her handprint on the flag, she was not excused from having to vet a visitor who arrived at their doorstep.

Sky's first face-to-face encounter with a potential threat was a woman who approached the fortress carrying a rifle. She fired randomly at the fortress, but outside of her Wyatt Earp-style entry which presented as an attention-getting strategy, she seemed frail and nonthreatening. Shark didn't want to kill her, as he knew this was no ordinary situation. Ace argued with Sim about killing her. The stranger was screaming about losing her children and was seemingly out of her mind. But Sim was quick to caution her.

Until you disarm her, and we know she is someone we can safely admit, you have to be ready to kill her.

Sky proceeded to the street and met the woman, who then lowered her gun. "An angel," the woman said. "I see an angel."

"No," Sky said. "I'm just a kid."

"Heaven sent," the woman said. She dropped the rifle to the ground and fished through the right-side pocket of her tattered sundress. As she did so, Sky kicked the gun away from her then turned back to the others at the door and nodded. She came out with a picture and handed it to Sky, who looked at it with empathy. It was the woman in better days, sitting in a field with one child on her left, a boy, and one child on her right, a girl. They looked to be about five. She couldn't help but think of her own family...long gone from this world.

"Those are my twins," the woman said.

"Won't you come inside?" Sky asked. "We have a place you can stay. It's safe there."

The woman peered into the heavens as if not hearing Sky's question. "My babies."

"I'm sorry," Sky said to her. She then reached out her hand and took one of the woman's bony hands in hers. "Come with me."

They admitted the woman that night and brought her to the heights the next day.

That evening, Ace got out the paint to add Sky's handprint to the mural.

"I have to say," Sky said as Ace painted her hand yellow, "this is the strangest ritual you have here by far. Isn't it true that some of these handprints came along after people were killed?"

"Mine, anyway," JZ boasted. "Oh, and Leo's."

"Don't forget my guy," King said. "He did try to strangle me, though."

"I'm just saying," Sky said. "Shouldn't this banner commemorate something more positive? All I see is death when I look at it."

"If anyone died," Sim reminded, "it's because they wanted to hurt us. We must never allow people to steal our life or our humanity. We must always defend what's ours." He regarded the banner with a smile. "When I look at this banner, I am reminded of all the lives we saved from the streets by getting them safely to the heights, as well as our success in defending our dignity, lives, and honor."

"A glass half full, I suppose," she said.

After she applied her handprint, everyone gathered around and recited their pledge.

We, the orphans of the new world, pledge to: do our best, work together, defend our home, live and die for one another, love, lead, remember. We are the fortress, and the fortress is us.

Those days were but a distant memory. And all that mattered were the two little ones in front of her who she was charged with keeping safe during the siege. Miracle and Yamil. Sky read them a book while gunfire, explosions, and screams erupted from the lower floors. She kept their attention by ignoring the chaos herself, though profoundly curious about what was happening.

"I hear something," Yamil said. Sky had taught him English. He'd known only Spanish when Sim found him.

"It's like TV," Miracle said. Sky was befuddled that Miracle remembered the days of TV at all.

"It's not for us to worry about, boys," Sky said. "We must pay attention to the story, or we won't understand it."

"But we've heard this story before." Miracle sighed. "We already know it. The fish makes a friend with the crab even though they are different, and everyone is happy."

"Can we get a drink now?" Yamil asked.

"When the noise stops," Sky said. "When Sim says it is okay."

"What is the noise?" Miracle asked.

"It's our loved ones protecting our fortress," she said.

"We are the fortress," Yamil proclaimed.

Sky looked at him. He was so young, but Sim taught them all—or had Sky teach them, rather—about the code. About the world. It would be the only world they would remember.

Teddy, thirteen, burst into the room as the younger boys were becoming unsettled. Teddy was wild and crazy. He had at one point revealed his memory of being diagnosed with ADHD in the first world and wondered how he could be perfectly normal in the new world. He remembered how Sim had explained this to him.

Maybe it was the world that needed to change in some way back then, not you.

"I did it!" he cheered. "I blew them to hell with the cocktail. I never thought I would have a chance to do that, and it worked!"

"So happy to hear you were able to light some fires down there," Sky said. "Is everything okay now?"

"It's getting there," Teddy said. "These guys didn't have a chance. We smoked them."

The little ones looked at Teddy with wide eyes. Sky had no real idea of what was happening downstairs, and she didn't want to discuss it in front of Yamil or Miracle, so she directed them to play in the corner of the room where there were blocks, toys, and other fun things. The room was quite cozy, with a small carpet, a couple of battery-operated lights, some pillows, comfy seating, and lots of toys and books.

"What is going on, anyway?" Sky asked.

"I don't know exactly," Teddy said. "It was an attack. Lots of people. Twelve in all. We bombed them from the top and finished them from below."

Sky was puzzled. "We've never seen this before."

Teddy scratched his head. "I guess not."

"Is it over?" she asked.

"Hell if I know," Teddy said. "I'll go check and come back and let you know."

Teddy dashed off down two flights of stairs. Sky waited patiently for his return while the little ones played, obliviously so. Teddy returned a few minutes later. "It's clear."

"That's a relief," Sky said.

"We're all staying on the first floor tonight," Teddy said. "Sim said gather what you need, and we'll have a family night."

"Yay!" Yamil said.

They often had family nights where they gathered on the first floor and shared stories, jokes, and then fell asleep at each other's sides, but this felt different. There was more urgency and purpose to this gathering, and Sky could feel as much even without having personally taken part in the violent scuffle.

Five

UNDER THE FULL MOON, a man named Zagan lowered his binoculars and smiled. Several in his group gathered around and followed him as he backtracked to the side road on the outskirts of the fortress and headed south up the desolate road strewn with the remnants of years gone by including cars, trash, and random debris enshrouded with withering vines and weeds, whose death and regrowth cycles never changed in the years since most humans had died.

There were roughly ten men, including Steer, his right-hand man, who stayed close to him as he retreated from the area near the invasion. When Zagan reached the intersection at the top of the hill, he paused and took a breath. Three years ago, the intersection would have been bustling with traffic, waiting to go straight, turn left into the fast-food burger restaurant, or turn right into the local bank parking lot. But in these days, only wind whistled through the streets and the buildings that crowded the once busy area had long before begun to decay.

Zagan held out his arms in the middle of the intersection as his followers gazed upon him like he was a god.

"It's good to finally be home," he said. "Let's take a minute to remember our fallen comrades."

Everyone bowed their heads amidst the eerie silence until Zagan released them from their obligations. “They gave their lives for a good cause, gentlemen,” Zagan said. “Like the kamikaze pilots in the Second World War.”

“Then you knew they were going to die,” said a man in the circle that had formed around Zagan.

Zagan pointed. “*They* knew they were going to die!” He shrugged. “I had hoped that maybe some of them would make it through the line of defense, but that building they call the fortress...well let’s just say it’s just as well fortified as a fortress should be. Therefore, their deaths will not be in vain.”

“Why?” the man again challenged.

Zagan regarded him with a prolonged stare. “Because now we know what they are capable of as a unit. We know they are trained. We know they have guns, gas, knives, and spears. Most important, we know their resolve.”

“They’re just kids,” the man said impishly.

Zagan and Steer exchanged glances and smiled at one another. Zagan then looked back at the man. The others remained silent, watching with caution. “My dear fellow, there is no such thing as a child anymore. They’re killers...like us. Children...Do you know when I stopped being a child?”

The man said nothing.

“If not before, then after I entered juvenile detention,” Zagan said. “I was eight. Precocious. Angry. But no match for what was in store for me.” Zagan approached the vocal man stealthily. “There are no children. Just people. Some with the luxury of taking their sweet ass time waiting for their bodies and minds to grow while parents pamper them, and others having to jump right into it without those conveniences. Make no mistake, once this world befell us, children existed no more.”

“I had a child before this,” the man said. His lip was trembling.

Zagan, a bit taller than the newcomer to the group, leaned over and peered into his eyes. “Many did,” he said. “You’ve heard the rumors of that place like all of us, which is why I came back here after all this time. Tonight, we saw the truth etched in blood. The blood of our own men." Zagan pointed down the hill in the direction of the fortress. "Those are fighters in that house, and if you think this is the first time in history when people their age have been trained to fight, you would be wrong. They are soldiers. And so are we. Soldiers fight." Zagan pulled back and regarded the entire group. "We need at least one hundred footmen!" he yelled, his voice echoing through the hollow streets. "More would be better. We need ammo. We need explosives. We need a plan. For before the season's end, there will be another ruler of that fortress."

"I still don't understand the purpose of this mission," the man said, causing Zagan to turn around.

Zagan shook his head, frustrated. He then offered Steer a nod. Steer pulled out a revolver and shot the newcomer in the right knee. The man let out a terrified scream as he crumpled to the ground. Zagan approached him as he sat holding his knee in pain.

"There are two kinds of people in this world, my friend," Zagan offered quietly. "My people, and everyone else. Everyone else dies. Near and far and most especially people who exalt themselves as the kings of a fortress while the rest of us fight for the scraps. You see, the people of the fortress have their rules, and I have mine. It's that simple."

Steer raised his gun unflinchingly and fired three more shots into the man's body and head.

"To everyone else, there will be no taking this crew out one by one. Our victory will be more glorious than that of random cowardly acts. They deserve as much. We will start planning our siege on the fortress tomorrow. It is a lighthouse sitting on top of bedrock that oversees the gates of the city and therefore is a prize to behold. For tonight, we will celebrate our newfound knowledge by visiting that house on Reynolds just down the road. The people hiding there will most certainly not offer the same kind of defense and it has been a tremendously stressful day losing so many men. So, I must vent. What better way to let off steam than to hunt and kill the helpless and weak?"

Zagan burst into a fit of maniacal laughter, and though there were a few chuckles from the crowd of followers, they largely remained quiet as they followed Zagan up the empty street to Reynolds Avenue.

When they arrived at the ranch-style house, on what has been a quiet street then before it was a quiet street now, they stood upon the lawn. Zagan had his hands on his hips, gazing into the home through the picture window, where a faint candlelight stirred.

"This is it, people," he said. "Go get them."

His followers, under the cover of darkness, charged into the house. Zagan waited on the lawn as his crew pillaged the home. He heard screams and relished their pain. He knew who was there. Three men, two women, and a boy of no more than fourteen. They were all soon dragged from the house and tossed to the lawn weak, tired, and defenseless.

Zagan approached the boy who had risen to a defiant stance. He was small in stature, reaching Zagan's neck in height. The others who were with him in the house had remained on the ground, expectant, but not defiant, for they surely knew who had control.

Zagan eyeballed the boy up and down and smiled. "You know, I've been watching you people squat here for a month now, and it made me remember simpler times. Why this place?"

"I don't know," the boy shrugged. "I was just following them." He turned to regard his fellow squatters on the lawn.

Zagan nodded. "Makes sense."

"I thought so," the boy said.

"Then tell me, why is it that you are on your feet and the rest of your...friends...are on the ground?" Zagan asked.

"Because I died before," the boy said. "They might be scared of something bad happening, but if the worst thing is death, then I already know what that's like and they don't."

"Trust me, sir, there are much worse things than death. But I do think I want to adopt you," Zagan said, scratching at his beard and laughing wildly. "Though, there are no more children in the world. How old are you?"

"Thirteen," he said. "If I've kept track right."

"Mother nature tells a boy when he's thirteen, so if you say thirteen, then you are probably right." He sized the boy up once again, this time with his pocket flashlight. "I have an important job for you."

As he said this, one of his men approached with a box of cereal in his hands. Zagan recoiled as the man crunched down on the cereal with loud chomps. "Jimmy, that is fucking annoying, you know."

"Sorry, Z," he said as he began to step away.

"How the hell did you find cereal that still has a crunch after three years?"

The man shrugged while chomping down on another fistful of flakes. "The bag was still sealed."

"Christ," Zagan said. "Never mind. It gives me an idea." He turned to the boy. "Your name is Kellogg now," he said.

"What do you mean?" the boy asked.

Zagan put an arm around the boy's shoulder. "That's your name when I send you off to beg for asylum at a fortified locale not too far from here."

"Kellogg?" the boy said. "My name is Anthony."

Zagan shook his head. "No. That's not going to work. You must use the name Kellogg. Trust me."

"What the heck am I supposed to do?" he asked pulling a coin from his pocket, which he then began to twirl with his fingers.

"Well...we deliver you to this property and you find out everything you can about its inhabitants and then report it back to me. Pretty simple."

"Why me?" the boy asked.

Zagan laughed. "You're...young. This place is a warehouse for lost...young people, of sorts. I'm still trying to figure it out."

"That doesn't make too much sense to me," the boy said. "If there are just kids in there—"

Zagan held up a finger as he recoiled. "Don't say the 'k' word, please. And your job is not to second-guess my motives. Just follow my lead."

Kellogg nodded then looked back at his cohabitants on the lawn. "What about them?"

"My young friend," Zagan said. "We didn't come here for a picnic. Without a purpose...they are just...in the way."

"Why can't they join you?" the boy asked.

Zagan looked at the motley crew affixed to the lawn with disregard. "Yeah, no. As much as I would love to take everyone I meet under my glorious wings, there must be someone to kill. It may as well be them. But you're lucky. *You* made the cut."

"It's this coin," the boy said, flipping the coin he had taken from his pocket into the air and catching it. "Where is this place, anyway?"

"Follow me," Zagan said.

As he and Kellogg walked away from the home, gunshots echoed through the night sky as Steer finished the job Zagan had set off to accomplish on Reynolds Avenue.

Six

JIMMY WAS THIRTEEN AND when people started to die, he had little to think about apart from wondering if he too was going to die. Then he watched as everyone around him deteriorated while he moved from place to place doing what he had gotten accustomed to. He ran away from home when he was twelve. His mother was a drunk, which he could have tolerated, but when her live-in boyfriend started to beat him, he decided he'd had enough. He left home only a few months before everything changed, and in that time, he begged and borrowed, slept on the street and at friends' houses, and a few times in abandoned cars.

When Sim found him, he was in such a car, sleeping with one eye open. He sprang from the seat when he realized someone was watching him. He dared not move while Sim regarded him. In those three lost months away from home, Jimmy had run into some unsavory people.

"It's okay," Sim said, offering a smile. "I know you."

Jimmy did not respond other than to widen his eyes, his body entering fight or flight mode. He was no lightweight, and he was not afraid to fight back. It was what helped him survive when he was on his own. "I don't know you," Jimmy said. "And you don't know me."

"I do," Sim said. "Can I open the door so we can talk?"

"Fuck you," the boy snapped.

"Fair enough," Sim said, patiently. "I have a place where other children such as yourself are safe. It's a fortress. It's stocked. It has weapons. It's what you need right now."

"I haven't needed a Goddamn thing from anyone in the last six months," he retorted bitterly.

"Six months?" Sim said. "It's only been three since...So you were a runaway?"

"I've been on my own before all this and I took care of myself fine. I don't need a fortress."

"Because you *are* a fortress," Sim said. "I get that. My children, together, we are the fortress, like you. Whatever life was like before all of this...whatever life is like after...it can be better. Love teaches different lessons than hate, son."

"I'm not your son just because my father is dead, and how do I know you won't just kill me?" Jimmy asked.

"Because I would have already," Sim said. "And I'm not interested in killing you. I want to protect you. In many ways, I *have* to protect you. It's the only thing that makes sense."

Jimmy let down his guard and opened the door for Sim. Sim remained there smiling. Jimmy slid his body toward the open door, eyeing Sim distrustfully. "Does anyone know how to play chess at this place?" he asked. "I used to play with my dad."

"And what was your favorite piece?" Sim asked.

"The king, of course," the boy said. "My dad was the real king, though. He used to call me his prince. He died when I was six." Jimmy slid out of the car and stood before Sim, his height reaching only Sim's chest.

"You are a prince no more," Sim said. "You are the King now. And we will play chess at the fortress. You will teach everyone how. You will have love. Again."

King nodded. "My mother never even looked for me after I left her."

Sim returned the nod, careful not to encroach on the boy's space. "It's her loss. If my daughter ever ran from me, I would never stop searching for her. No matter what."

Maybe she should have run, Sim, and she would still be alive.

The thought made Sim cringe.

The two walked off together. They found a store along the way and picked up a game of chess, which they brought with them back to the fortress so they could teach the rest of the orphans how to play. Ultimately, only Big Will committed to the challenge, and that would a special bond he and King would share until the end.

The group spent the night downstairs after the raid. They all worked together to close and lock the shutters and bring all the blankets and pillows to the living room area. They kept three soft battery-operated lights on, and it was cozy, though a little uncomfortable. They all visited the outhouse as a group and went in one at a time, as the rest of the group kept watch.

In three years, there had never been a siege on the fortress. Sim had prepared them for such an inevitability, but it was unclear if he really believed it would ever happen. Sim was hard to read. He wanted everything done in a particular way without negotiation, but the means were always to some unknown end.

And so, they gathered, alert, yet recalling those many nights prior where they would all convene in the living room for fun and family stories. They admitted to loving such tradition, but on this night it was different. Sim paced the floor, his hands in his khaki pockets while Sky tended to the little ones on the couch, where they fell asleep in her lap while she tousled their hair. Still others were camped out on the blankets that were strewn about the floor while Ace stood at the main doorway visible from the living room, contemplative.

It was Sky who broke the silence after they were gathered. "We need a new couch. So, next time you see Charlie, perhaps come back with a good one."

Charlie was their local ally overseeing the nearby heights community, which was a fortified apartment complex. Charlie had been a student of Sim's in the old times.

Teddy broke out in wild laughter while he lay on his back, staring at the ceiling. "We'll be lucky if we can go anywhere after this, and you're talking about getting a couch."

"Ha-ha-ha," Sky mocked.

"Okay," Sim said. "So, let's discuss the elephant in the room, then."

Yamil perked up, raising his head off Sky's lap. "I saw an elephant once."

"I'm sure it was an amazing sight, Yamil," Sim said. "But I was using an expression." He kneeled in front of the couch and patted Yamil's dark hair. "It simply meant we have big things to talk about." Sim then stood. "We'll do some scouting tomorrow. Take it slow. Play it safe. None of us goes out with fewer than four of us at a time and we bring our guns."

"We have a lot of digging to do in Restland tomorrow," Flip said.

"No," Sim said. "This is too much to bury. We'll dig a hole and burn them beyond the fortress border."

"What happened here tonight?" Ace asked, his black shirt unbuttoned just enough to reveal the dressing he had applied to his upper chest. "It makes no sense."

"It was a probing attack," Sim said with confidence. "They were testing our defenses. I would bet there were others observing the siege on the outskirts."

Everyone peered at Sim, their concerns clearly heightened. Baby sat with Big Will and Gigi in a shabby love seat, trying not to seem panicked. Misty sat with her back against the wall, her legs pulled up into her chest while Shark, King, and JZ clustered together in ready position near the doorway closest to the back of the house. They would be the last ones to fall asleep.

"Who?" Ace asked.

Sim shrugged. "I don't know," he said. "But they're here and this isn't the end, you can be sure."

"What are we going to do?" Shark asked.

"We're going to kill everyone that attempts to attack us," Sim said. "Like usual."

There was a silence.

"You're scaring the little ones," Sky said as she comforted Miracle and Yamil on her lap.

Sim looked at her through the artificial light, with a curious eye, as if wondering whether it was Sky who was scared. "These are scary times, Sky. If we pretend otherwise, we could die or even worse."

"I'm just concerned that you *want* us to be afraid," Sky said.

"Chill, Sky," Ace said.

Sim appeared not to panic at Sky's utterance. "Yes, I do. Because fear builds awareness. Let's not pretend, here. If Baby had not gone out there today fearing the outcome of her encounter, what might have happened?"

"But it is no way to live," Sky said.

Sim nodded. "How should we live, then?"

"Alertly," she said. "With appreciation for each day with the understanding that each day is a gift, but not panicked that any day could be our last."

"That's a tall order," Sim said. "But you understand living with this particular idealism...we would have all been slaughtered, if not long before this day, then most definitely in the last hour."

"We can't live like it's yesterday," Ace reminded her.

"And anyway," King said, "you live *here*. *We* are the fortress. This isn't *your* show."

"*We* know whose show it is," Sky said, eyeing Sim. "If we are the fortress, then why don't *we* get to have an opinion on anything?"

"Sky," Sim implored. "I know from experience how bad things can get when we become complacent and think we are untouchable. Bad things happen. People don't change. Our best defense is always to dig in and—"

"Hide?" she said. "It should be the maniacs hiding...like before. Not us."

"We're not hiding, Sky," Sim said. "People know we're here, and they also know our resolve if they try to weaken and plunder us."

"Let's have a story!" Flip shouted, breaking the tension.

Sim peered at Flip with a smile. "What kind of story, Flip?"

"A 'days-gone-by' story," he said.

Sim turned to the wall behind him. He pushed a button light that illuminated the hashmarks that were carefully marked on the wall under the words, "Days Gone By," which were scrawled in big letters with a Sharpie marker.

They added a hash mark every day at sunrise after opening the shutters. Presently, there were two hundred groups of five hashmarks and three individual hashmarks. A grand total of 1,003 days since the new beginning. Sim had multiple lines pointing out in all directions from individual hashmarks. Each one had an annotation next to it. A memory. The wall had become a daily journal over the years. But a mystery journal, at that. All the orphans along with Sim would write hints about the stories they would one day share. Some stories had been told, and others not yet revealed. Like an advent calendar from Christmases long ago, when little children would open a new door each day to reveal the latest surprise.

"Okay, then," Sim said as he backed up to the wall. He pointed to one of the annotations toward the beginning of the crude timeline. *The cow.* Sim smiled. "It's time for the cow story."

"No way," Flip said.

"It's about time," said Misty. "Maybe next time you'll share your 'before the end' story."

Sim glanced back at the wall and regarded that annotation scratched into the wall denoting a starting line before any hashmarks were added. He turned back to Misty. "No doubt. But for today my memory is of a cow."

"You were gone for days," Ace smiled. "I remember that much."

Sim reflected. He then took a seat on the floor and crossed his legs over one another. "I walked eight miles in that stretch just to find a cow so we could have milk. At last, I found a pasture and there they were, a whole bunch of them, wandering around, looking lost."

"That's very sad," Baby said.

"Anyway," Sim continued. "I picked the healthiest looking cow in the pasture and headed off with it in tow. The thing was so slow. Three days slow. You can't even know how agonizing it is to walk with a cow for three days. It still had that bell around its neck, too, and by the third day I thought I would go insane listening to it. I tried to pull it off its neck, but I couldn't unfasten that leather strap for the life of me."

Sim laughed, as did some of the others.

"I was so excited to be bringing this cow home. To be able to provide milk for all of you. That's the only thing that kept me going."

There was a brief silence.

"But...as I was almost home, I reluctantly had to leave it behind."

"Why you gonna leave that cow behind after pulling its big carcass through the city for three days?" JZ asked, eyes aglow.

"Because I realized it was a bull," Sim said.

The older children laughed while the younger ones missed the punchline.

"You didn't lift up its skirt before you left the pasture with it?" King asked, laughing.

"I didn't notice anything," Sim laughed. "It had been castrated and I was just so excited to see cows and thankful we would have milk. I guess I wasn't thinking clearly."

"Forget about milk," Shark said. "We could have cooked that thing and had meat for a month."

Sim shook his head. "It was in the middle of summer and no way to keep the meat from spoiling," Sim said. "It wasn't worth the butchering for a single meal."

"So, you left that fool cow in the middle of the road just like that and walked away?" JZ asked.

"Just like that." Sim snapped his fingers. "I was spent."

"After all this time, the story is finally told," Ace said.

"Milk," Sky said, wetting her lips and thinking back to Sim's story. "Oh, what I wouldn't do for some."

"I almost forgot about milk," Leo said, his eyes distant as he sat upon the hardwood floor. "I loved chocolate milk. My mom would make it for me every morning before school."

Teddy crinkled his nose. "Milk was gross," he said. "Even if you did end up bringing home a milking cow, I don't think I would have had any. It's not like milk from the store if it comes right out of the cow and into your cup."

"I liked milk with cookies," JZ said. "We would leave some out for Santa."

Everyone grew silent. The luxury of Santa Claus had long been given up on.

"I miss Santa," Baby said.

"There may still be cows out there," JZ said. "We should go look again. This time we could get the girl variety. Mmm, hmm."

Sim smiled. "Maybe."

"It would be nice to have something other than deer meat once in a while," Shark remarked.

There was a collective silence before a loud thud. Everyone froze and listened.

"It sounded like something hit the basement door," Misty said.

Then came the shattering of glass. The living room window. The wooden shutters stopped the projectile after it cascaded through the glass. The older children sprung to the wall, flanking the window. Baby ran with Big Will to either side of the front door where they had earlier taken up position.

"Where do you want us?" JZ asked Sim.

"Come on children," Sky said to the little ones. "We'll go to sleep on the third floor."

"No!" Sim said. "Stay here."

More projectiles struck the other windows on all floors, and the sound of breaking glass echoed around the house from the upper windows down to the lower ones. The group stood firm in the living room and waited as the assault continued.

"What are they doing?" Leo asked.

"Trying to scare us," King said. "But it's not going to work."

"Yes it is," Leo said, hugging himself.

"Let them try to come in," Shark said. "I should just go out there now and waste them."

"Quiet," Sim said. "Let them have their fun for now."

As he said this, objects continued to pelt the fortress. Some of the impact was only faintly observed as the objects hit the brick walls.

"What if they try to come in?" Flip asked.

"They can't get in," Sim said. "They'd be stupid to try."

"There could be dozens of those fools out there," JZ said.

"Stay calm," Ace said. "We were trained for this, and the fortress is impenetrable to rocks. They would need an army and explosives to get to us, and based on what we have seen tonight, they aren't prepared."

Sky sat back down with Miracle and Yamil and tried to distract them with a song, as objects continued to batter the fortress. Ace and King remained by the windows while Baby and Big Will stood poised by the doorway. Sim stood in the middle of the living room as the others huddled together in various clusters on the floor, hunkering down in the absence of any kind of directive from Sim.

"Why we gonna just sit around instead of taking our positions?" JZ asked.

Sim returned a whisper. "Because there is no sense in trying to go on the offensive in the dark of night. There is nothing they can do right now outside of throwing some rocks, so let them waste their time if they wish, and we will go about our business." He took in a few steady breaths. "We should all be ready at the break of dawn, though, and in our positions."

"What do we do now?" Baby asked.

"We try to sleep," Sim said as glass shattered against the front door, as if someone had hurled a bottle against it.

Big Will and Baby, startled, jumped back and Big Will raised his weapon. "Let me open this door," he said, teeth clenched. "They'll be sorry."

"No," Sim said. "That's what they want. They want us to panic. They want us to react. But we won't."

"It's like psychological warfare," Teddy shouted with an arm pump. "I get it."

"Shut the hell up, Teddy," Flip said. "You're really annoying, you know."

"It's going to be a long night," Misty said. "This reminds me of a time when I was little when we had thunder and lightning storms all night long. I was so scared and couldn't sleep a wink. Not even when I went to my mom and dad's bed. Just when I was about to nod off...kaboom!" Misty clapped her hands together.

"Shhh," Leo said, putting his pointer finger over his lips.

"They'll stop as long as we don't react," Sim reassured. "It was the author Tolstoy who said the two most powerful warriors are patience and time." He smiled through the soft light.

Artificial light at night was a luxury in these days, and it was Sim's forethought to stock up in the beginning on not only weapons, but batteries and battery-operated light sources of all kinds from local stores. They would have light for years before having to resort to fire to keep them out of the dark. They used fire for heat. Sometimes they used it to cook and other times they used a propane grill.

"If you say so, Sim," Ace said. "Then it's true."

Sure enough, the mayhem did conclude after some time, without the orphans having to take up positions or answer to the taunting. Half of them stayed alert while the other half slept. When the younger ones complained of having to use the bathroom, they peed in buckets, not daring to visit the outhouse.

Before long, the sun had risen, and a new day had begun.

Seven

WITH FIRST SUNLIGHT, EVERYONE was stationed in their places. Shark was positioned on the uppermost rooftop, which offered a 360-degree view of the property. Perched on his knees, he peered through a set of binoculars to the front of the house. The streets were clear from the top of the hill to the intersection at the bottom. The alleyways next to the homes across the street were clear. Then he focused on the east side of the house. The grass lot was clear, as well as the side street that ran parallel to it. Next, he turned to the back of the home. Their expansive yard was clear. Finally, he cleared the west side of the house, careful to check for movement on the tree-studded hill that led down to their property. He then lowered his binoculars, peered into the blue skies, and sighed at the beauty of this ugly world.

Shark was twelve when Sim found him. Shark, then Scott, lived a suburban life with all the benefits that came from privilege. His mom worked for an insurance agency and his father was former military. They had a nice house. It was white with black shutters and had a pool in the backyard. His father became sick first and Scott watched him quickly succumb. He remembered his last conversation with him. He had grabbed Scott's hand while coughing and spitting up blood. His mother watched them from the other side of the bed, covering her mouth in sheer panic as she attempted to contain a light cough of her own. A sign of things to come.

"Listen, Scotty," he said. "If this sickness doesn't get you, you'll be on your own in a world you aren't prepared for." His eyes widened. "We sheltered you from what would have been normal challenges. But *these* challenges...who would have ever known?"

"What do I do?" Scott implored.

His father swallowed hard. "You hide. You hold tight to my guns and find more." He squeezed Scott's arm as he coughed. "You know where the police station is. That's a good start. Go through every house and every drawer with caution. You must not delay on this. Stay sheltered, eat the food you find, and wait until you run into someone you can trust. Don't let your guard down. Not for a second."

Scott recalled crying. "I'm so scared."

His father locked eyes with him. He was a strong man, a former Army sniper. "You can be. We're all scared. But I taught you *some* things."

His mother coughed. "Can't we just go together, Joe?"

He turned to her feebly. "That's not the lesson I want to teach my son." He turned back to Scott. "You'll fight to survive. You'll live or die, but to be alive even in an uncertain world is a gift. A privilege now. Honor your life."

Honor your life. Scott heard those words echo through his mind daily.

He never did make it to the police station for a long time after his mother passed away. He spent the first weeks after the electric grids shut down scouring neighborhood houses for food and weapons. He found rifles, shotguns, pistols, first aid materials, food, and other items of value, and carted them back to his house in a red Radio Flyer wagon. In those days, he ran into people only sporadically but tried avoiding the other survivors where possible.

He ran into Sim after finally making it to the police station. There were no weapons because after eight months of apocalyptic hell, others had gotten them. Including Sim, who proudly admitted he was among the first raiders, Elizabeth at his side in those days.

"Smart move, coming here," Sim said to him. "But a bit late."

Scott, remembering his father's advice, aimed his rifle square at Sim's head. Sim was standing ten feet away, remembering when Ace shot him and hoping this boy would not do the same.

Your instincts will kick in. "Are you a good guy?"

"What do *you* think?" Sim asked.

"A lot of times I can tell," Scott said. "But I don't know with you."

"Then I'm bad," Sim said.

"You don't look bad," he said, his gun wavering in his hands. "I try to avoid other people, but I've seen bad things."

"Of course you have," Sim said, stuffing his hands into his long coat. "I was talking to another boy about your age today about the state of the world and he thought we were near the end of the age, but I reminded him that we are beyond the end of the age."

"Another boy?" Scott said, only hearing those words.

"Yes," Sim said. "He is with me now. I have other children too that live at my fortress. You might say it's serving its purpose."

"Is this like an...orphanage?"

Sim nodded. "Maybe. But some say children don't exist anymore. But I think that no matter what children must do to survive nowadays, they are still children. The last children, perhaps."

"And you want to protect them?" Scott asked.

"I have to," Sim said.

"Why?" Scott asked.

Sim looked beyond Scott momentarily. "Redemption."

Your instincts will kick in. Scott lowered his weapon. "I'm a good shot, you know. I could have killed you even from a long way off."

"How so?" Sim asked.

"My father was a sniper," Scott offered. "When he was dying, he told me he didn't prepare me, but he forgot that he showed me how to shoot. He taught me the value of my own life. So, he was wrong when he said that."

"He wasn't wrong, son," Sim said. "He was scared. Because he knew how precious you were. He knew you were a fortress."

He then remembered telling his father how scared he was. *You can be.*

"Yeah."

"Come with me then," Sim said. "And with me and some new friends, you'll fight for a new world. A world that remembers good. That's why you are still here, after all."

"Why are *you* here?" Scott asked, before closing the gap between him and Sim. "If you knew there was nothing left at this place."

Sim smiled. "I've been following you since last night. I've seen how you have helped others from the dark using your sniper skills."

"You could have killed me?" Scott asked.

"I'm not a predator," Sim said. "I observe and act accordingly. I'm doing the only thing that makes sense to me. That's all."

"Then show me this fortress," Scott said.

Scott followed Sim at a distance back to the fortress, his gun often pointed at Sim's back until the fortress was revealed. The truth. After thirty days, he revealed his name to be Shark, because he remembered as a small child being fascinated with sharks after visiting an aquarium in Atlanta. Sim found this ironic.

"What does that mean?" Shark asked at the time.

"Well, great whites in particular hunt prey at the surface from below. Snipers hold a higher ground. Like our rooftop, in your case."

"But sharks are predators," Shark said. "We are not. We are prey, defending ourselves."

"Then why call yourself 'Shark'?" Sim asked.

"Because I like sharks," he said.

A child's answer. Sim laughed.

Shark had shifted onto his stomach and traded his binoculars for the scope on his rifle as he continued to carefully survey the land, remembering all the years of practice it took for him to become such a marvel at distant shooting. Sim told him it was genetic. Talent often was.

Shark could see nothing as far out as the creek bed beyond Restland. He thought of Tak. The pike bearing the head of Tak's killer was still there at the edge of the property, the head itself nothing more than a skull at this point. All was quiet.

Downstairs, the crew had drawn open the interior shutters that Sim had installed to protect the windows on the first floor, and he observed that much of the glass panes had been shattered.

"How will we fix all these windows?" Ace asked. "With the changing weather coming, it'll be as drafty and cold as hell in here."

"We'll measure the frames and scour the local residences for replacements," Sim said. "There are some people at the heights who are skilled in this area. We have to be resourceful in these times. Windows are one of the easier fixes. We also need to find a store that still has walkies. Ever since the other ones petered out on us, we've procrastinated in getting new ones, and this is not the time to be saddled with communication problems within the house."

"When do we get to go out?" asked Big Will.

"As soon as we get clearance from Shark," Sim said.

Just then, Shark barreled down the wooden stairs, rifle in hand, huffing and puffing. JZ, Flip, and Teddy were on his heels. "We really need to get new walkies," he said.

The others laughed and he looked at them crookedly. "What?"

"Never mind," Sim said. "What's the lowdown?"

"The area looks clear from a distance, but if anyone is within five feet of the house, I wouldn't know."

"Makes sense," Sim said. "Let's carefully take this party outside. I want JZ, Flip, Teddy, Misty, Shark, King, and Ace to join me."

"I can go," Baby muttered, batting her long eyelashes and carrying her knives as if they were surgically attached to her hands.

Sim hunched over to meet her height. "You have to add another tally to the wall," he said. "That's your job now."

"That will only take a few seconds," she said.

"Don't argue, Baby," Sim said. "You can watch from the window."

"Misty! King! Let's go!" Ace yelled.

The two appeared from the kitchen, each gnawing on an apple collected from the trees in their yard.

"What the hell are you doing eating now?" Ace chided. "Go get your guns."

The fortress was stocked with lots of guns and ammunition. Sim boasted that, prior to his gathering of children, he raided homes, stores, military reserve bases, and police stations within a fifty-mile radius to build his arsenal full of pistols, semi-automatics, automatics, rifles, grenades and shotguns. He had found Big Will's AK-47 in an evidence locker along with several other firearms that were likely seized from gangs during normal times. It was easier to get places before the gasoline soured in the thousands of abandoned vehicles that peppered the lands, now only relics of days gone by.

"I can't scout on an empty stomach," King said.

Misty giggled. The two grabbed their guns from the dining room table and Big Will, who lived at the front doors, opened the right for them with one hand while he clutched his weapon in the other. Baby opened the left side door and the scouting crew exited in close formation until all were out. Then King and Ace split to the right and left corner of the fortress, respectively. The others looked up and down the street that cut in front of the fortress, guns poised. They waited. They listened. All was quiet.

"Clear," King whispered from the west.

"Clear," Ace said from the east.

Then came a rustle in the woods on King's side. Everyone turned, prepared to open fire.

"Wait," Sim said. He always commanded the orphans to not waste ammo. In three years, they had barely fired their weapons outside of target practice. "It's probably just an animal. Do not fire unless I say."

They waited for thirty seconds and heard nothing more. Sim directed them around the west front corner of the house and into the narrow driveway that separated the side porch from the treelined hill. "Stay as one."

The group, huddled together but each facing a different direction, moved in cluster formation down the driveway path and diligently followed it into the backyard, which ran into the side lot on the east side of the house.

Sim paused the group in the middle of the driveway just beyond the porch as the trees offered up more noise. Everyone turned toward the wooded hill again and waited. The trees, covered in orange and yellow leaves, rustled and stirred.

"There's someone up there," King said.

"Maybe more than one," Ace said.

"Stay calm," Sim said. "It could be just some squirrels."

"Can we wet our pants if we want?" Misty asked.

Flip chuckled.

"Classic," Teddy said.

"Shush," Ace yelled with clenched teeth.

From the woods, tree branches snapped and fallen leaves shuffled.

"Who's out there?" Sim yelled. "Come out of there now or we'll fire."

More shuffling.

"Let's just shoot up the forest," Teddy said.

"You don't even know how to fire that thing," Flip teased. "Last time we practiced you could barely hit the tree standing two feet away."

"That's not true," Teddy said. "In that last Nerf gun fight I hit you eleven times!"

As the pair bickered, a person revealed himself from the woods. He stepped out from behind a tree and stood there.

"Come down from there now," Sim demanded.

The person stood frozen halfway up the hill. Sim fired a shot into the air. "Now!"

"You'll kill me," the voice said, shaken. It was a boy's voice. "They said you kill everyone who comes close."

"Well, some of them, anyway," King stated. "Little shits that snoop around."

"*They*," Sim said inquisitively.

"The men that killed my friends last night," the boy said.

"How about you come down from there and we'll talk about it," Sim said.

"If you promise not to kill me," the boy said.

"I'm not going to promise you that," Sim said. "We vet people here before we decide if they should be killed. So, if you come down, you'll have a good fighting chance if you don't do anything stupid."

"Just come down, you coward!" Teddy yelled. "Before we fill you with holes."

"Enough, Theodore," Sim said.

Ace slapped Teddy on the top of the head.

"I'll come," said the boy. He then shuffled down through the trees and brush to the outer edge of the driveway until he was standing only a few feet away from the group.

Sim lowered his gun, as did the others when they saw him: a boy no more than thirteen. His hair was long and greasy. He had on blue jeans and a black T-shirt that was ripped vertically along one side, exposing his ribcage.

"What's your name, boy?" Sim asked.

"Kellogg," the boy said.

Sim turned to the others with a curious eye. "Kellogg?"

"Your name isn't Kellogg," Ace snapped. "Why the hell do you call yourself that?"

"Because I like...Frosted Flakes."

"Who gave you that name?" King demanded.

"My friend, Damien," Kellogg said. "He was killed last night when these people raided the house we were in."

"Why not just tell us your real name?" Sim asked.

"Jimmy." The boy dropped eye contact with them. "Jimmy Stapleton."

Sim prolonged his response. "What do you want, Jimmy Stapleton?"

"A place to live," he said. "I heard them talking about you while I was hiding. They described this place, and it sounded like a place I could live."

"What the hell did they say?" Ace demanded.

"They said it was a place where children lived."

Sim raised his gun and pointed it at the boy. "Were you throwing rocks and bottles at our house last night?"

The boy flinched and shielded his face with his forearm. "No, I swear. It was them. I followed them here. I watched them. They left just before dawn."

"He's lying," Ace said. "Don't trust him. We don't need him."

Sim kept his rifle pointed at the boy.

Ace moved closer to Sim and whispered into his ear. "Not all kids are good. This is probably a trap."

Make a child safe. Save a life.

Sim listened but did not acknowledge Ace's warning. "Are you the fortress?" he asked instead.

Ace shook his head, discouraged, while the others gawked at the boy, realizing that he would soon be one of them.

"I don't know," Kellogg said. "What does that even mean?"

"Yes or no," Sim said.

The boy seemed confused. Lost. "Yes, I guess. If you want me to be a fortress, I'll be a fortress."

Sim contemplated this response while holding his gun at the firing position. After thirty seconds of silence, during which Kellogg likely wondered if he would live or die, Sim lowered the weapon.

With the tension diminished, they scoured the remaining grounds for signs of trespassers and then returned to the fortress. The others were waiting anxiously at the door.

"Let me see him!" Leo yelled as they entered the foyer.

"See who?" Sky asked.

"The new kid," Leo responded, never turning back.

"He's not a specimen," Flip said. "He's just a dirty kid."

Sky pulled Yamil and Miracle to her sides. "New kid?"

"I saw him through the window," Leo said. "He's ugly."

"His name is Jimmy," Sim said. "And he knows the drill. Thirty days to settle on a new name."

Sky shouted from behind the crowd of orphans that were huddled in the foyer in front of the staircase. "Are you crazy?"

The chatter immediately ceased. All eyes were on Sky as she pushed her way to Sim. Jimmy was beside her, eyeing her curiously with an upward gaze, as she was a bit taller than he. She too reviewed him from head to toe with a curled lip before reverting her attention back to Sim.

"After what went on last night and you think this is a coincidence?" she huffed.

"He's a child—"

"I don't care!" she snapped. "We should at least sequester him until we interrogate him before we let him loose in the house."

"We did so outside," Sim said. "Trust me. It was a proper vetting."

"Surely, three years after the fall the criteria for letting children live at the fortress has to be based on something more than their age," Sky said.

Kellogg stepped to her side. "I promise I won't do anything—"

Sky turned on him like a lion. "Your promises mean nothing to me, boy. I don't know you, but I do know you sprung out of last night's chaos. And though this is not my house, I promise you this: should you go near my children or give me any reason to suspect you are anything other than a victim, I will kill you in your sleep and I will cut your body into pieces and feed them to the coyotes."

"Whoa," Kellogg said.

"Sky," Sim said. "This *is* your house. And it's *our* fortress."

Sky regarded Sim and then Jimmy again. "It's feeling less so with these kinds of decisions being made without anyone else's input."

"Sim makes the decisions here," Ace reminded. "Maybe you need some time to yourself right now."

Unexpectedly, Sky lunged at Ace. Shark intervened and kept her from reaching him, but she fought to break through his grasp.

"You're acting crazy!" Ace shouted, stepping back.

"And you're woefully compliant," she hissed, Shark still holding her back. "You know this isn't a good decision, but you sit there silent like a twit. Grow a pair of balls, Ace."

Sim stepped between them. He held out both arms. "Stop this nonsense, Sky," he said. "I'm in charge of this house and demand your respect, regardless of whether you think I'm right or wrong."

Sky pulled away from Shark and composed herself. She regarded Ace, Kellogg, and finally Sim. "For the record, I think you are wrong in this instance, and if our voices and opinions don't influence your decisions, then what point is it to speak at all on *any* matter that involves this fortress?"

Before Sim could reply, Sky moved toward Yamil and Miracle and shuffled them off to the bathroom. Sim pursued her outside.

"I want to talk, Sky," Sim offered while she stood outside the makeshift outhouse. Yamil was pressed to her side.

Sim rubbed the top of Yamil's head and smiled at him.

"You know my opinion about this new boy," she said. "What else is there to discuss?"

"You are too emotional," Sim retorted. "And you act on emotion, which confuses everyone and causes disorder. If you want to be a leader, then you must find other ways to be heard outside of yelling at us all when you aren't getting your own way."

"Tell me how you wish I would have handled that," Sky said.

"Privately," Sim said. "Not in front of an audience that depends on me to make them feel safe."

"What good would a private conversation do, Sim?" she asked. "Would you have kicked him out had I addressed the situation privately?"

"No," Sim said. "But the means to the end are important. I would have listened and heard you. I would have respected your opinions more. Nobody respects a leader who lacks self-control."

She stepped closer to Sim. "I don't want to be *you*. I just want to protect the little ones."

"That's admirable, Sky, but the children...including yourself, are *my* responsibility." Sim reminded. "That's why I'm still alive."

Just then, Miracle exited the outhouse. The wooden door sprung shut with a bang.

"You function under my authority and under the protocol of the fortress."

"It doesn't sound very democratic," she said.

"I never told you we were operating under democracy here," Sim said.

"But you forget," Sky said, "some of us are young adults now. Maybe it's time to start letting us *be* adults. If you treat us like seven-year-olds forever, you will see unfold the exact opposite vision you have for this place with us as its future."

"Maybe my only vision is to keep you all safe until my penance is fulfilled," Sim said.

Sky regarded him with a crooked glance. "It sounds like you allow your personal demons to guide your decision-making. You may want to consider this."

With that, she walked away, her little ones in tow.

Eight

THERE WAS NO FURTHER action against the fortress that day or evening. Shark had reported nothing from the rooftop for the duration except that all was calm and quiet.

Like lemonade.

This is how Misty described the sound of nothingness. Flip taunted her, of course, when she said such a thing, but she justified it quite nicely: *The sound of emptiness reminds me of sitting on my front porch in summertime drinking a glass of lemonade. My mother made the best lemonade. She squeezed the lemons herself. It actually wasn't nothing at all. It was quite something.*

Then Flip stopped taunting her because she had reminded him that the world hadn't always been like this. There were other memories of years ago that were easy enough to forget if you didn't think about them often enough. Misty was the best at remembering.

While Shark stood his post and the others milled about expectantly on the first floor, Sky was reading to Yamil and Miracle in their third-floor playroom. Sky always sat facing the entryway to the room, so when Kellogg pushed open the door, she immediately noticed and lowered the book. Yamil and Miracle, lying on their tummies, shimmied to attention, each taking a crouched position on either side of Sky.

Kellogg had cleaned up and put on fresh clothing, which was transforming in Sky's eyes. And though she reflected upon how she reacted to him initially, she was steadfast in her opinion of him.

"It's okay, boys," she said. "He was just leaving."

Kellogg did not take her cue, but rather advanced into the room stealthily, a slight smile etched across his face. "Whatcha reading to them?"

"That's none of your concern," she said. "And I think you heard me well enough when we were all downstairs that I didn't want you near these children. Not until you have earned our trust. I am tasked with taking care of them, and you'll have a different role in the community, one which you will be told soon enough. Because that's how it works here."

"I like a good story, though," Kellogg said, still smiling, but stopped halfway between the trio and the entryway door.

"Then go find a book and read it," Sky sneered. "We have a library on the second floor, you know."

Kellogg ignored her comment and closed the gap between them. He knelt before her and the boys, but only passed glances between the Yamil and Miracle, as if Sky wasn't there at all. "Do you guys like shiny things?"

Yamil revealed a grin that boasted a few missing teeth while Miracle clasped his hands together excitedly. Kellogg pulled a silver dollar coin from his pocket and held it before them. It was shiny and glimmered under the button light. It wasn't too often they saw coins. Money was useless in this world, not like toys, books, batteries, or guns, and so there was no occasion to have it on hand.

Kellogg twirled it round and round with his thumb and index finger. "There was a time when this was worth something."

After a brief silence he stood. "What do you eat around here?" he asked.

"Food," Sky retorted. "If you have any questions about the gardens or any of the operations of the fortress you can talk to the others. Now please excuse us so we can continue the story."

Kellogg nodded and left, and Sky continued with her story. It wasn't until a couple of hours later after she tucked the boys into bed that she crossed paths with Kellogg again as she was proceeding down the main stairwell from the third floor. Kellogg was going up the stairs, which made her curious, because aside from the annex where the younger boys played and slept, there was only Shark on the rooftop accessible through the attic space, and Teddy, Leo, and Flip's room, which was currently empty because they were among the larger group who were gathered on the first floor.

"Where are you going?" she asked.

"Can't I explore the house?" he asked. "Sim never suggested that I would be a prisoner, even though you wanted to questor me."

"The word is 'sequester' and it's just a single vacant bedroom, the playroom that you have already seen, and the attic'" she said, "which leads to the rooftop."

"Then I'll pay a visit to Shark," he said. "I haven't been to the roof yet."

"You know, when I first came here, I was afraid and anxious," Sky said. "I had begged my way in, and when Sim opened the door, I could hardly breathe. I could hardly move for days."

"What's your point?" Kellogg asked.

"Why are you here and what do you want?" she asked.

"The same things as you," he said.

"How on earth do you know what I want?" she asked coldly.

"Look," he said. "We may not see eye to eye, but I've already noticed not everybody does here. They handle you with gloves, that's for sure. King, like you, believes Ace is too much a kiss-ass, and Shark would rather spend full days on the rooftop than interact with anyone. Big Will wants nothing more than to open fire on someone...anyone. Baby has panic attacks at the sight of her own shadow, and Teddy is oblivious, as if he can't tell this new world from the old one."

If his intent was to rattle her cage, Sky did not take the bait. "It's a bit arrogant to think you know us all after a single day, but it makes me curious as to why you would even be focusing on our apparent weaknesses, not even considering that we are all on edge after a terrifying assault on our home last night, after which you conveniently emerged."

"It's not a coincidence," he said. "My home was attacked too. By the same people. Only the people I was with didn't survive."

Sky regarded him with curiosity, as if trying to read his inner thoughts. Could she be wrong about him?

"I'm sorry about that," she said. "But that doesn't mean I trust you."

The two locked eyes. Then JZ shouted up from the first floor, which distracted them. "I hear you up there! Are you coming down for conversation? Leo is telling us a days-gone-by story. 'The garden.' And turn off that light on the stairwell when you come down."

Sim was always after them to make sure lights were only turned on as needed to optimize battery life.

"Well," Sky said, "are you coming down for a story? You said you liked stories, after all."

"I do," he said. "I used to like fairy tales, but the only stories that make sense nowadays are tragedies."

"You haven't been here long enough, then," Sky said. "It's not always quite so chaotic. Normally everyone just follows Sim with obedience, and all is quiet."

Kellogg tilted his head, feigning curiosity about this girl who was everything but predictable. He reversed his course and followed her down to the first floor where everyone was gathered in the firelight save for Shark, and the little ones who were fast asleep.

Leo. Full of surprises. As he recited his story of the garden, overly anxious to reveal that it wasn't animals or marauders stealing the food they were growing, but him, consuming far more than his share, the mood became somber. It was as much a confession as a story, and of course Sim forgave him. He had learned that Leo, despite having a loving family in the other world, often hoarded food back then because his family had gone through rough times when they couldn't provide for his basic needs. He often came home from school to an empty refrigerator and cupboards. He had learned to take food when and wherever he could get it, even if he didn't need it.

"You know you wasn't gonna eat all that food," JZ remarked.

"He didn't," Sim said. "I found it all in the eastern corner of the property at one point, in a pit beyond Usland."

"And you didn't say anything?" Leo asked, slack jawed and squinty-eyed.

"I saw your annotation on the wall and knew one day *you* would tell *us*," Sim said.

"You didn't think it was a coincidence that we took you off food gathering detail," Ace laughed.

Leo slapped himself on the forehead. "That's when you assigned me outhouse cleaning detail." He kicked into a fit of laughter as he put his hands on his thin belly, doubling over.

Everyone started to laugh as well. Of course, nobody knew what Leo had done up until that point except Sim and Ace.

Sim turned to Kellogg amidst the laughter. "I found everyone here except Sky, who found us. I know their stories. What of yours?"

Kellogg leaned his back against the wall. Sky crossed the floor and sat down underneath the window. She watched Kellogg closely, wanting to hear his story more than ever. The fire crackled in the fireplace.

Kellogg appeared frozen in time. The muscles in his face tensed as he shoved his hands into his pockets. "I died before."

Nobody responded. They only watched him struggle to find words.

"Before everyone," he said. "When I was ten, I was skating on Tomhannock Reservoir and fell through. I hardly remember the struggle to breathe, but I remember dying. It was actually...beautiful, but weird. Like looking through a kaleidoscope. Warmth, light, and lots of colors. Some that I've never seen before in this world. My sister, who died when she was a baby, came for me, but she wasn't a baby at all; she was like our age, yet I knew it was her. I knew it was real. They said I was dead for eight minutes."

"That's incredible," Ace said.

"I told my parents when they were dying, a short time after that experience, that Aubrey would come for them and it would be peaceful. It meant so much to them to know that I had crossed over and could tell them...I knew I wouldn't die with everyone else because it wouldn't make sense." He scanned the room. "I was meant to live."

"Why?" Sky asked.

"Because some of us are," Kellogg said. "I lived because I've already died."

"Inspirational," Sim said. "But let's not get cocky. You are flesh and blood and like everyone else, are vulnerable as anyone."

"Wasn't the world always dangerous?" he asked.

Sim nodded. "Yes, it was, but at least rules and laws used to protect us. Now, we have only ourselves to rely on for that. That's why we live as we do."

There was no point to argue this. The world was much more dangerous than it had been, as people didn't behave for the sake of it. People were only as good as they needed to be in many cases, but not all.

That night, while everyone slept except Misty, Flip, and King, who were on rotational guard duty, Kellogg slipped out through the basement door and crossed the green lot, went past the garden, and to the tree line. Once confident he had eluded the watchers, he traveled down the empty street on which the fortress sat, turned onto another road that connected to it, and made his way halfway across the Troy-Menands bridge which passed over the Hudson River. There waiting were Zagan, Steer, and the cereal boy. They were sitting on the rails of the green bridge, the moon the only source of light in the darkness. Zagan stood when Kellogg arrived and spread out his arms as if to welcome an old friend he hadn't seen in years.

"Dear Kellogg," he said. "How was your first day in this...fortress? I'm wondering how true the rumors are that brought us here."

Kellogg shrugged. "Interesting."

Zagan offered a curious look to Steer and cereal boy, a kid in his late teens, perhaps a little older than Ace, Kellogg surmised. "Do tell."

"For one thing," Kellogg said, "I'll probably be killed when I get back. At least one of them suspects I'm a plant and always has her eyes on me. They have guards alert around the clock, a rooftop sniper at the ready, about a dozen others trained to fight and kill, and a fortified house made of solid brick and stone."

Zagan looked at his soldier again over his shoulders. "Did I tell you this kid was a genius?" He put his hands on Kellogg's shoulders and shouted. "A fucking genius! Are they all young? Who leads them? What is their mission? I need to know everything."

Kellogg shook his head, not impressed with Zagan's flattery. "In my opinion, this goal of yours is not worth it. They are secured, and though I didn't see any type of arsenal, I suspect they have a strong one somewhere in the house. They have high ground, which means they can see you coming from a mile away and even if they don't see you coming, they still have the advantage. What is the point of all this?"

Zagan's smiled faded and his eyes turned feral. "Don't tell me you are falling in love with them already," he said.

Steer took to Zagan's right side and pulled back the hammer on a revolver he was holding. Kellogg could hear the river flowing and thought for a second that they might shoot him and hurl him over the side of the trestle bridge and watch his body be swept away by the current. He was terrified but was obliged to seem otherwise.

"Let's get something straight," Kellogg said. "I'm not in love with them. But I'm not in love with *you,* either."

Zagan's eyes narrowed, and he peered at the boy, and Kellogg thought this would be his last moment on earth. Though, he had been dead before, so at least he knew what to expect. In fact, he started to think about how a bullet might feel in his gut or in his head. How the cold river water would feel on his body, or rather the cold concrete if they decided to leave him there instead of pitching him into the water.

Instead, though, Zagan started to laugh hysterically. This gave cause for Steer to laugh as he tucked his revolver into his waistband.

"You are too much, kid!" Zagan said. "You slay me, in fact."

Instead of a bullet to his gut, Zagan offered a surprise punch. A solid right undercut to Kellogg's abdomen that sent him hurling to the ground, coughing and struggling to find his breath. As he attempted to recover, Zagan kicked him in the face with his booted foot and Kellogg fell hard onto his back. He lay there still, a rag doll, peering into the night sky, not feeling the pain. Not caring if it was his time. After all, the anticipation of death was scarier than death itself.

Zagan knelt before him and whispered. "The point I was going to make, dear Kellogg, was that love has nothing to do with this. Love is dead. And if someone suggests otherwise, he must also die. Because where there is love, there is someone who pretends, and I'm not one for living in fantasy. Me. I am reality." He stretched his long neck backward, and like a coyote baying at the moon he screamed. "I am reality!"

Steer stepped over to where Kellogg lay on the ground and yanked him up to his feet. Kellogg could feel the blood running from his forehead. It was pouring into his eyes. His legs were weak. Cereal Boy took to Kellogg's other side, and he and Steer held him up so he would not collapse.

Zagan positioned himself so that he was only an inch away from Kellogg's blood-soaked face. Kellogg could feel Zagan's hot breath on him. It stank of death. "I will see you here in two days, my friend. And if you don't show with more information on their arsenal and fortifications, I will hunt you down. I will spare no man finding you, and I will tear you apart limb by limb. Then my men will feast on your corpse after we turn it on a spit over a raging fire."

Zagan wound up and threw another fist into Kellogg's soft face. Kellogg offered a moan as Steer and the other soldier let go of his body. The boy dropped to the ground with a thud and the trio disappeared into the night.

Kellogg listened to the water some more. *Mom. Dad. Aubrey.* The fall wind whipped at his face as tears spilled from his eyes. Or was it blood? Then he noticed the stars. Millions of them. Like the people of long ago. Dancing. Sparkling. The universe was forgiving. The world, not so much. His pretend confidence did not stand the test of time, but he had had a good run.

He had no intention of moving. He had every intention of lying there watching the stars until they were no more; though, he didn't think this would happen as the result of a couple of punches to his little body, but perhaps in two days when Zagan returned. He could rest until then. On the bridge. In the cold. Maybe he would freeze or starve.

But then a face appeared over him. She offered a look that was a cross between pity and betrayal. She tried to pull him from the concrete, but he resisted.

"No, please, Sky," he said. "Kill me."

Sky sat down beside him and leaned her back against the rail. "I will do no such thing."

"I wanted to die again with the virus, you know," Kellogg said as he began to wail. "With my mom and dad." He cried out to the stars. "Why the fuck did I live after I drowned? For this?"

Sky slid her hand down Kellogg's frail arm and found one of his limp hands. She took it into her own. It was ice cold. She said nothing.

"You know why I came into your room today?" he said, spitting blood from his mouth. "I wanted to see you. That's all."

Had he been looking at Sky, he would have seen her smile. "So, you were trying to steal my heart with your silver dollar?"

He laughed through a coughing fit.

"You can leave me here, Sky," he said. "The coin is in my pocket. You can have it. My mother gave it to me on my tenth birthday. For luck." He offered another short laugh. "And two days later, I drowned. And three months after that, my parents died."

"It sounds more like a curse to me," Sky said. "And this is the coin you wish to give me?"

"I believe in it, though. There is still time...for it to be lucky," he said.

"Then it will remain yours," Sky said. "Until that day comes."

He turned away from the stars for the first time to look at Sky. "I'm sorry."

Sky shook her head. "I'm just glad I was right. Sim simply doesn't understand teenagers. I don't know if he understands himself. He probably wishes we were eternally ten years old. Or that everyone was like Ace, following his every little command without question."

"Maybe together we can turn him around," Kellogg said, wincing through pain, shivering through the temperature.

Sky then said, "I know why you lived back then."

Kellogg shivered and his lips trembled. "Why?"

She turned to him and smiled. "Because you are the fortress, and the fortress shall be you."

Kellogg cried, but his body warmed as his spirit made noise from deep within, firing with electricity like a car starting in the middle of winter.

Nine

THE NEXT MORNING, WHILE Baby was scratching another tally on the wall downstairs, and after Sky wrote "into the night" as an annotation on the days-gone-by wall, Kellogg was recovering from his beating in Ace and Shark's room. He was in Shark's bed and a small fire was alight in the fireplace. Next to the bed was a nightstand with a bowl of vegetable soup sitting on top. Sim paced the floor but stopped when he saw Kellogg stirring. Ace and King were also there, and Sky soon entered.

Kellogg swished his eyes back and forth from face to face, unable to decipher the mood of the older children who stared back at him blankly. He assumed they were unhappy with him, and though he should have felt guilty about this, he did not, as he never expected to return. He had accepted a fate on the bridge that would not be realized because Sky had dragged him back.

"Look, I've already been beaten and never expected to come back. I accepted death on the bridge last night and so there is nothing more you can—"

Sim held up a hand. "Stop," he said. "Let's not think about what's done. Let's think about what happens next."

"That wasn't my thought," King said, stepping closer to the bed so he was hovering over Kellogg.

"Maybe you'll listen to me more closely next time," Sky said.

"Who is he?" Sim asked Kellogg, ignoring Sky's comment.

"Shouldn't we allow him time to eat and rest more before we interrogate him?" Sky asked.

"This coming from the one who wanted to kill him the second he entered the fortress yesterday," said Ace.

"We do this now," King said, poised to throttle Kellogg even in his weakened state.

"So, who is he, then?" Sim restated, not with impatience, but urgency.

"He's just some crazy-ass guy," Kellogg said. "He wants to take this place down for no apparent reason than for the thrill of it. He's got a crew. I don't know how many."

"Well, you'll make up for what you've done by telling us everything you know about him."

"I only met him two days ago!" Kellogg said. "What I told you was the truth. He dragged me and the people I was traveling with out of the home we were using not too far from here. His men ransacked it, burnt it, stole Frosted Flakes, and killed everyone I was with. The only reason he kept me was because I was a kid, and he thought he could use me to—"

"We know the rest," Sim said. "So, he stills plans to keep with this hit-and-run game?"

"Yes, he does," Kellogg said. "I told you, he's crazy."

"This doesn't make sense," Ace said. "He could do any number of things to interrupt our livelihood without having to plan an invasion. He could catch us on runs, burn down our fruit trees and gardens, or even sabotage our well."

"He may, at that." Sky said.

"The well is secured, so we would know if anyone tampered with that." Sim rationalized. "And the basement garden will provide ample staples if they disrupt our outdoor production flow."

"The storage pantry is full because we already prepared for winter," King said.

"I told you we should have walled this place in a long time ago," Ace said.

"Doing so would have simply drawn unwanted attention to us," Sim retorted. "We've been over this."

"Because *us* being here is such a big secret," King responded.

"If it were your personal idea, Sim, we would have had the wall done in a month," Sky said.

"Enough is enough, Sky," Sim said. "You're exhausting me. It's a moot point now because we can't build a wall around the fortress overnight. We've done plenty to prepare ourselves against this threat. Anything more we can do in the months or years to come to better position ourselves here we can discuss after we deal with this lunatic."

"Maybe he just wants to play games," Ace said. "We could always go to the heights for a while until this all blows over. He won't pay the fortress any mind if there is nobody here to antagonize."

Everyone in the room turned and stared at him quizzically. Even Kellogg.

"We stay here," Sim said. "This is where I need to protect you. It's your home."

"Isn't that *our* choice?" Sky asked.

Sim ran his hands through his hair, which is something he did commonly when he was frustrated. He ran his hands through his hair a lot when talking with Sky. He rarely yelled. He rarely perpetuated a power struggle. "Yes, Sky! Yes. You have a choice. But I'm begging you to always let your choice be the fortress. No matter what. That's the pledge!"

"You just better hope Zagan doesn't keep at this," Kellogg said. "He's dangerous."

Sim spun around and put his hands on the bed's footrest. He arched his body over the bed. "Zagan?"

"Yes, that's the whack-ass name he gave himself. He's evil. I'm telling you. Scares the hell out of me."

Sim's eyes bulged. He stroked his neatly trimmed goatee in thought.

"What?" Ace asked.

"I knew a man, once," Sim said solemnly. "It couldn't be, though...could it?"

"You knew a man named Zagan?" Sky said. "It couldn't possibly be a coincidence. How many people are named Zagan?"

Sim shook his head. "I served with a man who called himself that."

"You were in the military?" Ace asked. "That explains a lot."

"Let's pretend that it *is* him," King remarked. "What do you know about him?"

Sim pushed off the bed rail and continued his pace around the room. "He won't use cheap tactics to take us down. Nothing short of a glorious assault and victory over this place will suffice for him. Which would explain why he doesn't want to take shortcuts. That could be a good thing for us. We can exploit his egotistical mindset. Plus, once he finds out I'm the one running things here, it's only going to encourage him more."

"Can I eat my soup now?" Kellogg asked.

"Shut up!" King snarled. "Or I'll dump it over your head."

"Why don't you have Florence Nightingale over here feed it to you," Ace said.

"Stuff it, Ace," Sky seethed. "It was me who told you numb nuts right from the start about this boy and now this nutjob knows everything about us."

"He doesn't know anything that he didn't already know," Kellogg defended. "That's why he beat me up. I could have told him where your cache of weapons is stored, or about your indoor gardens or well. I tried to persuade him to leave, in fact. He wasn't overly obliging to that idea."

"Bringing you back was the best thing we could have done," Sim said.

"We?" Sky said. *A simple thank you would be nice.*

Sim eyed Sky and then retrained his thoughts. "Zagan will still think you are providing him with real intelligence, and he has no idea about my identity, so that also gives us an upper hand. Maybe when you go back to meet him, we can take him out at the bridge and end things quickly. His men will be nothing without him."

"Go back?" Kellogg said. "Are you nuts? He threatened to make me the center of some ceremony and tear me into pieces and eat me after putting me on a spit over fire."

"He's a cannibal, too?" Sky put her hand to her heart.

"He's just trying to scare you," King said. "Don't be a pussy. Even Big Will would go if you gave him the chance."

"Big Will is as crazy as Zagan," Kellogg said.

"Don't worry," Sim said. "We'll be right there with you the whole time. All Shark will need is one good shot."

Kellogg swallowed hard. "That's all Zagan will need too."

"Wasn't it just you telling us that you didn't expect to live?" Sim asked. "That you considered yourself dead on that bridge last night?"

"Well, that was before I knew you weren't going to kill me," Kellogg said. "Now I want to live."

"Everyone here has to vet someone," Sim said. "This situation is no less dangerous than any other orphan had it when their turn came to face the music."

"What does this man even care about our home?" Ace said.

"Okay!" Kellogg said, pounding his balled-up hands into the mattress. "But if I do this, it will prove my loyalty once and for all and nobody will ever doubt me again."

"Well," Ace said. "It'll be a step in the right direction."

"Risking death and having my body eaten over a campfire for a step in the right direction hardly seems worth it." Kellogg crossed his arms and pouted.

"Just start inventing your script for the next meeting," King said. "We'll take care of the rest."

"And if you kill someone at the meet, you'll get to add a handprint to our fortress flag," Sky mocked as Sim passed her leaving. "We sure enough aren't inviting Zagan back to our home."

"What?" Kellogg said. "What kind of sick place is this?"

"The nicest sick place you'll ever be," Sky said.

"Will you stay and help me with my soup?" Kellogg asked.

Sky curled her lip. "There's nothing wrong with your hands or arms, boy, and I'm still angry at you, so do it yourself."

Ten

Sim found yet another boy at a shelter for animals four months into his search. He barely recognized him as a person, as he was dirty, emaciated, and curled up into a fetal position alongside a large brown retriever.

The boy was asleep when Sim arrived, and Sim waited patiently thinking how peaceful the boy was among the animal. He couldn't be more than six and was sucking his thumb. Sim could hear the swishing sound of the saliva in the boy's mouth as he marinated his own thumb, surely soothed. It was heartbreaking for Sim to watch, but he felt a surge of happiness that he would be able to make things right again for this child.

The retriever licked the boy's face while he slept, as if he was one of her pups. This was also endearing and if the boy had slept forever more, Sim would have watched him 'til the end of time in this state, thinking of days when sleep was a way to rest the body and not a way to escape the world.

The boy woke up eventually, and right away he spotted Sim, who was staring at him intently with an endearing smile. He didn't speak and though the dog showed little defensiveness over her charge when Sim arrived, she must have sensed the boy's growing anxiety because she immediately started barking ferociously after the boy saw Sim. She bared her teeth and growled fiercely. There were other dogs in the facility that started to bark and yelp from their cages in response to the retriever's cries.

"Easy," Sim said. Though he wasn't sure if he was talking to the dog or the boy.

The boy rubbed the sleep from his eyes and scurried to a seated position on the floor. He wrapped his stubby arms around the retriever. "It's okay, Gigi," he said.

"Is that what you named her?" Sim asked.

"I can't find my mommy," he said. "She has brown hair and is taller than me."

Sim wanted to cry, of course, but he would not. "She sounds beautiful."

He swished air from cheek to little cheek. "She worked here. I came to look for her, but nobody was here."

"Lots of people are not here anymore," Sim said. "But I'm here."

"Who are you?" the boy asked, letting go of his hold around Gigi's neck.

"I'm Sim. What is your name?"

"William," he offered. He then scooped a handful of dog food from Gigi's bowl and shoved it into his mouth.

"You amaze me, William," Sim said.

"Why?" he asked, crunching down on the hard food. He scooped up another handful and fed it to Gigi.

"You are a strong fortress. Will you live with me?"

William tilted his head, curious. "Do you know my mom?"

"No," Sim said, tears welling in his eyes. "But she would want you to go with me. I know that much."

"Why are you crying?" William asked, not understanding the heartbreak.

"Because I am happy I found you," Sim said. "I was meant to find you."

"You were?" William looked at him crookedly. "Were you looking for me?"

"No," Sim said, drying his tears with the sleeve of his long coat. "But I want you to come with me."

Sim remembered his daughter, Sara, every time he found a new child and it was like finding her spirit each time. She lived on, despite his careless actions. He couldn't change the past, though. He could only believe that Sara was pointing the way to the children he found. She had to be. Perhaps Elizabeth was with her as well and they were playing together in heavenly peace.

"Can I bring Gigi?" William asked.

"Sure, you can," Sim said, never having been presented with the notion of entertaining a pet at the fortress, but there was no way he was going to get William without Gigi.

"What about the other doggies?" William asked. "There are lots of animals here. I feed them every day and talk to them."

"Well, William," Sim said. "It may just be time to set them free and let them discover the world for themselves."

That is what they did. They released the cats and dogs from their cages and all except Gigi scampered and darted off into the twilight. Sim knew that many of them would die, but it was not unlike how the lives of humans played out. Those that were meant to live, would, and the others would embrace another world.

Sim carried William on his shoulders the whole way back and William was enthralled. He laughed and called to Gigi from his human pedestal and was delighted.

As time went on and William became comfortable at the fortress, Sim began introducing his orphans to the variety of weapons that he had on hand to be used in defense of their home. There were all kinds, as Sim and Elizabeth scoured for weapons at his former military installation, police stations, private homes, and anywhere else he thought of to get his hands on artillery, including dynamite, C4, and other explosive devices that he could use in the name of self-defense. He tried to deter William from going with an AK-47, but the little guy was insistent. He let Gigi pick it out, which might be part of the reason. She kept barking every time she reached the AK-47 sprawled out on the ground with all the other options.

"I get it, William," Sim said. "Gigi likes it. But look at the thing. It'll knock you on your bottom. You don't even know."

"I can try it," William insisted. "If I train with it, I can learn."

Sim shook his head and allowed William to practice with the weapon. Of course, William had no idea how to control the thing when he started firing with it and bullets whizzed everywhere as the gun spun him around in every direction. But William stuck to it day after day and slowly it was him who began to control the gun. Replenishing ammo for it was the tricky part, but when Sim found it, it was in a police evidence locker along with loads of ammunition, so they had plenty, since it didn't get regular use.

William didn't even use it for his first vetting, which earned him his handprint. He used a revolver. A man came knocking at their front door and William, seeing through the window that the man had a gun of his own clutched in one of his hands, ever so casually opened it, fired a shot between the man's eyes before the man had time to utter a word, then slammed the door shut as the man's lifeless body crumpled down the stairs.

"Jesus, Will," Ace said as he turned to Sim, who was equally stunned. "Didn't you say he was sucking his thumb and eating dog food out of a bowl when you found him?"

"That he was," Sim said. "I guess we won't be sending him to the heights."

"I still suck my thumb," William said, handing the revolver back over to Sim. "But the name is *Big* Will. Now where's my *real* gun?"

Eleven

THEY WERE PREPARING FOR the meet up and everyone was on edge. Baby, Flip, Misty, Teddy, and Leo were the least concerned, devoting their attention to a card game while the others got ready to leave. Big Will, the resident doorman, of course argued about being left behind.

"You're needed to guard the house with JZ," Sim said. "Plus, you know if you leave, Gigi will go nuts and be heard half a world over."

Gigi whimpered as if understanding what Sim said and Big Will patted her head. "It's okay, girl. I know it's cuz you love me."

Kellogg was the most nervous of all and he didn't make any bones about letting everyone know. "My heart is pounding. Can you hear it?"

"You've already died, Kellogg," King reminded. "So, it's not like you lack any experience with the worst-case scenario."

"I don't want to die again," he whined. "I mean, I did want to die the other day, but that was then. But now, I want to live."

"I don't know how you survived two minutes out there with that whacko, let alone two encounters, quite honestly," King said. "I probably would have killed you the second you opened your mouth."

"Because I pretended. I'm a hack. That's all. Plus, I was in shock when I first met him and I don't even think I knew what I was doing. Sort of like I was on autopilot."

"It's fine, Kellogg," Sim reassured. "Zagan won't be there for an hour. Me, King, Shark, and Ace are leaving now and we'll be well planted under the cover of darkness by the time you get there, no more than 100 feet away on the hill overlooking the bridge. Just keep it cool and as soon as Shark shoots, you hightail it out of there."

Sky appeared with Kellogg's coin in hand. "Don't forget this," she said.

Kellogg regarded it warily. "I don't know, Sky. Are you trying to kill me?"

"Shut up and grow up," she chided, stuffing the coin into his pants pocket. "What happened to that boy who survived three years of this hell on his own? Who so boldly crossed the threshold of my room fully well knowing I had it in for you? And the boy that sneaked out into the middle of the night to meet a cannibalistic madman on his own? That's who you need to be right now."

Kellogg made himself rigid. "Okay then. Actually, I'm not leaving quite yet. But it was a good pep talk, Sky."

She eyed him crossly as the others prepared to leave. "We'll see you soon."

Baby ran up to Sim and he lifted her into the air. "Why do you have to go? The others are cheating at the game. Shall I use my knives on them?"

"My God," Ace said. "You created a monster." Ace teased her blonde locks, which were a mess with tangles. "We only stab enemies, Baby. Not housemates."

"We'll do your hair when I get back," Sim said.

"You see, this is why we need a mother here," Ace said. "Sim doing hair...it just doesn't fit."

"True, it wasn't what I envisioned my grand purpose to be," he said. "But I had daughter once."

Until you killed her.

"What am I?" Sky asked. "Chopped liver?"

"You only like little ones," King said, smiling his wide-mouthed grin that boasted a browning front tooth. "I need a mother too, you know."

"I'll bet you do," she said.

Sim placed Baby softly on the ground and ushered her back to the card game. He then set off with his oldest boys to position themselves for the kill that would end this feud.

Big Will opened and shut the door behind them and Gigi whimpered as she usually did when people left the fortress. Gigi knew as well as regular people what kind of world it was, and that leaving could mean never returning.

Sky and Kellogg went over to the card game and played a few rounds with the middle children. They laughed, accused each other of cheating, and Teddy stripped off his shirt and was sticking the cards to the sweat on his armpits causing everyone to turn green, while Misty insisted on trying to keep the game organized by reminding everyone of when their turn was. In the corner, Yamil and Miracle played patty cake until Flip grabbed Miracle and rolled around with him on the floor as if he were a stuffed toy. Miracle laughed of course and it was the perfect evening for them. The older orphans did not reveal to them much of what was going on. Only Big Will and JZ were aware that there was a mission.

JZ watched them depart from the third floor and tracked them as far as she could, all the way down the barren street to the intersection and around the turn off to the trestle bridge. She sighed when she lost sight of them. From the window, she could see pieces of the river glimmering in the moonlight, but not the bridge. She pulled up a chair to the window and cracked it open so she could hear. It was one of the few windows that hadn't been broken during the previous assaults. Now all she had to do was wait for the single shot.

Misty came in as JZ anxiously stewed in her chair, staring into the darkness.

"They'll be fine," Misty said. "They're always fine."

JZ turned to her and smiled awkwardly. "You gave up on cards?"

"It's a zoo down there," she said. "Too many boys and they all need a bath."

"Do you really think it'll be that simple?" JZ asked, her hands folded together tightly on her lap. "One shot?"

Misty shrugged. "They didn't tell me much about what they're doing, so it's hard for me to say. But I can say that things do work out the way they are supposed to. I remember my father always worrying about how he was going to pay the bills. But he always figured it out. In the beginning of each month, he was angry, but by the end of the month he was laughing and planning big trips for us to take. I remember one of those trips to Niagara Falls. It was so cool. The falls lit up at night in all the different colors."

"Shoot, I never went nowhere outside of here," JZ said. "I did go to the hair and nails place a lot with my auntie and I had me my own smart phone. I would always see these places on the Internet and thought how cool it would be to go there."

"You would have gone many places," Misty said. "Had the world lasted long enough. You can still go one day. Because even the death of man doesn't stop the waterfalls from flowing."

"But what about those lights?" she asked.

"You'll see them in your head," Misty said. "I see them now."

JZ smiled. And she too could see them.

Kellogg left the fortress on his own once again, careful to leave through the basement even though there was hardly any need to be secretive for the sake of those at the fortress. If Zagan suspected a setup, however, he might have scouts watching the fortress, so Sim felt it was best to keep Kellogg doing what he had previously done to leave the fortress under cover.

Kellogg played the part well too. He ducked and shimmied and crossed the field as if avoiding detection from the guards who were not even there because they were set up near the bridge waiting for Zagan. Kellogg didn't know how to feel about being so close to where all the action was going to go down. He didn't feel ready to see a man's face blown off right in front of him. He had been around death since this new world unfolded, but rarely up close. And what if Shark missed? That thought caused him more anxiousness than the idea of seeing a man's life snuffed out before his eyes.

He popped out of the tree line at the bottom of the hilly street toward the intersection. As he walked that stretch of road away from the fortress, he turned back and wondered if Sky was watching him. Once he got to the intersection, he paused and regarded the fortress, an impressively massive structure that shadowed all the other rundown homes that dotted the street.

This is it. The end of the day or the end of me. He wasn't a fool. He knew it could go either way, but he had people who would miss him now, and that made him feel somewhat complete and more anxious to do his part. He felt the bruises on his face and head, still raw and hurting, and it made him think of the man who put them there. He never saw it coming. He thought he could say and do anything in the name of confidence and that he would be celebrated because Zagan had said such nice things about him, until he didn't get what he wanted.

As Kellogg approached the bridge, he could hear the river flowing and it sounded as cold as it did two days before, though the air temperature seemed a bit warmer. He moved across it confidently, not wishing to appear hesitant, which could tip Zagan off that something was amiss. He waited at the halfway point and then leaned over the rail staring into the void. The sky was black. The Hudson was black and the tree line where Shark was waiting to kill Zagan was equally dark and foreboding. Earlier, Shark had showed him how his night vision scope worked to reassure him that he could still see to shoot even at night.

Come on, come on. Where are you? How the hell did you think I would explain all these bloodied bruises and cuts on my face in going back to the fortress? As this thought crossed his mind, he saw them appear from the same direction from which he had just traveled. Three of them again. He immediately recognized Steer, the large beefy bald man with a face that looked like granite. Black eyes. Nothing behind them. Zagan was in the middle, his wild gray beard a giveaway. And then there was Cereal Boy.

The encounter felt different from the previous one, and he couldn't tell if it was because he knew it was something more or because he was preoccupied thinking that *they* knew something more. How could they, though?

The trio stopped about fifty feet away, only after taking a few steps onto the bridge. This was strange to Kellogg, of course, and he prepared himself to bolt in the other direction if anything went awry. He dared to say not a word because last time he opened his big mouth he was pummeled for it. Tenderized.

"Glad you could make it," Zagan yelled. "Why don't you come down here, off the bridge."

"Why?" Kellogg yelled back. "This is where we agreed to meet. You can see this bridge from the third floor on the fortress and I, for one, do not want to be spotted by them talking with you. I'm standing in the only blind spot, and I know this for a fact," he lied.

Their voices echoed through the air, and it reminded him of when he went to the Grand Canyon and how his voice sounded trapped every time he spoke. It was haunting hearing your own voice bounce around, frantically trying to escape the world. There was something unnatural about it.

"The breeze off the river was a bit too chilly for me last time," Zagan hollered. "We'll take our chances."

"I don't trust you," Kellogg said. "Not after the other night. I'm exactly where I said I would be, so if you want the information I have, you'll come here."

"You drive a hard bargain, Kellogg," Zagan said. "But that's why I like you!"

The trio embarked onto the bridge and continued forward, which relieved Kellogg because he was certain Shark was in a position that aligned with Zagan being *on* the bridge, not at the edge of the bridge.

One shot.

As the men got closer, time seemed to stop, like slow motion video capture. With every new step, it became clearer to Kellogg that the men were decoys. Too late to do anything about it, however. They stopped a few feet away from Kellogg and they must have noticed him staring at them crookedly.

"Don't worry about us," said the Zagan lookalike. "We just wanted to make sure you didn't have any tricks up your sleeve. Zagan will be right along, and we'll get down to business."

Oh fuck. Oh fuck. Kellogg turned helplessly to the tree line to offer some sort of signal but had no idea exactly where Shark had taken up. And what would he do anyway to alert Shark that this was not the real Zagan? The decoy looked as Kellogg had described him to the others.

He had no time to consider the epic fail this night would assuredly be because the shot came like a lightning bolt from a sudden storm. The bullet tore into the side of the fake Zagan's head and he was dead. The bigger guy who looked like Steer cursed under his breath and attacked Kellogg while the cereal boy decoy attempted to run. Another one of Shark's bullets cut the smaller one down before he could get off the bridge.

As Kellogg tried to fight off the Steerish-looking man, he could only imagine what was going through the mind of the real Zagan who was likely not too far away. Kellogg saw himself turning on a spit as he did his best to defend himself.

The man tackled him to the ground and his beefy body was on top of him in no time. Kellogg delivered a knee to the man's groin, which caused him to topple off him in a heap. Kellogg scurried to his feet and started to flee to the opposite end of the bridge toward the highway. The man got to his feet and gave chase and for a bigger guy, he was light on his feet. He soon caught up to Kellogg and thrust him into the rail and wrapped his meaty hands around Kellogg's tiny throat.

Kellogg thought of the lucky coin in his right-side pocket, and it reminded him of the knife that he had put into his other pocket before he left. He pulled the switchblade out, pressed the release button and jammed it into the man's thick abdomen. The man grunted but held his grip strong to Kellogg's neck. Kellogg pulled the knife out and thrust it back into the man's body. The man offered another grunt and Kellogg felt his grip loosen.

I'm winning! Then came the whiz of a bullet streaming through the night air. The projectile landed true, and the large man's forehead popped like a balloon that was filled with too much air. Blood and brain matter spattered across Kellogg's face and upper body. The man collapsed, but his grip, still taut around Kellogg's neck, did not loosen, and consequently Kellogg was pulled to the ground with him.

Kellogg remained there, examining the stars once again and felt it annoying that he ended up the same way as he did on the last encounter. Sim, King, Shark, and Ace rushed over to him from the trees, but it took them a few minutes to get there. He heard them coming, or so he hoped it was them, and decided to lie in wait until they arrived.

"Kellogg?" Sim yelled.

"Is he dead?" Ace asked.

"Fuck if I know," King said. "Who cares?"

"I'm not dead!" Kellogg bellowed. "Just get this fatso off me."

King and Ace grabbed him and pulled him off Kellogg.

"It all worked just according to plan," Shark boasted. "I guess it'll teach them to mess with us."

"It wasn't him," Kellogg said, holding his neck while pulling himself up with help from the bridge guardrail.

"What?" Sim said.

Kellogg pointed at the bearded man lying on his side ten steps away. "That's not Zagan. He was a decoy. I guess they prepared for the possibility of a trap."

"Well, where in the hell is the real 'Zagan'?" Ace asked.

Kellogg was attempting to brush the debris from his clothing, to no avail. "They said he was coming, but the next thing I know bullets came flying."

"So, if Zagan saw the trap sprung, he could know the fortress is not properly defended and decide to—"

Sim kicked into full speed back in the direction of the fortress. The others followed behind and didn't stop running until they returned. Big Will opened the door when he saw them approaching. They all stopped, out of breath when they saw Big Will and Gigi at the gate.

"So, is it over?" Big Will asked.

They were all relieved that Zagan had not exploited the situation by attacking while they were away, but they weren't clear as to whether Zagan observed the ambush. If he had, they assumed it would incite him further.

JZ appeared from behind Big Will, breathless, and behind her came all the middle children, including Sky.

"Thank goodness," JZ said. "I was so worried. I heard more than one shot from the bedroom."

"There were three guys," Shark said. "So, three shots."

"If that's what it took, then so be it," Sky said. She regarded Kellogg's brain-spattered clothing with an upturned lip. "Disgusting. But I guess it's good you're alive and this is over."

Sim glared at the group assembled at the doorway. He didn't have the heart to tell them they had failed. None of them did. Instead, they panted heavily and when they were sufficiently calm, they retreated inside and locked the doors behind them.

Twelve

STEER ENTERED THE SOUTH Troy Diner, a relic from years past, and found Zagan sitting at one of the dingy yellow tables, occupied long ago by patrons in need of eggs, bacon, or pancakes to start their day. He took his seat in the dusty booth at the other side of the table and waited for Zagan to snap out of a self-induced trance. He knew well of the dangers of waking Zagan while he was in the zone. Zagan's head was cocked back, his eyes fixated on the light hovering above the booth, seeing nothing but what was behind his eyes until finally he lowered his head.

"This used to be one of my favorite breakfast joints, Steer," he said quietly as he gazed longingly around the small dining room. The shoebox diner was once a staple of the small urban area, nestled on the river a mile from the bridge where Zagan narrowly escaped his demise.

Steer glimpsed around the place and then brought his attention back to Zagan. "It looks like it was a shithole."

Zagan lunged forward. "Exactly!" he yelled. "A greasy spoon. That's where you get *real* food. I remember the guy who owned it. Jimmy Stix. Fucking guy was hilarious and cooked a hell of an omelet, Steer. A hell of an omelet!" He relaxed back into his seat as he played with one of the old menus as if intending to order. "I suppose you liked Cracker Barrel or some shit like that."

"I hate breakfast," Steer uttered in monotone. "Greasy bacon and slimy eggs. And what the fuck is a grit, anyway?"

"Yes, well, it's a moot point now, I suppose."

"Everything is a moot point now," Steer said. "Then again, what was the point of life before?"

"A good breakfast," Zagan lamented as he breathed in a deep breath. "That's what I'm saying, Steer. Maybe all I needed in this new hell hole was this diner in good order with a line cook. Or a movie theater. A steak. One Goddamn thing, and everything else...forget it."

Steer pursed his thick lips while considering Zagan's words. Then he cautioned his friend. "It might not be too wise to speak public about how killing everyone in sight is the next best option to a good breakfast and scrolling through Facebook on your phone while you take a shit."

"I guess now I know how you spent *your* pre-apocalypse days," Zagan huffed as he leaned over the table. "Anyway, if I was meant to just sit back and eat eggs and bacon in this world, then there would be some to eat. No, not me. Me...I was chosen for what I am compelled to do. It's the only thing that makes sense, Steer, or I would have died with everyone else. I was spared to bring death and defeat to those who survived. To take away hope. To destroy what has been built back up and deliver this land into the hands of Satan. Whoever oversees that fortress on the hill will discover his final days in the wake of my wrath, along with all those who ally with him."

"How do you know a man is running the show over there?" Steer asked. "I mean, it would make more sense that it was a woman, being a caretaker to children and all."

Zagan considered this. "Could it be? No. The stories never mentioned a woman. It was always a man. A man and his small army of children who built a mighty stronghold upon a hill and whose gates they defend with deadly force and precision against the evil spirits who prowl about the world. Steer, this is a man. My antithesis. My ultimate purpose."

"And the children his," Steer reminded.

Zagan shook his head. "Children...the very word annoys me. Their purpose enrages me. Their myth vexes me."

"Speaking of children," Steer said, redirecting the conversation. "I guess you were right about Kellogg,"

"That I was, Steer," Zagan said. "Had I listened to you we would both be ugly dead right now. Each with a hole in our head. Thank God for willing decoys. One day in that happy home with that pied piper bastard is all it took to swipe away from me my ultimate spy. I guess the stories were true."

"In case you have forgotten, you did punch him in the stomach and kick him in the face," Steer reminded. "I don't suppose that helped in convincing him that Team Zagan was the way to go."

"I was mad, okay!" Zagan hissed, throwing the plastic menu card across the room. He would only accept such retort from Steer. "I get a little crazy when I'm mad. What can I say?"

"So, what next?" Steer asked.

"We get as creative as they are," Zagan said. "And we stick to the plan."

"We have at least seventy-five bored, depressed, angry men and women taking up shop at the steelworks building looking for some purpose," Steer said. "Most are a bunch of fucking rednecks, but a lot of them had their own guns and know how to hunt for food. They'll do whatever we say if we keep supplying them with booze."

"I guess they're too dumb to know there are a hundred liquor stores out there with shelves lined with alcohol. Maybe they all just want to serve a purpose."

"I think you're giving them too much credit," Steer said.

"Regardless, we need one hundred more," Zagan said. "Preferably men. Women will get one look at those orphans, and they'll turn against us. This siege has to be as glorious as the stories of this fortress, so that new stories are told throughout the lands, and I don't want anything getting in the way of my victory."

"Most of the women are there to distract the men," Steer said. "I didn't even count most of them in the seventy-five. And the ones I did are as fucking bat shit crazy as my ex-wife."

Zagan shook his head. "Ironic you say that, considering you are the one who strangled *her* to death as soon as you got word that the world was ending."

"I'm an opportunist," Steer laughed. "What can I say?"

Zagan laughed. "Nothing more."

"What if they track us to the steelworks?" Steer said. "These orphans are like rats. Clever rats, at that."

"They'll stay put," Zagan said. "That place is their Alamo. Which is a convenient comparison because that is exactly how I intend this story to end. It seems like they have everything they need right there, as if they had a magic fucking wand to make food, water, weapons, medicine, and anything else they desire appear without having to take two steps from the property. In the meantime, we have to dream about eggs and bacon and drink from the dirty river to stay alive." Zagan balled up his fist. "Anyway, we can keep that shitty steelworks as an outpost, but we need to relocate to a more ideal setting to house these people. Maybe to that school on First Street, or the prison, better yet."

"I'll send out a scouting party in the morning to search for a better encampment, as well as more weapons, and more men."

"You do that, Steer," Zagan said. "And when the scouting parties depart, come find me. I have a special job for you."

Zagan locked eyes with Steer and offered a most devious smile.

The next morning, everyone gathered in the living room so that they could witness Kellogg add his handprint to the mural. Sky begrudged having to pause her lessons with the younger and middle children, but she put up little fuss about it. Ace had taken the banner down from above the living room mantel and laid it across the hardwood floor. Baby brought the paints in and put them on the floor beside the banner, remembering her special day.

The mood was somber, as the group had navigated some of the toughest days and nights it had seen since the dawn of the new world. Ace still nursed a nasty chest wound, Kellogg's face was bruised and battered, and Big Will, along with Gigi, did not dare tear themselves away from the door. Nor did Shark leave his post.

On the roof, Shark kept a supply of homegrown fruits and vegetables to snack on during the long hours and pissed over the side as needed. He loved it up there. Sim didn't know if it was the serenity from being alone that appealed to him or being ever so much closer to the larger world, but the reason mattered less to Sim than Shark's contentedness. In fact, Shark had not opted to join the handprint ceremony and Sim did not press him to do so, given the events of the previous night. They were all on high alert.

Kellogg regarded the banner with wonder. Sky had already told him about Tak and Elizabeth, the two orphans handprinted and no longer with the group. It was a lesson that life in the fortress was not a free pass to escape the horrors of the new world. Perhaps that is what he was thinking. He had, after all, nearly escaped death himself and his treachery was out of the bag.

"Hey," Baby said. "How come nobody had to come down when *I* had my handprint on the banner?"

"A lot of us were here, Baby," Sim said. "But it was pretty chaotic with the attack."

"Don't be a baby, Baby." Teddy mocked. "When I got my handprint, only Sim was in the room, and I shot *my* intruder eight times. It was epic."

"Teddy," Sim said. "We aren't proud of killing, remember. That's not what this is about. And you wasted ammunition that day. I'm not even convinced you vetted him proper."

"He had a gun," Teddy reminded.

"It was a squirt gun," Sim reminded.

"It looked real," Teddy said.

"It's just a rite of passage," Misty said. "The movie stars used to get their handprints in concrete outside this theater in Hollywood. I went there once, you know. Most of the names I didn't recognize."

"But none of us here are famous," King said. "Not yet, anyway."

"More importantly," Sim said. "Each handprint is a story of having saved someone or protected us from those that would harm us."

"If you say so," Sky muttered. "Anyway, from what I understand, Kellogg here didn't even kill the man that was attacking him. Shark did. Plus, he never had a chance to vet him properly."

Kellogg looked upon her with insult. "I think it was safe to say that once the guy started choking me that he wasn't going to come live with us. Anyway, he was nearly dead when Shark shot him. I never asked Shark to blow his head off all over me. I would have preferred he not. I had gotten two good stabs in that would have surely done the job. Regardless of some bullet to the brain."

"Go ahead then and get your handprint on there already," Sky said. "Let's just hope in years to come when we become civilized again, you are all ready to explain the nature of this tapestry."

"History is never pretty," Sim said. "It's almost always forged in death, tyranny, destruction, murder, and mayhem. Take the Declaration of Independence: it was signed by men before they had even become free. Men who knew that if they lost the war that they would be hanged as traitors. Anyway, by the time the world becomes civilized again, we'll be long since dead, I'm sure. They'll debate our tapestry but will not be able to hold us accountable for it. Let them judge us if they want and without ever knowing what this world was like."

"We'll probably be dead by the end of the week after what we did to that lunatic out there," King said. "I can't even imagine how pissed he is right about now."

All the orphans turned to King and stared. The room became quiet.

King shrugged. "What?"

"Are we really going to die this week?" Baby asked. She clutched her chest. "Oh, God. I don't want to die."

"We aren't gonna die, Baby," Teddy pronounced. "We're gonna kick butt!"

Then Big Will stepped into the room from the foyer.

"I'm not going to let anything happen to you, Baby," he said. Gigi, as always, stood beside him, tongue out, panting. "I have this gun here. The biggest gun at the fortress. And I will shoot anyone who tries to get in."

"I'll open the door for you," Baby said, taking in deep breaths. "We're a team that way."

Big Will nodded. "There's something I never remembered to tell you, but I might as well share it now. It's on the wall where I wrote 'shelter story.'"

Misty and Teddy turned to the wall and, sure enough, the words were there on the timeline. He had etched them there some time ago.

"When I couldn't find mom, I went to where she worked. There were lots of dogs and cats. I took care of them. Fed them. Hugged them. All they had was me and all I had was them. But one day a man came in and he didn't see me, but he was really not nice to the animals. He was poking them through the cages with a stick and talking about how he was going to eat them. He was laughing and I was scared. But he didn't know I was there, so when he went into one of the big cages to fetch a scared dog, I locked it behind him. He wanted me to open it, but I said no. He tried to get me to let him out for a long time, but I wouldn't. And after a lot of days, he was quiet. He wasn't moving. But I fed the dog that was in there with him at night, while the guy slept, so even after the guy died, the dog was alive."

"Wow, Will," Sim said. "I never saw the remains of any person when I found you. I never knew."

"That's because the dog ate him after he died," Big Will said.

Sim cringed.

"This boy don't play," King said.

"How about we get down to this handprint business and be done with it," Ace said. "Go on then."

Kellogg shook his head, and then knelt, grabbed the paintbrush, and dipped it into the green paint that was contained on a small plate lying on the floor. He painted his hand and then affixed his print to the banner thereafter, then stood. Those who were in the room recited the pledge.

We, the orphans of the new world, pledge to: do our best, work together, defend our home, live and die for one another, love, lead, remember. We are the fortress, and the fortress is us.

As the pledge concluded, Sim placed his hand on one of Kellogg's shoulders. "You did good out there last night. Follow my lead, strictly, and you'll be fine."

Kellogg nodded and Sky headed for the stairwell. "I need Misty, Teddy, Flip, Baby, Big Will, JZ, and Leo to the library."

And so they went, packed into the second-floor room containing shelves of books and two tables with four seats at each one. It was where Sky generally conducted reading lessons, using the books they had collected from stores and homes. She would tell them that they mustn't become ignorant, and that if more stories were to be told, that they would have to be written, but before they could be written, the storytellers would have to know how to read and write.

Once the group had assembled, it was clear that one of them was missing. Flip was not accounted for in the roll call, and it raised an eyebrow because Flip was always the first one there, ready for lessons. Not Big Will, who, like Leo, was more interested in constructing things and figuring out how things worked; or JZ who would rather exercise, do her nails, or practice her axe throwing skill; or Teddy who could scarcely sit still for more than a few minutes; or Misty who loved art more than anything. Baby and Flip were the scholars, each one excelling quite naturally at reading and writing and loving every minute devoted to such studies.

Sky's biggest challenge with those two was keeping up on the books and finding more for them to read.

"Where the heck is Flip?" Sky asked.

Everyone looked around as if they might spot him in the corner or sitting like Rumpelstiltskin on top of a shelf.

"Hell if I know," Teddy said. "He wasn't with us downstairs either when Kellogg was stamping his hand on the mural."

Sky scratched her chin. "Come to think of it, you're right. Maybe he is on the roof with Shark and forgot what time it was."

"I'll run and see," Teddy said. Always the runner. When he reached the top through the attic he yelled back down from there. "There's something happening!"

Sky stepped to the entryway of the library. "What is it, Teddy?"

"Shark said there are people approaching from the bottom of the hill," Teddy screamed.

Sky then yelled down to the others. "We have company!"

Ace immediately took up to the east side of the house, as did King, who would normally be on the west side, but there was nobody approaching from that side. It wasn't like the other night, which was wild and chaotic. The men on this day approached slowly up the street from the intersection.

When they got close enough, Ace, King, and Sim saw what Shark had probably spotted through his binoculars seconds earlier.

Flip was at the forefront of the parade of men, the back of his neck clutched in the hands of a skinny man with a wild black and gray beard. Flip was wincing, but otherwise looked unharmed. The man who held him had a pistol in his other hand pointed into Flip's back.

As the men arrived at their doorstep, they spread out along the street, but remained in clear view. Each had a gun of some sort, a mix of pistols, rifles, and shotguns.

Kellogg, who had cracked open one of the shutters in the front of the house to peer out, took a step back when he recognized Zagan as the man holding Flip.

"It's him," Kellogg said, voice panicked, continuing his backward step until he hit a wall. "I mean it's *really* him this time!"

"Yes, it is," Sim said. "Yes, it is."

Sim backed against the wall and closed his eyes. He remembered the child he'd been and his days serving with Zagan in the Army and sucked in a few deep breaths to stave off a potential panic attack.

"So, you *do* know him," Ace said, peering through the cracks of the other front window shutter.

"King, tell everyone to report to the front of the house on their respective floors and be ready to fire if need be."

King dashed off rumbling. "We really need those damn walkies."

JZ arrived from the kitchen. "It's clear back there."

"How the hell did they get him?" Ace asked. "How the hell did they get Flip?"

"He must have broken a house rule," Sim stated matter-of-factly. "Same as Tak."

"What do we do now?" Big Will said.

"He's here to negotiate, clearly, and not engage a battle, so let's take first things first."

Sim made his way to the door and Baby put her hand on his arm. "I'm scared."

Sim smiled. "That's good, Baby. But it's not time to freeze up."

Baby let go of his arm and Sim opened the door. The morning light poured through the gate and washed the tiled floor with intense whiteness. With such a light in the world, Sim often wondered how there could be so much darkness.

He stood at the top of the concrete stairs with a hand on either side, observing the situation with much pity for Flip, who appeared deathly frightened, and it was right of him to feel this way.

Zagan stepped off to Flip's left side as Sim exited the fortress. *Too close to the house for Shark.* Big Will stood behind him, his AK-47 positioned to open fire. Gigi ran out and started barking at the intruders, but Sim hushed her.

"Well, as I live and fucking breathe," Zagan said, with a slight smile. "It cannot be you. All those stories. I would never have dreamed they were about you."

"It's me, David," Sim said.

Steer, who was on Flip's other side, turned his head from Sim to Zagan twice over, trying to understand the connection. Zagan was taken aback, like a deer in headlights. A rare state for him.

"I cannot fucking believe it," he said. "Actually, yes, I can."

Sim nodded. "Now how about we stop all this nonsense and go our own ways," Sim suggested. "You have life. I have life. We have both survived this awful catastrophe and many others before. Just let me do my part before the end."

Zagan laughed as he tightened his hand around Flip's neck. "You forget from those days in the shit...I *thrived* in awful catastrophe. I *am*...catastrophe."

"And I never judged you when others did," Sim reminded.

"That's true," Zagan said. "But still, just the sight of you." Zagan called out to his men, "We were in the middle of war. Our men dying in front of us all the time. All I wanted to do was kill those Hajis, and all *this* man wanted to do was play soccer and give candy and bubblegum cards to all their little shit kids. Until one of those...little...Hajis...blew his best friend to pieces...and here you are today. Still handing out candy and bubblegum cards during the shit."

"One thing has nothing to do with the other," Sim said.

"I think it does," Zagan said. "I think you know it does. Mister simulator. Do they all know how 'Sim' was born? Tell them how good you were at playing Call of Duty and winning games, but when it came time to go to war...not so good. Spineless, in fact. Did you ever even fire your weapon in those days? Christ, why did you even join?"

Sim kept his composure through Zagan's cage rattling. "If you're intent on going to battle over this place, you'll see how different things are now, as you may have already observed. I wanted to die not too long ago, Zagan, but I have a purpose to fulfill now in keeping these kids safe."

Zagan nodded. "You figured it out, then. Wow. Touching."

"I want my boy back," Sim said, changing the subject. "If you harm him, we'll shoot you all down like dogs in the street."

The random footmen that Zagan brought along with him stirred a bit, which was telling, but not surprising.

"Damn!" Zagan said. "You *have* changed. Maybe you actually can defend yourself and these...street urchins. Well, what about a little trade? Your boy, for my boy?"

Inside the fortress, Kellogg heard those haunting words echo, like his own in the night sky, and they still sounded trapped as if yearning to escape the world. He began to feel panicked, and Baby took his hand.

"I know how it feels," she said. "But Sim will protect you."

"He's not *your* boy," Sim said. "He's mine. I want my boy and then I want you to leave and never come back. I want you to do this because you don't know my world anymore. You never did. And I knew you in the other world. I did not hate you. You were you, and I was me, and afterward we would smile and nod in passing and remember those ugly days but keep them buried. We had respect and mutual understanding."

"You kept them buried," Zagan said solemnly. "I lived them. I live them. And unfortunately, as you see your current purpose in life as a grand protector, I see my purpose as that of a destruction artist. And it's not about good or bad. It's about seeing the world for what it is. Most everything was taken away, now I just want to finish the job." He offered a short laugh. "It's nothing personal, Sim."

"Then don't *make* it personal," Sim said, "by hurting my child."

"Then give me Kellogg!" Zagan yelled. "Give me mine and I will consider finding another town or city to shift my attention to. It's a win-win. After all, you tried to blow my head off last night, so I think the least you could do to honor this history you mention, is to give me Kellogg. I made promises to that boy that I want to keep."

Sim took in a few deep breaths and felt the warmth of the fall sun on his face. It wasn't a bad deal that Zagan was offering, though Sim understood that offering Kellogg to his old acquaintance would end in the boy's painful death. Even for someone as fresh to the fortress as Kellogg, it was impossible for Sim to negotiate such a deal.

Before Sim could utter a response, Kellogg appeared at his side. "I'll go."

"Yes," Zagan said. "A simple trade. For old time's sake. Then this is over."

Kellogg started down the stairs, but Sim grabbed his arm. He locked eyes with the boy who looked not frightened, but sad. "*You* are the fortress. And the fortress is *us*."

Then Flip did what he had been trained to do. What he had done to squirm out of a similar predicament with JZ a few days earlier. He raised his leg and brought the heel of his foot down on top of Zagan's foot, which caused the man to howl. Soon, a hail of gunfire rained down from all three floors of the fortress on the men and they fled like cockroaches for cover. Kellogg ran back into the house as Flip reached the stairs. Zagan was able to fire off a shot from his revolver as the boy fled, however, and the bullet ripped through Flip's back and he collapsed on the stairs. As the children continued cover fire and the men ran in varying directions, Sim ran down and slung Flip over his shoulder and got him back into the fortress.

"Flip!" yelled Baby. "No, Flip."

Flip was limp and Sim collapsed with him onto the tile floor. Sim took to a seated position on the floor and thrust Flip across his legs on his stomach. He turned up Flip's shirt and saw the small bullet wound between his shoulder blades, just as Flip began to cough and sputter.

"No," Sim cried.

Ace was watching out the window as the rest of the men fled, including Zagan and Steer. He ran to Sim's side as Flip lay there, coughing.

Sky came down the staircase in awe. Blood stained the tile in large pools and smears. Baby was crying.

"Get the others," Ace said.

Sky clutched her mouth and retreated. She returned with Leo, Misty, and Teddy. Everyone was gathered in the foyer, and Shark was the last to arrive, slow-stepping down the stairs, his face taut. Sim turned Flip over onto his back and brushed the sweaty hair from his eyes. JZ sat beside him and took his hand in hers. She could not hold back her tears.

Keep a child safe. Save a life.

"It almost worked," Flip said.

"Yes, it did, my boy," Sim said.

Sim found Flip at his house, which was nestled in a quaint rural area only a few miles from the urban center. In normal times, he had many provisions. His house was a raised ranch that sat on several acres of land that included a small pond with a dock. Sim hadn't been searching for children that day. He was looking for cows for milk, but happened to spot the boy doing all kinds of crazy flips and cannonballs off the dock into the water. Sim watched him for a while before approaching. The boy was drying off with a towel at that time and from afar, nothing seemed amiss with this child's life. It was as if the death of the world had not yet found him. Maybe his parents were in the house cooking dinner. It seemed possible.

Sim hollered to him from across the pond, not wanting to alarm him by getting too close, too soon. "Hello there."

The boy wrapped his towel around his waist. His body was thin, and Sim could see his ribcage protruding from his small torso. His parents were not cooking dinner, Sim decided. The boy appeared not to be alarmed or suspicious.

"Can I help you?" he asked.

"Are you...okay?" Sim asked.

"My parents are inside with my brother. We're all fine."

Sim knew this couldn't be true. Statistically, it was impossible to believe that his entire family was spared from the fate of the world. "Can I come in and see, just to make sure? Or maybe have your mom or dad come out here so I know."

"They don't like to come out," the boy said. "They think it's in the air. They haven't gone out since people started dying."

"But they let their small child out?" Sim responded.

The boy eyed him curiously, partly annoyed. "What do you want?"

"I want to offer you a safe place to live," Sim said. "A home. I'm bringing lots of children there and we are going to live together."

"I can't," the boy said.

"Why?" Sim persisted.

The boy shook his head. "I just can't." He then turned away from Sim and walked back to his house.

Sim understood that something was not right, so he proceeded around the pond and back to the boy's house. He knocked softly on the door and waited, thinking what a lovely house this was, out of the way and perhaps a sanctuary of its own. Until the wrong person found it. There was always someone looking. Scavengers. Pillagers. Heathens.

The boy cracked open the door and peered at Sim through that small space. His brown eyes spoke curiosity, fear, and wonder. "I told you—"

"I know what you told me," Sim interrupted. "But that's a lie. I only want to help. Believe me. For certain, the wrong people are going to come soon enough, and they won't knock first."

The boy opened the door and led him into a first-floor bedroom. There, lying in the bed was a young boy of four or five, nestled under the covers, a stuffed dog tucked under his arm. He looked ghostly white, was bloated, sweaty, and his eyes were closed.

"Is it the virus?" Sim asked.

"He has the same symptoms of my mom and dad before *they* died, but he didn't get sick right away. I thought he might be like me."

"I'm sorry," Sim said. "When did your parents die?"

"Two weeks ago," the boy said sadly. "I was taking care of Sam and for a while it was working fine, and then he got sick, and we ran out of food."

"He looks near the end," Sim said.

The boy nodded. "He's my best friend."

Sim locked eyes with the boy. "You did the best you could. Better than I ever did with my own daughter. Can I wait with you for a few days, and when Sam's time comes, you can leave with me? I'll protect you. We'll protect each other."

"Will you help me bury them?" the boy said with guilty eyes. "I had to put my parents on a sheet and pull them out into the back. The house was starting to smell."

"You did that all by yourself?" Sim asked.

"It was hard, but I wouldn't let Sammy help, because he would be too sad."

"I understand," Sim said. "What's your name?"

"Ollie," the boy said.

"I'm Sim," he offered. "And Ollie, I must say, you are a fortress."

"What does that mean?" Ollie asked regarding Sim with a crooked gaze, accentuating his pale, sharp features.

"It means the Spirit and the gifts are yours," Sim said.

For the next week, Sim stayed at the house, amidst the family photos, several of them featuring Ollie at gymnastics tournaments; televisions that didn't work; empty cupboards; a full bar in the basement that had plenty of vodka and whiskey in store; and a garage with two SUV's—pretty to look at, but otherwise useless. The only way to get around these days was by walking or horseback.

Sam never regained consciousness and died quietly at dawn on Sim's eighth day at the ranch. Sim helped Ollie bury his brother and parents and after taking everything of value from the ranch, they walked off together back to the fortress.

Thirty days later, Ollie became Flip.

Flip coughed up more blood and Sim held him tight. The orphans gathered around him, as many as could fit.

"It's okay, Flip," Sky said. She began singing a tune that silenced all noise. It was one she made up as a lullaby to sing the kids to sleep after the old songs got stale.

I see you in the morning, waking

I see you in the daytime, happy

I see you in the night, peaceful

I love you all the time, darling

Flip squeezed Sim's hand and turned to them, sputtering. "I...am...the...fortress...and..."

He coughed one last time and his chest heaved outward, then inward again. Then, he was gone.

Sim's lip trembled. King, Ace, and Shark hovered over them in shock while the others cried. After several minutes had passed, Sim slid Flip's body off his legs and gently placed him on the foyer. He rose to his feet and snatched Big Will's AK-47 from his hands.

"I'll be back," Sim said. "Well bury him in Usland when I return."

Usland is where he buried Amanda, Sara, Elizabeth, and Tak. It was where they buried their own. On the other side of the lot, they buried the rest. *This is the spot where we will bury Us. And over there is where we will bury the Rest. So, it shall be Usland, and Restland.*

"What are you doing, Sim?" Ace asked. "You can't go after them."

"And you said *I* let *my* emotions cloud my judgment," Sky said. "Now look at you."

"This is different," Sim said. "I'm going to end this."

"You're going to die!" Ace said.

Sim, face hardened, eyes full of water, replied, "You all know what to do if that happens." He looked lovingly at his orphans. "What I taught you to do."

"Take Gigi," Big Will offered.

"No," Sim said. "But thanks."

With no more said, Sim dashed out the front door.

Sky directed her attention to the group, wiping tears from her eyes. "Let's wrap Flip in the cloth and prepare him for burial. I need a few volunteers to help clean up."

"What's wrong with you, girl?" JZ cried. Nearby, Baby and Leo whimpered. Teddy took to a corner and was rubbing his arms up and down, talking to himself. "Flip is dead!"

"And we will mourn him properly," Sky said, quietly and sympathetically. "I loved him too. But this mess needs to be cleaned. I don't want Flip's body disrespected any longer by lying in a pool of blood on our foyer floor. Let's not lose our heads."

"Come on, JZ," Ace said, as he helped her from the floor. As he did so, King passed behind them and departed the fortress without a word.

Thirteen

SIM RAN DOWN THE hill in the direction of the fleeing men who survived the encounter. He was well behind and didn't know which direction they went at the intersection, but he assumed they didn't proceed over the bridge to the highway, and he also estimated they likely chose the route closest to the river, so that is the direction he pursued.

He remembered his reaction to Tak's death as he ran. Flip was only the second orphan that had been killed by an outsider and he took it personally on each occasion. He promised them protection. He promised them safety. Was he wrong about his purpose in living if he could not protect these kids? Each time one of them died, it was like putting a bullet in Sara's head all over again.

The morning was crisp, and the skies were blue. He looked to them for answers as he ran, panting, hoping to get a glimpse of Zagan on the road ahead. What then would he do? The man needed to die. He would not allow him to take another one of his orphans. He would not allow him to wreak havoc upon his society. He would win.

Zagan didn't seem much different than he had in the military. Always looking to engage. Always looking to kill, deriving some pleasure from the requirements of the job. He was a psychopath, and nothing mattered to him but creating mayhem. How did it figure that fate had spared this man from the death of the world, but had taken so many other *decent* people?

Zagan did not become this man with the onset of the new world. He *was* this man from the beginning.

Oh my God, Flip. I'm so sorry I couldn't protect you.

Adrenaline pushed him forward and he finally spotted Zagan several blocks ahead passing a row of houses created by the Habitat for Humanity group back in the day so that urban families could own homes. They were walking casually, never thinking that they would be pursued. Sim stayed with them but kept under cover as the half dozen men made their way to a steelworks building just past the row of weathered homes.

Sim didn't want the crew to make it all the way there, as he guessed there would likely be more men inside waiting. Instead, he opened fire with the AK-47 from behind and took down several of the unsuspecting men with bullets to the back. He even clipped Steer in the shoulder and when he ran out of ammo, he tossed the weapon aside and tackled Zagan to the ground as he attempted to run to the entrance of the steelworks building. The two crashed to the ground and Sim pummeled Zagan's thin body with closed fists as the man wailed and struggled to get free.

Two of the men who survived the initial hail of bullets moved to pull Sim off Zagan, as did Steer, who only had one good arm. Eventually, they dragged Sim away from Zagan, who struggled to his feet, surprised, but laughing wildly. Sim roared like a feral animal.

"My God, Sim," Zagan said. "You really have fucking changed."

"And you haven't," Sim hissed. "You killed that boy!"

Sim struggled to break free from the hold the two men had on him, but when he realized the futility of struggling, he settled down. Steer punched him in the face with his good arm.

"Steer!" Zagan said. "For crying out loud, leave the man alone." He placed his hands on his hips and shook his head in disbelief.

"You bastard," Sim said, spitting out blood.

Zagan took two steps forward. "I didn't fire the first shot!" he yelled. "Your orphans did. You trained them to kill, remember? And not only did your boy die because of it, so did most of the men that were with me. And all I wanted was *my* boy."

"You were going to torture and kill him," Sim said through heavy breaths.

Zagan offered a quizzical glance at Sim. "Well, yes," he said. "But that's only because I told him I would if he betrayed me. You don't get to be a traitor and live in this world. For fuck's sake, they used to do it in war all the time. One of America's most celebrated heroes is Nathan Hale."

"Who the fuck is that?" Steer asked, nursing the grazed skin on top of his shoulder.

Zagan sneered. "I only regret that I have one life to give to my country..." Zagan saw that it was not registering with Steer. "Never mind, you idiot." He turned back to Sim. "The point is, he was supposed to set *you* up, not the other way around. I could have been killed. That's twice now, so you tell me who the real threat is? You are trying to kill me preemptively. What fun is that?"

"I remember you killed plenty of people preemptively in war," Sim said. "And anyway, we aren't at war. He was just a child."

"That's debatable," Zagan said. "Anyway, I tried to offer you a way out. Hell, Kellogg was going to make it easy for you. This could have been over. I would have moved on. It wasn't even my idea to come back to this shithole after three years of roaming the countryside, but I was intrigued by the news I heard about your fortress on the hill. I even left a group I was happily wed to in order to check it out. I'm quite sure they miss me."

"Who wouldn't miss you?" Steer said.

"Just leave, Zagan. Please...just leave. Or leave us alone."

"I'd love to," Zagan said. "But I feel like we have reached the point of no return. You see, I'm really interested to see if we can take down that fortress of yours. I've not met a bigger challenge since these whole end-of-the-world shenanigans, so it's very refreshing. And the good news is, I want to make sure you are alive to defend it. Otherwise, what fun will that be? So, go back and bury your dead, old friend, and we'll see you soon."

As Sim was about to spit in his face, the sound of gunfire shattered the still of night. Zagan ducked, as did Steer, and the two holding Sim dropped him to the weathered pavement. The four men ran off as King continued to fire while approaching Sim, who was stirring on the ground.

"Sim!" King said, kneeling beside him. "Do you have a deathwish or something?"

"He could have killed me," Sim said. "But he didn't."

"He went to that steelworks," King said. "At least we know where they're hiding out. Maybe we can plan something."

"Let's get back for now," Sim said. "And I have to get William's gun on the way."

The pair walked the half mile back to the fortress at a slow clip. Neither spoke, but it would be unlikely that they were thinking of anything else other than Flip and how he was gone and how such an event would change things. For it wasn't over.

In fact, it was only beginning.

The orphans spent the day crying, cleaning up the carnage that lie in the front of the fortress in the form of five dead men, and preparing a burial spot for Flip in Usland. JZ and Teddy did the digging, and it was JZ who broke down first.

"We was just out here the other day rapping a taste," she muttered through tears. "He got away that time and that boy was fearless."

Teddy's eye twitched, which was a normal thing for him. He could never keep any part of his body still, not even the muscles in his face. "He was my friend," Teddy said. "When I was in school, I never had many friends.

Nobody even came to my parties. But Flip, he was a real friend. A true friend. We had a secret handshake. Do you want to see it?"

JZ wiped tears from her eyes and stood. "Sure."

Teddy led her through a series of hand motions that included slapping the front and back of their hands, fist pumps, fist shakes, and a high five to end it. When he was done, Teddy seemed proud. "That was it. Oh, and we winked at each other too."

JZ laughed at Teddy's cuteness and winked back at the boy. She had nearly forgotten why she was sad, and though it soon came back to her, she stayed on her feet and continued to dig the burial plot with Teddy. This was a much harder feat than digging holes in Restland.

As they were nearly completed with the job, Teddy looked at the hole with wide eyes. "How long do you think it could be before someone else will be digging *our* holes?"

"We're not gonna worry about that," JZ retorted swiftly. "The truth is, whatever he did, he got caught and made a bad mistake." She turned to him, impassioned. "If we *don't* make mistakes, we live."

Teddy continued gazing at the hole. "Everyone makes mistakes from time to time. It shouldn't cost us our lives."

"That was in the old world," JZ reminded.

Everyone gathered in the living room after lunch for a house meeting. Often, it would be unknown what was on the agenda for the meetings, but it would be no mystery what details would be covered in this particular gathering.

Everyone was in attendance. Sky sat with Yamil and Miracle on the little couch, while Misty, Teddy, Leo, and Baby sat together on the larger couch. King took to the lounger while JZ sat in the corner of the room, knees drawn to her face. Big Will sat on the floor with Gigi and Kellogg while Ace, King, Shark, and Sim hovered.

Sim, wearing his long overcoat and pacing the floor, started the meeting with "welcome," as he typically did. He began rather abruptly, and it was no surprise Flip was the first order of business.

"Does anyone know how Flip ended up alone and out of the way of protection?"

"The last I saw him, he was going to go pee," Leo said.

"Did anyone see him after that?" Sim asked.

The room was quiet.

"And you didn't see anything from the roof, Shark?" Sim asked.

"I don't spend the entire day gazing through my scope," he said. "Someone must have gotten on the property unnoticed and snatched him."

"Aren't you up there to make sure that kind of thing *doesn't* happen?" Ace said.

"Fuck you, Ace," Shark said. "The only thing you see at any given time is the hair on Sim's ass because you have your nose up it. Even Big Will spends more time on guard than you."

"I'm just saying you spend your whole life up on that damn rooftop and you missed seeing an intruder sneak onto our land in broad daylight and leave with Flip under his fucking arm."

Shark bellowed and went into full charge, but Sim was between them, and held him back. "Stop it!" Sim yelled. "All of you!" He shoved Shark back and raised an arm at each one of the boys. "Is this what you want now? To fall apart when we need each other the most! This is only the beginning."

Again, silence filled the room until a little voice emerged.

Yamil offered, "Maybe if we invite him to dinner and story time, he will be our friend."

Everyone turned to him at once. JZ broke into tears and Shark's shoulders fell. Shark walked over to Yamil and lowered himself to stand eye-to-eye. "You're a smart little man, Yamil."

"You are, indeed," Sim said. "But the other person must want to be friends too, darling. And this man, he does not want to be our friend."

Yamil stared at Sim wide-eyed and Sim could only offer him a smile, as he was a testimony that children were still children and nothing more.

"We should go to the heights to gather people and attack them," Ace said. "They'll help us, and we know where he is assembling men."

"They will help us, yes," Sim said. "And you and I will go there tonight and do just that. But we aren't attacking them on their territory. We are defending our home when they come, because this is where we will have the best advantage."

"Then we just sit back and watch while they gather an army of pig-headed mongrels who will join their cause just because they are bored?" King asked.

"Exactly," Sim said. "Because Zagan thinks he is gathering up soldiers, and it will be his mistake when he sees that numbers aren't everything. Did any of you learn about the Battle of Thermopylae back in the day?"

The orphans stared at him, waiting.

"It was a famous ancient battle where only a few hundred Greek warriors held off a Persian army consisting of over one hundred thousand men using their excellent training and skills," Sim said.

"Did they get *their* training with Nerf guns?" Sky asked, garnering many angry stares. "Anyway, there aren't hundreds of us, and *they* lost."

"Well, Sky," Sim said patiently. "There aren't over one hundred thousand of *them*, so in fact, our odds are better. And, yes, they did get beaten, but they achieved much more than victory at the end of things."

"What's that?" Ace asked.

"Honor," Sim said. "Ace, you're coming with me to the heights tonight and we'll have a chat with Charlie about this crew. We'll bury Flip in one hour and all will attend. Tomorrow, we'll double up on our training and response and inventory our arsenal and fortifications. When Zagan comes, we'll be ready."

Sim knew it was a lot on them. They had lived a relatively peaceful existence over the past three years and everything had abruptly changed. From the siege to Kellogg entering their lives in such a way, to Zagan revealing himself and his intentions, to Flip's death. This Sim realized and though he wanted to grieve Flip as badly as everyone else, he knew that if they let his death get under their skin for too long, it would work against them. He had to keep them strong. He had to keep them focused. Even when he, too, wanted to scream.

Flip's burial was quiet. Even Shark attended, which meant nobody had an eye on the perimeter, but this was not the moment that any of the orphans wanted to miss, so they took their chances on Zagan not being nearby.

The orphans surrounded the mound of dirt that covered Flip's body, heads down, as quiet as Sim had ever known the entire group to be when all together.

"I remember the day I found you, Flip," Sim began. "You stayed with your brother to take care of him, and your bravery never faltered. You lived for your brother, and you died for your brothers and sisters by not forcing anyone to make a choice. You made the choice for all of us. We'll always love you. Deeply. And we will never forget the love and light you brought to both worlds. A light that those who did this will never know. Your name and your flame will carry on forever. You are a fortress. Our fortress."

Each orphan took a moment to offer their memories and sentiments through many tears. Each concluded by placing a fresh cut flower on top of the mound of dirt. Yes, beautiful flowers still grew in the darkness of a new day.

Finally, they gathered in a circle around the gravesite and held hands as they recited their pledge, which even Kellogg had learned by heart.

Fourteen

ACE RAN INTO JZ in the kitchen as she was finishing up a bowl of vegetable soup and the sun was dipping below the horizon. JZ gazed at him affectionately as he was checking his healing wound.

"Is it all better?" she asked.

"Not quite," he said. "But every day it heals more. I'll live, anyway." *Not like poor Flip.*

"Why you gotta go tonight?" JZ asked, staring at him with puppy dog eyes. "I don't like it when you go there because I know what you up to."

"What do you care what I do at the heights?" Ace asked.

"I just do," she said. "Those nasty girls are disgusting."

"You know nothing about those girls," Ace said. "And besides, what difference does it make?"

She put her hand on his forearm, as it lay across the table.

"Stop it, will you?" he said, pulling away. "You're just a child and like my sister on top of that."

"I'm almost fourteen," she said. "And I'm no more your sister than that gutter trash you spend time with up there."

"I know how old you are," he said. "I love you, JZ. Just...not like that."

She sulked at the table as Sim entered. "Am I interrupting?"

"No," Ace said.

"Yes," JZ said, at the same time.

"Well, regardless, it's time to go," Sim said. "JZ, eyes sharp. We'll be back by dawn."

"Yeah, yeah," she said. "Say hello to Uncle Charlie for us."

Ace leaned in and kissed JZ on the cheek. "See you, kid," he said.

She wiped his kiss away with the sleeve of her shirt and Ace smiled. Sim shook his head and the two of them headed out the kitchen door, which led directly to the wooded side of the house. They climbed the tree-laden hill to the top and traversed a small field to a side road that wound a half mile around before greeting yet another road that would lead the rest of the way to their destination. The heights was roughly two miles away from the fortress and ideally navigable.

The compound was named for its former glory: an apartment complex overseen by the city's housing authority, called Grizzland Heights, home to low-income families, many in dire poverty trying to figure out how to make a living day-to-day. In the end, it didn't matter.

Back in the day, the tenants were known in derogatory fashion as "Grizzies," and not held in high regard. Though in the end, death did not abide by class designations, as Charlie loved to point out. The Grizzies were not unlike anyone else when disease bent people the world over to their knees.

Charlie oversaw a group of survivors who occupied many of the buildings at Grizzland Heights. A Grizzy his entire life, Charlie held a strong post-apocalyptic community as well, albeit without the same self-imposed moralistic obligations as Sim. They were a passive group, at least, and not hell bent on conquering other domains.

The Grizzies were happily engaged in the new world and built a foundation rooted in meeting the needs of the most basic human instincts. Their larger preoccupation outside of keeping a strong defense was sex, food, and shelter. The only children that lived there were the few that had been living there when everyone died and a few that had been conceived and birthed by the inhabitants since the fall of humanity. Charlie catered to them as he invited others to join him. After three years, and thanks to some of the vetting of visitors at the fortress, he had a community of roughly one hundred and fifty survivors that lived throughout five complex buildings clustered together in an area roughly one quarter the size of the entire Grizzland Heights compound. The rest of the buildings on the grounds remained vacant, but Charlie and his crew tended to them in hopes they would grow into them. He wanted the heights to be in the wake of death, what they never could be in life.

Sim and Charlie had a history that helped in forging a symbiotic relationship as the pair grew their separate communities, often working together. Sim supplied the heights with occasional people and weaponry and taught them how to grow food. And, in return the heights supplied him with furniture and other resources, sexual liaisons, and the promise of extra numbers if needed. Charlie's crew were on call for such occasions, and it was Sim's intent to create a rooftop contraption to serve as a beacon of distress to the heights, but he had not gotten around to it.

Sim first took Ace to the heights a short time after he turned seventeen. He knew what Charlie could provide to satiate his budding sexual instincts, and Sim needed to give that to him in this more organized way. He did not want Ace out in the world alone seeking this and he did not want Ace's urges and needs to conflict with the nature of his relationship with the other orphans. It was a game plan he intended on sticking to as all the orphans came of age. King often nagged him about joining them on these journeys, but Sim consistently denied him.

When the time is right, Sim would say.

For you, or for me? King would reply.

Sim, too, found time for himself when he visited the heights, and though the present visit was not for such purposes, he would surely take advantage of the time there.

Darkness fell upon them as they neared the complex. Sim pulled a flashlight from his bag and flipped it on, illuminating the path forward.

The silence was often surreal for Sim. Even three years later. No cars. No horns. No sirens. No voices. No train whistles. The entire world at night had become a dark country road. Though it could be peaceful, sometimes Sim yearned for the sounds of something. Anything.

"It looks like JZ has a crush on you," Sim said, making small talk along the route.

"Yeah," Ace said. "She knows what happens when I go with you on these trips."

"No doubt King loves to tease her about it," Sim said.

"No biggie," Ace said in stride as they shuffled along. "One day, JZ will go too and find a cute boy to be with and then she'll marry and become the queen of the heights."

"Or she can rule as queen of the fortress," Sim said. "Though she may have to fight Sky for that position."

"Sky wants to be queen of the new world," Ace laughed. "You know, Sim, she...we do have a lot of good ideas. You should start listening to us more on things now that we're older."

If he heard Ace's statement, he didn't acknowledge it. Instead, he stopped and pivoted toward a small field off the road. He turned off his flashlight and watched as hundreds of fireflies that lit up the field in small flashes.

"I used to catch them when I was little," Ace said. "Me and my friends would put them in jars and try to save them as nightlights. I had this other friend, Cory, who smeared their guts on his face so his cheeks would light up."

Sim laughed. "My Sara loved them too. She would cup them in her hands and peer at them through the cracks in her fingers. She was mesmerized."

"That's because they are mesmerizing," Ace said. "A mystery like all the mysteries of the world."

It was no secret to Sim that children loved fireflies, but seeing them was a reminder of those times when humans and fireflies danced together. Did the fireflies sense things had changed? They weren't being chased, captured, or smeared on a young child's cheeks. They were, like all the animals of the world, immune to the death of humans...Free. It was their turn to own the world.

The pair continued their walk until they reached the edge of the heights. They halted on the road about thirty yards from a dumpster that was at the bottom of a fire escape stairwell, which led directly down from one of the apartment buildings. Sim knew there would be scouts watching and even though most of them knew him, it was dark, and it would be hard to tell who was lurking. Normally, he and Ace took the trip in daylight, but Sim did not want to risk leaving the fortress before dark with Zagan potentially watching their every move.

"Hello?" Sim called, keeping his shout-out short and sweet. "It's Sim!"

A few seconds later, he spotted the flashlights, the beams originating from either side of the building and eventually converging as they got closer.

"For Christ's sake, Sim," Jacob scolded as he crossed the street to greet them. "What the hell are you doing coming this late at night?"

"Nice to see you too, Jacob," Sim said. He turned to the other Grizzy. "You too, Sandy."

"We nearly opened fire," Sandy said in her gravelly voice. Too many cigarettes. "You shouldn't sneak up on the place at night."

"This isn't a pleasure trip," Sim said. "We need to talk to Charlie and didn't want to risk coming out in the daylight to make the trek."

Jacob and Sandy exchanged looks. "I guess they discovered you then."

"Who are you talking about?" Sim asked.

"That wild and crazy nutjob and his husky that showed up recently and are sacking houses wherever they find anything living inside," Jacob said.

"They've been here too?"

"Our scouts have seen them," Sandy said. "But thankfully, they haven't seen *us*. For their sake, anyway."

"Let's get you back to the other side so you can see Charlie," Jacob said. "He's a little drunk right now, though, you should know."

Sandy turned to Ace. "I suppose you want to see Willow?"

"It would be nice," Ace smiled. "But I'm just as much here to support Sim in this situation. It's a priority."

"Yeah, yeah," Sandy said, waving at him in jest. "Willow will want to see you, stud, so let's not feign nobility."

She turned to lead them back when Ace shouted, "One of my brothers died today! So, there is nothing superficial about today's visit, Sandy."

She turned back to Ace as Jacob regarded Sim with a stunned look. "One of your orphans was killed?"

"We need to see Charlie, Jacob," Sim repeated. "It's important."

"I'm sorry, Sim. Follow me and we'll get you to him. I'm sure this news will sober him up."

The two followed Jacob and Sandy past a multitude of single-level apartment buildings. It was a path they knew well that took them through yards, courtyards, a playground, and across narrow side streets. The heights was a city of its own, back in the day and in the new world as well.

Zagan was familiar with the complex too, as several of their military brethren hailed from the heights, so it was an oddity that the man in all his rampaging had never explored them in search of squatters or soldiers.

The five buildings used to quarter the people of the heights were clustered together in a horseshoe arrangement, with two buildings on one side, two buildings on the other, and a middle building adjacent to each right and left side pair. Charlie was housed in the middle building. He kept guards around the entire campus perimeter, however, so there would be as much warning as possible before unwanted intruders could get too close. Sandy and Jacob led Sim and Ace across the parking area that tied the buildings together. The lot was peppered with rundown vehicles of all kinds, remnants of another world. Here, but useless, except to use for campus defense.

Sandy and Jacob led Ace and Sim into the building, down a central corridor to apartment seven. They knocked three times, twice, then once. A young blonde with her hair tied up in a fanciful bun answered soon after.

"Hello, Susan," Sim smiled. Susan was Charlie's latest girlfriend. Each time they came, they never knew who from the community would open the door. Susan had opened the door for the last three visits. She was obviously special.

"Oh my gosh," she said, eyes bulging. "Surprising to see you here after dark." She glanced over the cluster of people by standing on her tiptoes to regard Ace. "How are you doing, sweetie?"

"I'm fine," Ace said, blushing.

"Well come on in," she said. "Charlie, you have visitors!"

Charlie was just behind her on the couch, a bottle of whiskey perched next to him on an end table and a glass in hand. No fewer than twenty candles shimmered around him. He raised his glass when he saw Sim and Ace walk through the door.

"Cheers, my friends," Charlie slurred. "I didn't know it was morning already. Damn, I have so much to do."

Ace and Sim took seats at a couple of loungers that were across from him as Jacob and Sandy closed the door behind them, departing.

Susan asked, "Can I get you guys anything? I have some canned soda or beer, Ace, but after three years who knows how it'll taste. We have plenty of liquor, though, if you prefer. God knows Charlie's scavenging missions always include a liquor store...any he can find in a hundred-mile radius.

That, along with baby formula and diapers. The residents of the heights are going to single-handedly re-populate the earth. And I can tell you I am not helping with that."

Charlie ignored her. "Yes, have a drink on me," he said. He stretched out his one lanky arm that was holding the glass and then brought it back to his mouth for a big sip. Charlie was tall. Each of his legs were bent at the knee and jutted out to the right and left of the couch, creating long wispy dark shadows on the wall. Like usual, and even in a stupor, he was wearing a silver ring on every finger and several chain necklaces around his neck. Though many years younger than Sim, his face was worn and wrinkled like an old sailor, but his eyes remained piercing.

"No, thanks," Sim said while Ace silently shook his head. "You need more batteries, Charlie? We have plenty and you won't have to use up your candle supplies. Can't help with diapers, though."

"No worries," Charlie said, as he twisted his long hair into a ponytail and tied it back with a rubber band. "I have plenty of batteries, but I try to conserve them. Besides, I like the ambience. It puts Susan in the mood." He then sat upright and gazed around the room. "But where's the sun?"

Susan sat beside Charlie and took the glass from his hand. "It's not morning time, you pervert," she chided. "Now get yourself together, because I'm quite sure they would not have come all the way out here in the dark unless it was important."

Charlie leaned forward, his eyes hardening. "Is everything okay, Mr. Ford?" he asked in a hushed voice.

Mr. Ford. He couldn't get used to hearing that name and it was only Charlie that referred to him by it.

Charlie was one of his sixth-grade students during his teaching days. Those were hard times for Charlie. His mother was despondent, holding down three jobs to make ends meet and his father was a local drug dealer, in and out of prison. Charlie was a loner, scared of his own shadow back then.

Sim, then Gabriel Ford, took him under his wing, as he often did the urban kids he taught. He had even started a club for bullied children and had twenty-two children attend weekly, including Charlie. Charlie was always fascinated with Mr. Ford, a soldier in the Army Reserve, two tours of duty in Afghanistan, a father, and a fun, dynamic teacher who cared more than anything about the children in his care.

"Flip's dead, Charlie," Sim uttered bluntly.

Susan put her hand over her heart and her jaw fell.

Charlie stared at Sim intently, his eyes wide. "Susie, babe, can you bring me a bottle of water, please."

Susan walked to the kitchen and back and presented Charlie with a bottle of water. Charlie cracked off the top and chugged the entire bottle down in one motion. He crushed the thin plastic bottle in his hand and threw it on the floor.

"What happened, Mr. Ford?"

"As you know, there's a man leading a crew around this area," Sim said. "They are ransacking places and killing anyone they come across. I know him, actually...from the old days. He's crazy. We tried to take him out, but we missed. He retaliated by kidnapping Flip, and Flip was killed trying to escape."

"They actually attacked the fortress as well, but we held them off," Ace added.

"But they are coming back after he gathers more men," Sim said. "Their goal is to sack the fortress and kill us all."

Charlie listed intently, his eyes moving between Sim and Ace, his body rocking slightly back and forth. When the two finished giving the gist to Charlie, the man propped his arms up on his legs, buried his face in his hands, and took several deep breaths though his nose before releasing his face.

"Fuck," he said. "I wish had I known you were coming," he snapped at Susan. "I need another water."

Susan retreated to the kitchen and returned with a second bottle of water, which Charlie downed in two gulps instead of one. Sim and Ace, understanding that the man was trying to quickly recover from being drunk, waited patiently.

"Maybe we should just take this up in the morning," Sim suggested.

Charlie held up a hand. "No. I'm sorry. I can't fucking believe Flip is dead. I just can't fucking believe it."

Sim bowed his head. "Yeah."

"How am I going to tell Shorty?" Charlie wondered. "Those two were as thick as thieves."

Shorty was one of the residents of the heights. He was the same age as Flip and although they didn't see each other often, they were good friends. Shorty took a lot of shit from his people at the heights for his short stature and scraggly frame. He shared that in common with Flip, so the two understood each other well. At one point, he pleaded with Charlie to live at the fortress, but Charlie wouldn't let him go.

"Look, Charlie, your people have said you saw this man in the area, so you have to know that while he's out there, we're all in danger."

Charlie poured the half inch of water that was left in his bottle into his cupped hands and splashed it on his face. Susan sat beside him and rubbed his shoulders while the three conversed.

"We've taken down a lot of stupid fools over the years, so if he comes near here again, we won't just observe him pass through. We'll kill him on sight."

"It's not that simple," Sim said. "He's no ordinary fool. He's ex-military. He's meticulous, sneaky, and he's amassing a small army to kill us all just for the thrill of it."

"Oh, my goodness," Susan said. "We were doing so good."

"Why don't you bring your people here, Sim," Charlie said. "This guy doesn't know about our community, and I've been hoping we could merge at some point. I have all those extra buildings on the compound and one hundred fifty residents here. Imagine what we could accomplish together in one place. The fortress can be an outpost."

"Maybe it's not such a bad idea, Sim," Ace said. "Even if it's only temporary."

Sim shook his head without pondering, as Ace expected he would.

"You're so isolated down there," Susan offered.

"I can't," Sim reminded. "It wasn't supposed to be that way. It has taken three years for us to grow our compound and we have a very specific philosophy that we adhere to. You know I love you, Charlie, but your lifestyle is different than ours."

Charlie laughed. "It sounds like the old days. The Grizzies and everyone else. But you don't know us as well as you think."

"That's not what this is, Charlie," Sim said. "You know that. Some of the men in my unit were people I knew my whole life and came from the heights, and some of my best and most endearing students grew up here, including you."

"Charlie told me it was the house you bought for your family before the shit hit the fan," Susan said, "but that doesn't mean you all have to die to save it."

"That's not what this is about," Sim said.

"Then what is it about?" Ace asked.

"Not today," Sim said. "I wouldn't even know where to begin. Sometimes *I* don't even know what this is all about. But I know I don't want to leave. I don't want to run."

"Then you definitely shouldn't," Charlie said. "What if we preempted this strike? Found out where he was and attacked him when he least expected it? Why the hell are we going to wait until he builds up an army and then attacks *you*?"

"We know where he is," Ace said. "He's not even a mile away from the fortress. On the edge of the river near the prison in that old steelworks building."

Charlie ran his hands through his greasy long hair. "You know where he is? Well let's take our men and go fuck him up!"

"Charlie, we already considered this, but it's too dangerous. We can't blindly attack this guy and expect any better odds than we have by staying put. He can bring two hundred men to the fortress, and I can't conceive how he'll be able to breach us. There is no way he'll have the firepower. We'll hold higher ground, and the place is all but impenetrable without heavy artillery. And though the orphans are just a bunch of kids, they are well trained and pretty fucking bad-ass. Plus, I had another plan that I thought you could help with."

Charlie sat back on his chair.

Susan shifted over and crossed one leg over the other. "Just let me know how we can help," she said.

"That's my girl," Charlie said, leaning over and kissing her on the lips. "So, tell me this plan."

"Well, we don't exactly know when he plans to hit us, so how to get word to you in a hurry when we see them coming will be the most challenging part of this plan. But there are three houses across the street from the fortress and even though they are only two-story homes, they still offer higher ground and plenty of coverage. If we station some of your men on those rooftops, we can create a deadly gauntlet on both sides of the road. They'll never expect that we'll be positioned there, and we'll be able to rain fire down on them from both sides of the street. We can probably take out half of them before they get within twenty yards of the fortress."

"How about we just send a dozen men with you now and they can hole up with you until this is over?" Charlie suggested. "Then the extra men you'll need will be at the ready."

Sim pondered for a few seconds before responding. "I don't know, Charlie; I don't have the room and last time I had a stranger stay at the fortress he turned the routines upside down and complained about everything we did. I'm sure you remember Walter."

"Indeed I do, God rest his soul," Charlie said. "Regardless, you need to take these men with you now and remove the question marks from the equation. The kids will adjust. It's not going to work any other way."

"The others will be fine," Ace said. "Look, I know you are very particular about things, Sim, and not overly keen on listening, but this isn't forever. This is a state of emergency. We can't have our cake and eat it too all the time."

Sim rolled his eyes.

Charlie laughed. "This man got some heavy motherfucking O.C.D.," he quipped.

Ace laughed.

"They're probably watching us, though," Sim said. "What if they see the extra men hanging around? I want to retain the element of surprise."

"You aren't going to be able to predict everything, Sim," Charlie said. "You said this guy is ex-military. He may try to set up his men on those roofs himself to get better access to the higher floors of the fortress. He may attack at night when you can't see him coming. This whole defense of the fortress is based on your assumption that he is going to walk up with two hundred men in broad daylight, trumpets blaring, when if he has half a brain, he'll attack at night and position his men strategically and covertly."

Sim shook his head. "No, no. For him to have any chance, his best strategy must be an all-out assault. Like Normandy. That is why he wants to amass as many soldiers as possible. Whether he makes his move in the daytime or at night, we should be able to see them coming from the roof."

"Regardless, take the men now," Charlie insisted. "Thirty days is nothing. We send crews out on supply runs for longer durations than that. They'll be fine. *You'll* be fine, you stubborn ass."

Sim pondered for thirty seconds more, perhaps trying to discover a new plan on the fly. "Okay, then. Maybe I can brief some of your people tomorrow before we go and give them time to prepare. Zagan's attack is imminent, but I don't think it will be within the next week. He's still building his numbers."

"Zagan?" Charlie said. "Is that what this dick calls himself?"

"Yeah," Sim said.

"Sounds like the devil," Susan said. "Well, if you need me to go, I'll be there. I would love to rain down some fire on these assholes when they show up."

"Babe, you aren't going anywhere," Charlie said. "I'll go and light this punk ass up for you, Mr. Ford. It will be nice to see the others. I'll also keep my men in line so you can keep your house in order."

Sim smiled. "That's fine, Charlie. Just don't get cocky."

Charlie shuddered. "Eh, this guy is just another schoolyard bully, Sim. Just like before. We both know them. He may be crazy, but deep down he is just a damaged little boy in a craggily middle-aged man's body."

Sim laughed, as did Ace, though it wasn't the kind of laugh that people had over enjoying a great time. It was a laugh invoked through ponderance of Charlie's insight. It was true. What man who behaved like Zagan—who *called* himself Zagan—could actually consider himself an adult? Yet, it was dangerous to denounce him as a lowly threat based on assumptions about his psychology.

Sim and Ace left apartment seven, leaving Charlie to his drink. Ace went to building four, while Sim retreated to building three. The two did not speak as they parted ways.

Sim visited his heights girlfriend, Gwen, as he hadn't seen her in two months and needed a shoulder to lean on. Ace headed for Willow's apartment.

The night wore on.

Fifteen

BACK AT THE FORTRESS, King, Shark, and Sky argued about who was in charge. Mostly King and Sky. Before Zagan and all the mayhem, their roles were clear and defined by Sim, but the unusual chaos over the past week had created rifts in the established order, which put Sim's authoritarian style of leadership to the test. This added another layer of conflict to the bigger picture and it was felt by all.

Before the usual bedtime hours, Sky did rounds on each floor of the house to make sure the rest of the children kept to their routines. She interrupted Leo, Miracle, and Yamil in the playroom. Leo was playing with blocks while the little ones were smashing up toy vehicles.

"It's time for bed, everyone," she said as she walked into the room. "We can't leave these lights on all night."

Leo walked up to her, leaving his house of blocks for Yamil to destroy, which he did in no time at all using a large plastic monster truck.

"Everything is blurry all the time," Leo said as he approached Sky at the door.

Sky grabbed his chin. "What do you mean?"

"I mean it's blurry," he repeated.

"Can you see me fine?" she asked.

"Yeah, I guess," Leo said.

"Now turn to the wall and read the poster," she commanded. The poster featured a young boy kissing a doll. He was wearing a shirt that read, *there is no wrong way to be a boy.*

"I already know what is says," Leo said.

Sky huffed. "Well would you be able to read it from here if you didn't know what it said?"

Leo turned and squinted. "I don't think so."

"It looks like you need some glasses, sir," she purported.

"Where do we get those?" he asked.

Sky was miffed. "I have no idea. I suppose we could scavenge for some with your prescription." She patted his head. "We'll do just that."

"Can we sleep with Leo?" Miracle asked. "His bed is big, and the mattress is really soft."

Normally, Miracle and Yamil slept in a room with Baby on the second floor.

"I suppose so, since Sim is away," Sky said, though thinking about the empty bed in the room left vacated after Flip's death.

"He pees the bed, though," Leo whined.

"I do not!" Miracle said.

Yamil laughed. "Orina en la cama todo el tiempo."

"What did he say?" Miracle asked.

"How the heck should I know?" Sky said, raising up her hands.

"Well," Leo relented, "how about Miracle sleeps in Flip's bed and Yamil sleeps with me?"

Sky paused, thinking about Flip again and how he was never coming home. His was not just an empty bed, she felt, and wondered if it was too soon before she allowed it to be filled by someone else.

"I don't think he would mind," Leo said, sensing perhaps that Sky's hesitance was related to this Flip dilemma.

She smiled at Leo's sweetness. "Very well, then. Off you go." She pushed a button on a mini receiver that was affixed to the wall and the light went out swiftly. The trio dashed off to Leo's room on the other side of the third floor.

Sky proceeded to floor two. She visited her own room that she shared with JZ and Misty and found the pair there, painting each other's nails.

"How are we doing, ladies?" Sky asked. "Prettying yourselves up right before bed, are we?"

"Do you want us to do your nails and hair?" Misty asked.

It was always odd for Sky to hear Misty speak of girl things. She was a bit of a tomboy, content to wear jeans and a simple T-shirt while having her hair tied back in a ponytail. Her face was freckled, angular, and she didn't mind being dirty, scuffed up, or even bruised like a pair of weathered sneakers. It was JZ who pulled her in with her beautification antics, as JZ was the opposite in all ways. Her hair was silky and dark, her face polished and glowing. She wore makeup and jewelry regularly around the house, if not to attract Ace's gaze, then to feel like a normal teenage girl.

Sky understood this, but did not deem it practical to approach each day with such an attitude, as many of the chores around the house were dirty and laborious. Sky remembered describing it once as like living on a farm. Building, growing, lugging, pushing, hunting, scavenging, and mending. This was not the life of a child before the end of things. Or at least not most of them, anyway.

Sky sat on her bed as the girls went about their leisure. In the end, purposeful or not, it was a way to bond and pass time. JZ's nails were a flashy purple and Misty's hot pink.

"I think I'll pass tonight," Sky said. "You look very pretty, Misty."

"Eh, once in a while I don't mind," she said.

Teddy walked in at that moment. "Do mine too!" he shouted.

"Whatever happened to knocking?" Sky chided.

"The door was wide open," he said, flopping beside her.

"I'll do your nails, Teddy," JZ said. "But no lipstick this time."

Teddy grabbed his belly and laughed. "I only did that so I could make lip imprints on the windows."

That he did. They had painted his lips bright red and put a bunch of imprints on their bedroom windows, fascinated by it.

Sky put a hand on Teddy's knee. "I will leave you all to it, but we must abide by the normal curfew, so when I come back it's lights out."

"Yes, mommy," Teddy squeaked in a sarcastic voice.

She turned around at the door. "Oh, and Miracle and Yamil will be sleeping in your room tonight and I suspect that Kellogg will probably take Flip's bed starting tomorrow to get him off the couch."

Teddy gave her a thumbs up and a big-toothed smile.

Sky continued down the hall to King and Big Will's room. Their door was open and the two were playing chess while Gigi curled up in a ball on Big Will's bed. It was one of those rare occasions in the last week that Big Will put down his gun and relaxed. He and King lobbied to be together in the same room, since Big Will was the only one who bothered to learn how to play chess, a fact that frustrated King. He tried to teach all the orphans at one point or the other, but for the most part, they weren't interested or couldn't grasp it.

"Well, well, well," Sky said. "You two look focused."

Neither raised his head from the game.

"And how many days has this particular game been going on?"

"Three," Big Will said, unflinching. "But it doesn't look like it will end tonight."

"It definitely won't if you don't take your damn turn," King said. "It's been twenty minutes."

"I'm thinking," Big Will said.

"I guess it won't help to try to engage you in small talk at this point," Sky said. "Let's remember the curfew. Last I looked at the schedule though, King, you were first on guard."

"I can't find the night-vision binoculars," King said without turning toward her. "That dingbat Teddy was running around with them last I saw, and he can't remember where he put them."

"I'll look around," she answered. "He probably brought them to the toy room."

Sky left them to the game as Big Will finally made his move.

She finished her check of the rooms on the second floor. She proceeded downstairs to see what Baby was up to on her own. Turned out, she wasn't alone. This was surprising because she assumed Shark was on the roof. Instead, he was sitting beside Baby putting together a puzzle in the dining room while they ate popcorn. It was a puzzle that had been in the works for as long as King's chess game. It was a depiction of Walt Disney World's Magic Kingdom castle, and it was nearly halfway complete.

"You're getting there," Sky said, her hands on her hips.

"I want to go there one day," Baby said. "My mother and father were supposed to take me, but they had to save up the money. I wanted to go to that room where you can dress like a princess."

Baby had her tongue out while she fished for the next piece of the puzzle.

"I guess it would be interesting to go and see what it looks like now," Sky said. "Once such a vibrant and full place. It's hard to imagine the silence there."

"Have you ever gone?" King asked, somber.

"Yes," she said. "But believe it or not, I always hated amusement parks."

"Why did you hate them?" Baby asked.

Sky shrugged. "I guess they look nice, especially at night, but I don't like rides because they scare me and make me sick. I wasn't a big fan of cotton candy or candy apples either."

"It sounds like you were a barrel of fun back then," Shark laughed.

Sky slapped him on the shoulder.

"I *was* fun," she insisted. "I played sports and loved animals, movies, and I played the clarinet. I loved school, most of all."

"That says it all," Shark laughed again.

"Oh, knock it off," she said. "It's nearly curfew, so wrap this up. You're on second duty tonight, so expect King to wake you after midnight."

"Yeah, yeah, I know the drill," he said. He pushed out from the table and stood up. He was taller than her, his sandy hair disheveled, and his teeth caked with film when he smiled. "You're okay, Sky. You can try to tackle me in a rage anytime."

She scoffed. "I'd be much more effective if I could convince you to keep your teeth brushed," she said, cringing from his breath.

Shark ran his tongue over the front of his teeth. "I just did."

Sky shook her head, but before turning round inquired about Kellogg.

"I'm out here," he said, hearing her inquiry from the living room.

Sky maneuvered around the corner and found him stretched out on the beat-down couch covered in a blanket. "Well why didn't you come out to the living room?"

"I'm already in bed," he said. "It's freezing in here."

"You could have stoked the fire," she said, walking over to the fireplace where she placed a log into the flames and poked at it until it breathed greater life.

"I told you I was too cold," he said.

"You're just sulking," she said. "About what, I don't know, but maybe you'll tell me."

Kellogg placed his hands behind his head and stared at the ceiling covered with a decorative white tin. "I just keep thinking what happened to Flip...It's all my fault, you know. And I'm supposed to take his bed now? I don't know if I can do that."

"I loved Flip," Sky said. "And what happened to him is a tragedy and we'll never forget him. We won't forget how it happened, either. We can't take anything for granted, Kellogg. Zagan had us on his radar before you were even part of the picture. What happened was perhaps...inevitable. I'm only worried Flip won't be the last."

"It's a scary thought," Kellogg said.

"Yes, it is," she said. "We'll see what Sim says when he gets back. Until then, rest, and try not to worry. In time, you'll be the best of us."

Kellogg smiled as the two regarded each other with kind eyes.

"Where is that silly coin of yours?" she asked.

"In my pocket where it always is," he said.

"Right where it belongs," she said.

Satisfied with the house, Sky returned to her room as Teddy was leaving, fanning his hands so that the blue polish would dry. The house went to sleep except for Shark, who did his rounds and perimeter checks before waking King, who would do the same, before waking JZ to finish the routine into the morning.

At daylight, the routine would begin again.

Sixteen

Ace entered building four through the main entrance—a pair of double glass doors that led to a dark hallway. He turned right and stopped in front of apartment six. After offering six distinct knocks in pairs of twos, he waited patiently for Willow to answer.

He and Willow met for the first time six months earlier on his first trip to the heights. At twenty years old, she was older than Ace, but she catered to his infatuation with her. Feeling a sense of flattery in these days was rare. Willow was well kept. She was not letting something as little as the end of the world get in the way of her enjoying life. While not everyone at the heights cared to maintain, Willow was a stickler for her appearance. She wore dresses, makeup, kept her curly brunette hair cleaned and cut, delighted in wearing bracelets and earrings and she smelled like the finest perfume. Aside from this, she was full-figured and well proportioned. Anyone into such beauty would be captivated by Willow. Not least, a boy of seventeen who was attracted to women.

When she answered the door, she was in a pink robe. She tilted her head and smiled, regarding Ace as if were a lost puppy dog. "Ace?" she said. "Ironic, because I've been thinking about you a lot lately."

"Why?" Ace said, swallowing hard.

"Because the only cute guys to look at around here are either too old for my taste or lost beneath three years of decay."

"Sim would never allow us to fall into that trap," Ace said.

"One of these days, you'll have to bring me to this fortress of yours and impress me with your devotion to remaining civilized."

Ace stepped over the threshold and paused at the gate. "It's not always sunshine and roses over there these days."

Willow turned to him, hands on her hips. "It never is. He's overseeing a dozen kids in the apocalypse. Most families I knew before the end could barely raise one child in normal times."

"Some of us aren't children anymore, though," Ace said. "Sim never wanted the interference of other adults at the fortress. He says he tried it once and it didn't work. But it's what he is getting anyway as we get older. Maybe he never thought about that."

"Well, he'll either have to treat you as equals, or kick you out and use your rooms to find other orphans." Willow sighed. "My parents couldn't wait till I was eighteen to send me packing. I guess some things never change."

"Or maybe, one by one, the orphans will just move out when they are old enough."

"The only difference is there were options back then for a young person needing to leave home."

"There are always options," Ace said. "They just aren't as ideal now as they were then."

Willow ran her hands through his hair and kissed him on the lips. "Maybe the heights will be an option for you someday."

Ace closed his eyes and relished her kiss. The thought of leaving Sim and the fortress for a life on his own never entered his mind until recently.

"We're under attack, Willow," Ace said. "And I don't know what to do outside of trusting Sim's lead."

Willow's face tightened. "What do you mean that you are under attack?"

Ace gently pushed her body from his but remained toe-to-toe with her. "This deranged man and his crew keep hounding us with hit-and-run assaults. He is planning a huge siege on the fortress, and they've already killed Flip."

Willow's mouth fell and her eyes disconnected from Ace as she pondered his words. "Flip," she muttered. She had never met him, but Ace spoke about all the orphans to her on his visits. "Why don't you just leave? You know Charlie would love to have you here at the heights."

Ace was shaking his head before she even finished the sentence. "It's more complex than that. Not like going off to college. We have a life there...a fully functioning compound, and Sim wants to defend it. I would never leave them. I would never leave him. Not now."

Willow turned from him and ran both hands through her hair, speechless.

"Sim just wants men from the heights to help us defend it," Ace said.

Willow quickly turned around. "Then I'm going too," she said.

"I didn't come here to recruit you, Willow," Ace said. "I just needed someone to talk to because for the first time since Sim and I met, I feel...afraid."

Willow wrapped her arms around him, and he rested his head on her shoulder as she enveloped his body. He cried in that moment for Flip, for his ignorance in feeling like life was always going to be so perfect, and for his concern about the future.

The fortress was an impressive compound, no doubt, and one they had spent years building; and maybe that is what Sim wanted to protect most of all: his property, the home he bought for Amanda and Sara. Or maybe, more importantly, he was protecting the virtues he instilled in all of them since they were young—another fortress, where good triumphs over evil. Or maybe he desired to, simply put, win this pissing contest against his old wartime nemesis. But at this point, even to win, there would be a cost. There already had been.

Willow pulled back and took his soft face into her hands. "This may not help, but I am going to tell you what my mother told me before she died. She said, 'Do not be afraid, because our fate cannot be taken from us.'"

Ace considered this through his tears and nodded. He was still only a boy, after all.

"If you are meant to fight to protect your house and cause, then we'll fight. If we're meant to die, then we'll die. If we're meant to live, then we'll live. Tomorrow is promised to no one, so let's fight for today."

Who was this girl, Willow, Ace wondered? Only a few years older than him but holding the secrets of the world. A lover and a friend. How beautiful to have both in a relationship. The two became one that night, and it was different from other times because there were now lives at stake, so every minute carried with it an edge, a thought that could not be escaped about what the future would hold. A notion that Ace always found predictable in spite of their preparations and despite Sim's teachings that everything they did as a community was to prepare them for some unknown and frightening end.

Despite the mood and urgency of their visit, Ace slept reasonably well with Willow beside him, so well that he didn't want to leave the next morning. He would rather have pretended that life with Willow was his only life. A fairytale. Alas, it was only an escape from the uncertain future.

Ace wandered into the front yard roughly an hour after the sun rose and Sim was already there with Charlie and a dozen men and women from the heights compound who were waiting on Sim for directions. They were only told to assemble but had no idea why. Shorty was among the group as the only child, his tiny little frame supporting a larger-than-life personality. He wasn't invited, but he was always up with the sun running errands, playing in abandoned vehicles, and on many occasions, driving everyone mad with early morning crows like Peter Pan. He had learned the value of freedom in this world and was not shy about being himself. Nobody had yet told him about his friend, Flip.

"Come out of there for a minute, Shorty," Charlie said, sipping from his flask while beckoning him from the bed of a pick-up truck. Shorty hurdled the side of the tuck and hit the pavement with a thud. He was scrappy, wearing ripped jeans and a white T-shirt that was three sizes too big for him. His hair was shaved, and his features taut and angular. He was pale, but not sickly so.

"What can I do for ya, matey?" Shorty said, offering a wink as he jeered like a pirate. "Are we going to play a game?" His eyes widened. "Hide and seek! I can hide and you can all try to find me. How about that?"

"Uh, no, Shorty," Charlie said. "We wanted to talk to you about Flip."

When Shorty heard Flip's name, his face brightened. "Where is he? Is he here? Is he hiding? Does he want me to find him?"

Charlie tucked his flask into his jacket pocket and leaned over and put his hands on his knees so that he was eye level with Shorty.

The boy examined Charlie quizzically and then crinkled his nose. "You smell like beer."

"Sorry about that, matey," Charlie said, playing with Shorty. "It was a long night...and morning. But, you see, something has happened to Flip. We wanted you to know."

Shorty peered at Charlie unflinching with his large brown eyes, awaiting more. The cool wind kicked up and leaves stirred around them. Charlie put a hand on Shorty's shoulder.

"A bad man killed him," he said.

Shorty's smiled faded and his eyes shrunk back into his head after filling with water. Then he smiled again. "I'll go hide. You can find me later. I won't go anywhere."

"Okay, Shorty," Charlie said. "I'll come find you."

Shorty pulled away slowly before dashing off.

Charlie turned to the crowd who waited quietly behind him.

"Will he be all right?" Sim asked, watching Shorty disappear around the back of one of the buildings.

Charlie nodded. "He is better equipped than most adults at handling the realities of this world. He'll be sad. But he'll be fine."

"Well, at this point, children don't know anything else but this," Willow said. "Most can't even remember what the world was like before."

Charlie took a deep breath, then raised up his arms as if to give a sermon. "Ladies and gentlemen, thank you for coming out here on this fine, brisk morning. You all know my dear friends from the fortress, Mr. Ford and Ace. They've come here because they need our help. And since they have done so much for us through the years, it is time for us to return the favor."

Willow stood beside Ace, bundled up in a winter coat and a beanie hat with a pompom and gloves. It was hardly less than fifty degrees out, but she was not keen on cooler weather.

"What do you want us to do?" Jacob asked.

Sim cleared his throat. "There's a man out there. I know him from the old days. He is ruthless and has his sights set on assembling men and attacking our home. He has already killed one of my children and he knows no boundaries. He's smart, methodical, diabolical, and relentless."

"Why don't you just leave?" a woman said, perhaps echoing the sentiment of many in the group. "He's giving you fair warning, so why stay?"

Sim was prepared for the question. "Perhaps consider if this situation involved the heights. Would *you* leave?"

His comment quieted her, but did not seem to inspire her interest in giving aid.

"You *know* what we would do, my friends," Charlie answered. "We need you to help fortify with extra numbers at the fortress until this threat is over. Sim has a plan, and the fortress *is* defendable. This is our home. From the fortress to the heights. We have staked a claim on this area and developed it, and nobody should be able to take that from us. We need to make a stand and let others know this is not a territory they can fuck with. If you would do it for the heights, then you would do it also for the fortress."

"I'm in," Willow said. "Just tell me what you need from me."

Nobody else in the group stepped forward with such enthusiasm.

"So, what now?" Jacob asked. "I'd be happy to help."

"Ace and I will be leaving shortly," Sim said. "We invite anyone who is obliged to leave here as well to join us at the fortress for upwards of thirty days, but we don't want to alert Zagan that we have recruits, so we'll need you to stagger your arrival to the fortress. These thirty days may be trying, as we will be keeping you indoors, but we have plenty of food and space to accommodate your temporary stay. We have a defense plan with specifics on how best to utilize you when the day comes, and we will fill you in on those details once you arrive."

"Y'all just fixin to sit around waiting for this fool to attack?" a thirty-something male asked.

"We never just sit around, Wyatt," Sim said. "Life is never a waiting game. We go about our business and when that day comes, we'll be ready."

"Well, it'll be a change of pace, anyway, from walking this cold-ass perimeter every night," Jacob said.

"Well, then," Charlie said, swigging from his flask, "It sounds like we have at least a few of us willing to put our best foot forward. Anyone else?"

"I'll fight till the cows come home if that's what you want, Charlie," Wyatt stated.

"Thank you, sir," Charlie said, holding up his flask in cheers.

The rest of the group disembarked slowly without stating their intentions and Sim took Charlie's hand in his own. "Thank you, Charlie. I am forever proud of you."

"I'm sorry about the lukewarm response," Charlie said. "It's a bit embarrassing because I know what they are capable of. It's just hard getting people to go above and beyond for a cause they may not understand. Most of them know only what is right here inside this compound and though I believe they would die for the heights, the connection with the fortress may be lost. We'll have to work to develop this in the future."

"I think it would be beneficial," Sim said. "And seemingly a gross oversight—like the wall King suggested we put around the fortress that I ignored. I've got to start progressing beyond my need to satisfy small details and start looking at a bigger picture."

"You're not perfect, Sim, and you don't have all the answers," Charlie said. "Once you realize that...you'll change the new world, not only the fortress."

"That's the thing," Sim reflected. "I never set out to change the world. I wanted to die back then. I *tried* to die, but then I brought all these kids into my life. Next thing I know...I'm in it for the long haul. The good, bad, and the ugly."

"You're doing it just fine, just like you did for me all those years ago," Charlie smiled. He emptied his flask to the last drop and stuffed it into his pocket. "See you, Mr. Ford."

Sim and Ace left a short time after the men and women dispersed. Sim could not hide his anxiousness from Ace about the impending arrival of the guests. *I wish there was another way. I wish they didn't have to stay. Maybe we can fix up one of the houses across the street with temporary accommodations. JZ is going to have a cow with Willow being there.*

"Just get over it, Sim!" Ace said at one point. "We don't have a choice and we're going to be good hosts because these are your people as much as the rest of us. Without you, the heights wouldn't have survived the first year. Some of Charlie's people are willing to give their lives for us so that means we owe them everything we have to offer."

Sim could not dismiss Ace's newfound wisdom, which only raw experience in the world could teach. He was waking up to leadership now.

Just in time.

Seventeen

Sim and Ace departed, with the expectation that the other volunteers would soon follow on a staggered schedule. In the meantime, Charlie and Willow sought out Shorty where they knew he would be. Shorty maintained real-estate of his own in building ten, which was otherwise not used by the heights residents, though it was the closest building to the cluster compound.

Sitting on the edge of a tree-filled lot, the building was immersed in shadow in the early part of the day. At the end of the day, the building would be aglow in yellow and orange hues, something the residents would complain about in former times as the sun blasted through their picture windows during dinner or when they were trying to watch television. It was the least popular building in the heights during its heyday.

As the two approached the building, they paused to make note of its eerie standing. Neither spoke, but they knew they were thinking the same thing: In the new world, the days were easily more haunting than the nights—a time when things were normally dark, quiet, and foreboding.

In daylight, in a place like this, there were memories of engines revving, people shuffling to work, distant train whistles, music, school bus pick-ups, arguments, road construction, and of the world, in general, bustling with noise and energy.

"At least we can hear everything else now," Willow said.

Crows cawed, small animals scurried in the woods, wind whipped, leaves whirled, and morning birds sang.

"You know," Charlie said, "when I was about ten years old, I put that window out with a sling shot." He was pointing to a picture window on the left end cap apartment and smiling.

"You were trouble," Willow said.

"I was," he said. "I couldn't even run because everyone in the complex knew who the only kid that had a slingshot was. Mr. Phillips would have just come for me anyway."

"What did he do?" Willow asked.

"He smacked me around a bit," Charlie said. "But I ran product for him throughout the complex, so he wasn't going to do anything too extreme."

Willow shook her head. "And they call these times crazy. It seems to me they aren't any different, just with less people."

Charlie sighed. "Let's go find our Shorty."

The two proceeded into the building and turned right down the cold, dank, corridor. Apartment one was the closest to the main entrance. They entered and found Shorty in his room sitting on top of his bed. He was holding one of his stuffed animals, a yellow cat wearing a baseball uniform.

Shorty, formerly known as Greyson Guy, grew up in the heights and lived there since he was a baby. His parents died and he was an only child. They had a hard time convincing him to leave his apartment to live in the cluster. *It's safer.* Ultimately, they agreed he could visit his apartment whenever he wanted, and they wouldn't allow anyone to touch his things. Thankfully, they never had large issues with squatters or looters because they firmly guarded the entire compound and invited many passersby to join the community in the cluster, unlike Sim who would train his orphans to dispatch trespassers. He and Charlie debated those tactics regularly.

"I would only have half the numbers if I killed everyone that stumbled by over the years," Charlie had said.

"I don't have the room to collect boarders and the fortress is only for children," Sim said.

"Then lead them to me if they have promise," Charlie said.

"That's not what I do," Sim said. "Besides, we have signs up all over to lay warning. If they abide by the warnings, they live. We see people all the time, but the only ones we kill are the ones that pose a threat by advancing on our territory. That's the rule and we act swiftly on it."

"How you doing, Shorty, my man?" Charlie said.

"This was Flip's," he said, holding the baseball cap to his chest. "He gave it to me when I saw him last."

Charlie sat next to Shorty on one side, his hand on one of Shorty's knees, and Willow on the other side of him, poised to snuggle the little guy. With his other hand, Charlie fished for the flask he had refilled prior to seeking out Shorty.

"I'm so sorry, Greyson," Willow said as she pulled the boy close to her. "Flip was special, and his other friends are missing him terribly as well, but you know how hard things are now. You have so much love, though, and so did Flip, so every single minute means something." She kissed him on the cheek.

"Yes, my man, indeed it does," Charlie uttered with an awkward smile, as if to convince Shorty that a few soft words should magically cure his heart.

The realization that the average mortality of a man, woman, or child was no longer based on whether one exercised, ate vegetables, or refrained from smoking was a fact of the new world that had to be reconciled. In these days, a tooth infection was a better bet to snuff out a life than a gun-wielding maniac. So connections that in prior days may have lasted years, in these times may last only days or weeks. Attachments came with a deeper emotional price tag without the acceptance of the potentially short nature of a given relationship. In fact, Shorty had only played with Flip on a few occasions, but it was enough to create an impact.

"I think next time we go to the fortress you should put that on Flip's grave in Usland. What do you say?"

Shorty nodded.

"He would like that," Willow agreed. "And be thankful, Greyson, that you are still here. Make it count."

It's not a message that was uncommon even in the days before the end, yet it meant something different now. There was never a guarantee for anyone that there would be a tomorrow, but such an idea was more coveted over the past three years. Once so easy to take life for granted, not so much so anymore.

The three walked from the apartment building hand-in-hand. Shorty was nine, but still wanted them to swing him as they walked, each of his hands in one of theirs. So, they acquiesced, hurling him over the entryway foyer and out the door, giving pause as they exited and encountered a gang of faces, led by Zagan and Steer.

Willow, Charlie, and Shorty, froze at the gate of the building. Zagan had a revolver stuffed in the waistband of his pants and Steer clutched a rifle, which he had slung over his shoulder.

"You know, I would fire all those people you have on perimeter duty, sir," Zagan said. "But I'm glad they suck at their job, because being here to observe this simple moment...it touches me." Zagan put his hand over his chest. "Damn, I don't know what it is with this area, but maybe children *do* exist, after all."

Zagan took two steps forward. "I think I may have even seen a baby back there," he said. "That is fucking awesome. Although, I don't know if I personally would want to be stuck with some baby in these times...actually, in any times."

"Who are you?" Charlie asked. "And more importantly, why the fuck are you on my territory?"

Zagan looked around as Steer and the gang of men laughed. There were about a dozen in total. "Well, excuse me for wanting to say hello."

"How about goodbye, instead," Charlie said as he dropped Shorty's hand.

Zagan shook his head. "You would like that, Charlie, wouldn't you? But I'm afraid we're going to have to stay and have a little chat about your best buddy, Sim. And I have about forty other people just around the corner ready to storm your shit-ass buildings if you don't oblige." Zagan held out his arms. "So, what do you say?"

Charlie smiled and held out his own arms and smiled, offering up a reverse attitude. "Well, then, how about we proceed back to my apartment and break the ice."

"That's sounds great, Charlie," Zagan said. "And I would love for the little lady and this...small person...to join us."

"He's a child, sir," Willow pronounced. "You can say the word."

"You know, dear Willow, in the Revolutionary War, the British wore coats of red not to look fancy, but so that when their blood spilled it would blend in and not be cause to panic the other soldiers who might otherwise turn away at the sight of it."

"I don't understand the relevance," she said.

Zagan smiled deviously as he removed the revolver from his waistband, pointed it at Shorty, and fired a single shot into the meat of the boy's thigh. Shorty cried out as he fell to the ground and though Willow and Charlie bellowed in unison at the horror of seeing Shorty shot, the others who were present stood silent and unmoving.

"What the fuck did you do?" Charlie howled.

"You see my men?" Zagan asked as Willow removed a belt from her waist and tied it above Shorty's bloodied wound. The boy cried out as Willow tightened the strap around his leg. "They don't run at the sight of blood.

They don't scream. When you have a clear goal and vision, the ends will always justify the means."

"You're wrong," Willow said with tears in her eyes. "You're so wrong."

Zagan's face hardened and his eyes glossed over, like what happens when sharks feed. "I once read that there are only two mistakes one can make along the road to truth: not going all the way, and not starting."

"And I once read that the road to tyranny begins with the destruction of the truth," Willow hissed.

Zagan regarded her utterance with a half-smile. "You're quite entertaining, you know. If you didn't have eyes for that boy from the fortress, I might make you my wife."

Willow spat at him as she embraced Shorty who lied on the cold ground moaning.

"It's time to go," Zagan said, as he extended his arm away from building ten. "Our goal in coming here has not changed, nor has our timeline, despite our philosophical debate."

Charlie scooped Shorty into his arms and he and Willow led the wayward pack to Charlie's building, with much apprehension, though not fear. Charlie's mind raced. He wanted a drink, but dared not reach for his flask lest it be mistaken for him reaching for a weapon.

Most of the men that had been with Zagan when they announced themselves waited outside. Zagan brought Steer and two other men in the building behind Willow, who was leading the way, and Charlie, who still had a grimacing Shorty folded into his body. At the apartment door, Willow knocked on the door—using the wrong door-knock code purposely to alert Susan—waited a minute, then entered.

She, Charlie, and Shorty were followed by Zagan and the two additional men who all piled into the small living area behind them. Willow and Charlie sat on the couch with Shorty resting in Charlie's lap while Zagan sat in the same chair Sim had occupied only twelve hours ago. Steer glanced out the picture window and signaled the other men before taking up position behind Zagan's chair. The other two men stood guard near the doorway.

Zagan crossed one leg over the other and took in a deep breath as he pulled at his coarse, dirty beard. He rested his head back on the chair and observed ten seconds of silence, during which the sounds of Shorty's whimpering was the only noise as his leg wound ran red, blood dropping from his shoes onto the floor.

Willow put a hand on the boy's arm. "I know, baby," she said. "We'll fix you up soon."

Her attention to Shorty snapped Zagan free of his trance and he leaned forward on the chair. Early morning sunlight flooded the living room through the picture window and illuminated the dust in the air.

"You know, Charlie," Zagan started. "It was a bit foolish of you to think we were unaware of your settlement here. I guess we didn't know you held allegiances to Sim and his orphans, but...now we do. My greater calling was to explore the depths of these stories I heard about the fortress. This place...peripheral...until now."

Charlie sat stone face, unblinking. "My allegiance is to my community. Everyone else is a sidebar."

"Hmph," Zagan said. "Yeah, I'm not buying that, Charlie, but if it's true, then you won't mind telling me what your meeting with Sim was about last night. In fine detail."

"Sim and his second come here on and off for the kind of fun that can't be had at the fortress. It's an escape. A vacation. That's it."

Zagan laughed and Steer along with him.

"Ironic," Zagan said. "Once the scourge of the city, now a vacation paradise."

"As good a vacation spot you'll find anywhere nowadays," Charlie said, flatly, finally finding the courage to remove the flask from his pocket, though as guns raised around him. “It’s just a flask.” He raised it to his mouth and took a drink.

Zagan raised a finger. “That’s true, Charlie. So true. And our friends in the east would agree; rules are for conformists. People who like control. Anyway, I know that last night’s visit was about more than just a little fling with the squeezes, and I just have to know what he has told you and where you have placed yourself in all of it.”

“Let me ask you something,” Charlie said. “Why are you so fixated on this man, his children, and his home, while you admittedly leave a community ten times the size in your peripherals. Your approach seems more cowardly than anything.”

Zagan smiled through his thin dry lips. “That is a loaded question, Charlie, but complicated, to be sure. Quite simply, though, when I learned there was a man that created what he called a fortress at the gates of my beloved city and that he trained young people to defend it...Wow. It was lit. Truth is, and you probably know it as well as I, Charlie, the fortress—now that’s a fight of all fights. A fight worth dying to win. Not for just the prize...the building...but the winner also gets to own the set of ideals that permeate the land moving forward. Truth is, me and my people have been looking for a new place to settle. And trust me when I say, government...progressiveness...it’s the last thing on our minds.”

“Well then what do you want from me?” Charlie asked.

“I want you tell me what you discussed with Sim last night,” Zagan said in staccato diction. “If you can do that, as well as refrain from offering him any support during this epic attack upon the enigmatic fortress, then I will lose site of the heights in my...peripherals, as you have called it. After all, this wasn’t a fight that involved you anyway, so there is no need to make it *your* fight. I want to see exactly what Sim and his team of orphan misfits are capable of on their own when push comes to shove.”

Zagan rubbed his hands together feverishly while his men listened in silence.

Charlie passed Shorty over to Willow and leaned forward on the couch, taking one last drink from his steel flask.

"You know, Zagan," Charlie said. "I have mad respect for Mr. Ford. Sim. Since I was a boy, in fact, but his idea that the fortress is a tightly wound, sacred place, while the heights is a loosey-goosey land of debauchery, excess, and chaos is ill-warranted. He's a good man, but the only thing he never realized is how much I learned."

"You know," Zagan said. "Putting a bullet in that boy's leg is a far cry from putting one through his skull, but that is exactly what I'm going to do, unless you tell me what I want to know."

Charlie scoffed. "You're not listening. But hear this: yesterday's meeting was indeed a call for help, to which we are obliged to answer because Mr. Ford is *our* people. We are the fortress, and the fortress is *us*, and together *we* will destroy any man or woman who attacks us, including you. So, if you thought you were going to stampede your way through a bunch of little kids with your bullshit ragtag outfit, you better fucking think again."

Zagan pulled at his beard and his eyes turned black. "It's a nice speech, but I'm just not seeing it."

Charlie clenched his teeth. "Maybe because I didn't want you to."

Steer's face tightened and he drew his weapon from his shoulder. "It's a trap!"

Willow dove to the ground with Shorty in her arms as Charlie roared. "NOW!"

Susan stepped out of the kitchen with a 12-gauge shot gun and fired. Half of Steer's face disintegrated, leaving blood and brain fragments splattered upon Zagan's body. Susan fired two more shots into the chests of each of the doormen before they had time to react. Zagan rushed Charlie and pushed him to the couch as he stood and then leapt through the picture window as gunfire erupted from the many windows of each of the left and right side buildings of the heights compound.

No fewer than a dozen of the soldiers who were waiting out front fell immediately to the hail of bullets and the other thirty or so men remaining ran between the buildings or took cover behind cars as bullets ricocheted across the campus.

Zagan crashed to the ground among thousands of glass shards as he plummeted from the window and Charlie jumped out behind him. When Zagan saw that Charlie was giving chase, he grabbed for a pistol he had tucked in his waistband and fired.

Charlie was on him swiftly and though he took a bullet in the side, the adrenaline had kicked in as he plowed into Zagan without even realizing he was struck. Zagan's gun flew from his hands as the two crashed into the side of an SUV. Charlie had him pinned against the vehicle hurling punches into his sides as gunfire continued to echo through the courtyard, some of the bullets striking the SUV.

Zagan hammered away at Charlie's injured side and eventually Charlie succumbed to the pain and fell to his knees. Zagan kicked him in the face when he went down to one knee and then rolled himself around the edge of the vehicle until he saw his pistol on the ground. The screaming of men getting mowed down by bullets permeated the morning sky. As Zagan was about to pick up his pistol, he was approached by one of his frantic crew members who was trying to escape.

"You're going the wrong way!" Zagan shouted.

The man grabbed Zagan and tried pulling him along. "We have to get out of here now!"

Zagan punched him in the face and the man recoiled, a look of shock on his face. Zagan then grabbed his pistol from the ground and whirled around and shot the fleeing man in the back. As bullets slapped the pavement around him, Zagan casually walked up to his fallen comrade and leaned over him.

"You have a gun, dipshit! You should have used it!" He brought his foot down on the man's head repeatedly until his skull split in two. He then grabbed the man's gun and headed back to where Charlie had fallen. A bullet caught his right shoulder as he stalked Charlie by following a path of blood back to his apartment, but it proved to be nothing more than a mild interruption. He turned around and fired off three aimless shots.

"Return fire, you idiots!" he shouted to some of his men who were cowering behind vehicles.

Zagan returned to the window he had crashed through only moments earlier and peered through the open space that was peppered with loose shards of glass around the frame's perimeter. It was dark inside and hard to see in, but to his surprise, Susan appeared at the window with her shotgun in hand. As soon as Zagan saw her peer her head out the window, he fired a single shot that entered one of her eyes and blew out the back of her skull. Her lifeless body fell forward and landed halfway out the window. Her shotgun fell from her hands onto the ground with a thud.

Zagan heard the screams of terror from inside and he fired two more random shots into the living room before kicking into a sprint away from the compound. Less than a minute later, Willow busted out the front door of the apartment complex, armed with an AR-15. She observed Zagan running in the distance and fired off an entire magazine of bullets hoping to get lucky. Gunfire from the buildings ceased as Willow made her way through the maze of cars looking for anyone who was still hiding. She found six such people with varying degrees of injury and wasted no time disposing of them with rapid fire.

When the battle was over and silence once again filled the air, twenty-four bodies, including Steer's, littered the complex grounds. Susan was the only heights casualty of the fire fight, which anguished Charlie, but he boasted pride for how much worse it could have been.

His bullet wound was clean, in and out, though Shorty required his bullet to be removed from the depths of his thigh, which was a painful extraction. Yet he lived. The heights had dominated, though Zagan escaped, likely demoralized, his men perhaps understanding that his lust for conquest was a conceit not worth indulging.

Time would tell.

Eighteen

WILLOW CAME ALONE TO visit Sim and the others at the fortress with a rifle strapped to her back and a small caliber handgun tucked into her waistband several hours after the assault on the heights. Charlie stayed behind to mend and lead his community in the cleanup.

Shark alerted the others that Willow was making her way down the wooded hill and Sim along with Ace, King, and JZ rushed to the kitchen entrance to let her in.

Ace ran onto the porch and hugged her while JZ looked on from the doorway with venom in her eyes.

"You came here alone?" Sim asked, stepping from behind Ace. "I thought I warned you to come in pairs and—"

"We were attacked," Willow said.

Ace took a step back and exchanged looks with Sim and King.

"Zagan followed you," she said.

"Oh my God," Ace said. "We thought we were being careful."

Willow shook her head. "He knew about the heights anyway, or so he says. It was only a matter of time."

"Well, what happened? Where's Charlie?" Sim asked. "Do we need to get up there?"

"We took out over twenty of their crew," she announced proudly. "Zagan escaped, though. Charlie is fine, but he was shot. Susan is dead, and Shorty was shot as well, but he's recovering."

Sim put a hand on his head and began pacing. "How does he keep slipping away?"

"When you prioritize yourself in every situation, it's easier to stay a step ahead of everyone," Willow said.

"Susan is dead?" Ace asked, as if not hearing correctly the first time.

"Yes, but not before she killed the big guy that is always by Zagan's side. Shot him clear in the face."

"Nice," King said. "Who is Susan?"

"Not now, King," Sim said. "I'm sorry, Willow."

"Don't be," she said. "Charlie wanted me to tell you that you were wrong about the heights."

"Wrong?" Sim said, crooking his neck, curiously. It had become an ongoing theme.

"We set a trap for them," she said. "They thought they had us where they wanted us. They shot Shorty to control us, and it didn't work. Our people at the heights destroyed them because Zagan underestimated our defenses, thinking that only you and the fortress were prepared to fight. He was wrong. *You* were wrong. We aren't just someplace where you come for sex and alcohol while supplying us with gardening tips and weaponry. We may be two miles off, but we are a fortress in our own right." She looked to the others. "We are all the fortress, and Charlie was quick to remind this psychopath of that."

Sim nodded humbly while JZ stomped off. She knew Ace's purpose for going to the heights, but hearing it was too much.

"I'm sorry," Sim said. "I never meant to send the message that the heights was weak and I don't go there just for sex and booze. Charlie and I have strong history, since he was a child, and he has amazed me time and again over the years with his resilience. So, in that respect, his success today comes as no surprise, as he has finally figured out how to fight back against his oppressors, but I understand what you're saying."

"Do you want to come in?" Ace invited.

"No," she said. "I have to get back and tend to Shorty and make sure the cleanup is complete. I worry Zagan could return to even the score."

"Take Ace and King back with you," Sim said. "And thank Charlie and tell him he has my praise."

Willow nodded. "And what about Zagan? Charlie will want to know if your plan is the same. We have Wyatt, Jacob, me, and even Charlie to lend support."

"It's hard to know how he'll react now," Sim said. "We can surely expect him not to tuck tail and run, but in having lost over twenty men, he'll have to regroup. Or maybe without his second in command—"

"Steer," Kellogg said from the door, flipping his coin. The others turned. "His name was Steer and I'm glad he's dead."

"I get the feeling Zagan has connections outside of that," Willow said. "There's more to this than we know."

Sim considered this. "I think we'll do something I was hesitant to do previously: a reconnaissance mission to the steelworks to see if we can learn anything. When things are settled there, if he can spare Jacob and Wyatt we'll check things out and go from there."

"Yes!" King said with a fist pump. He had been a major proponent from the beginning of hitting them on their own turf.

Sim turned on him quickly. "I'm not going there to initiate a fight, King. This will strictly be a covert operation to see if we can gather intel. But it is because of your urgence that I decided to run this mission."

King felt it awkward that Sim was pronouncing the motivation for his decision. Were the older orphans finally being heard? It hinted at progress.

Willow, Ace, and King left with provisions back to the heights while Sim returned inside to consult with Sky, who was in the dining room eating oatmeal with Leo, Miracle, Misty, and Yamil. She, along with the others, looked up when he entered.

"So, what was that all about?" she asked.

But before Sim could answer, Yamil dropped a spoon into his empty bowl. "More."

Sky sighed. "Misty, can you see if there is any more for Yamil?"

"Why do I was always have to wait on the little ones?" she huffed. "Make Leo do it. He always just sits around while the rest of us do chores."

"Not true," he said, insulted. "I do plenty of chores. And anyway, Yamil is little, but he's not helpless."

"He can't reach the pot, so rock, paper, scissors, you two," Sky challenged. "Loser gets the chore."

Leo and Misty smiled deviously at each other and threw out their hands and in unison cried, "Rock, paper, scissors, shoot!"

Leo threw out scissors while Misty threw out a rock and brought it down on Leo's two fingers. Yamil laughed. Leo frowned but slid out from his chair. It was always uncanny how losing an RPS battle never yielded complaint. It was an accepted and respected form of mediation among children and Sky deployed the tactic quite regularly in her management of the younger ones.

"Don't think you're just going to sit there, Yamil," Leo said. "You may not be able to reach the pot but I'm not bringing the pot to *you*. And I won't wait on you hand and foot, either. So let's get moving and bring your bowl with you."

The two passed Sim, each looking up at him with their large eyes, and he smiled down upon them. Sky shook her head as Kellogg entered the room and sat beside her at the head of the table.

"It's hard to believe that at a moment's notice they'll drop everything and throw firebombs out the window and kill anything that moves," Kellogg said with a chuckle.

"It's called discipline, Kellogg," Sim said. "Any parent will tell you that their child is a totally different person at school than he is at home. They do what's required, and when they aren't doing that, they are free to be...themselves."

"As long as they don't lose *themselves* along the way, it could be a fair trade," Sky said.

"It's the balance of all things that makes the difference," Sim said. "They will remain true to themselves as they grow in understanding that our love is most important and killing and death are only what is necessary to survive."

"In the story of Peter Pan, the lost boys killed pirates and Indians all the time and they remained good," Kellogg said. "Even without love and guidance."

"They had Peter," Misty said just as Leo was returning with Yamil in tow.

"Peter was a misfit, incapable of true love," Sky said. "That is why he could never get with Wendy."

"But there was Wendy, who was their mother," Kellogg said. "She loved them."

"But she was only there for a short time," Sky said. "I can see we're going to have to revisit this story."

"Why don't we have a mother?" Miracle asked, finally adding to the conversation.

The children fell silent and regarded Sim. In all the years, the question had not come up, and it was not ironic that the inquiry should arise from one of the youngest in out-of-the-mouth-of-babes fashion.

"You did have," Sim said. "But the sickness took them away. So, all we have is each other now."

"But mothers give hugs, and tuck us in, and sing to us when we fall asleep," Leo lamented.

Sim walked to the table and pulled out a chair next to Sky. He collapsed wearily into it. "True, I do fall short in those areas of outward affection, but I hope you all know I love you very much. When I took you in, though...it wasn't about that, I guess."

"Why did you take us in, then?" Sky asked.

Sim pondered. "It started with Elizabeth—"

"Sky tucks us in," Yamil said.

"She hugs us too," Leo said.

"Once she kissed me on the cheek," Miracle said. Everyone laughed.

"She never kissed me on the cheek," Kellogg said, hurling his cheek at Sky.

Sky shoved his face away. "In your dreams." She laughed and so did Kellogg.

"So, you're our mother then, I guess," Leo said.

"She's *motherly*," Sim said. "And maybe will be a mother one day. And a darn good one. But remember, she is like you. A child. And you are here to be children and survive to be adults."

"Then what?" Sky asked. "Where do we belong if this place is solely a haven for children?"

"I can't even think about what's in store for tomorrow, let alone in the next generation," Sim said. He then placed his hand over her arm. "Anyway, you'll always be my children. I just don't know how it ends."

JZ then entered and leaned on the wall. "What's going on in here? Did that ugly girl from the heights leave yet?"

"I don't know who you were looking at, but that girl was fine," Kellogg said, licking his finger and touching his skin while making a sizzling sound.

"Shut up," JZ said.

"That girl and the heights were just attacked by Zagan," Sim said. "He followed Ace and me there and when we left..."

"What happened?" Sky said, eyes wide. She cared more about people's well-being than anyone.

"The heights fought back with much success, but failed to kill Zagan."

"He's like a cat with nine lives," Misty said as her eyes glazed over. "I had a cat once, named Kelly. She was white and fluffy, and she used to climb the curtains and sleep in bed with me at night. Then she disappeared one day, not too long before everyone died."

Sim cleared his throat. "Sorry for that, Misty, but Zagan is not a cat. He is a man with only one life. And he will leave like your cat and never come back, or we will kill him so that *we* can live."

"I'll use my knives on him," Baby said as she, Big Will, and Teddy entered the room.

"Why is everyone in here?" Teddy asked. "Are we having a party? I love parties." He rubbed his hands together feverishly. "I wish Flip could be here for the party."

"We were talking about Peter Pan," Leo said. "Not having a party."

"I love that story," Baby said. "I want to be a mermaid when I grow up."

"You can't be a mermaid, no more than you can be a giraffe," Leo said.

"I don't want to be a giraffe, and Big Will said I could be a mermaid," Baby argued.

Big Will, a boy of few words, shrugged his shoulders.

"Listen, everyone," Sim said. "It's good that we are all here, because I can update you where we are in this situation with Zagan."

The last three to enter the dining room along with JZ crowded around the table. Sim was nearly ready to speak when Shark wallowed down the stairs in a series of thuds. When he entered the dining room, he regarded the crowd. "Whoa," he said. "I didn't realize you had called a meeting."

"It just happened," Sim said. "Everyone was here so I thought I would update you."

"Why did Willow come and why is she going back with Ace and King?" Shark asked.

"The heights was attacked," Kellogg said. "Whatever the heights are."

"It's a place with people that we know and care about," Misty said.

"Who is Shorty, anyway?" Kellogg asked.

"What happened to Shorty?" Shark asked.

"He was shot, but he's fine," Sim said. "They did well against Zagan, but the guy is still alive."

"Fuck it all," Shark said.

"Language," Sky chastised.

"What the hell is up with this guy?" Shark asked. "Is he the damn Terminator or something?"

"What's that?" Leo asked.

"A robot guy," Kellogg said. "My uncle loved those movies."

"He was a cyborg, not a robot," Shark corrected.

Sim held up his hands. "Enough of this babbling, everyone. Let's focus. Now, Ace and King are bringing back some friends from the heights and we're going to covertly visit Zagan's steelworks outpost to see if we can learn anything about his next move. The heights took out over twenty of his men, so if he is still planning to attack the fortress, I'm confident we have time, which is good, because we are going to brick over our windows and doors to make this place even more formidable. The heights just bought us more time."

"Brick over the doors?" Shark said.

"Yes, all entry points," Sim said. "We have piles of brick in the back from the old retaining wall, as well as concrete mix."

"How will we get out to use the bathrooms?" Sky asked. "The tunnel goes beyond the property line, and we don't want to go that far away from the fortress to use the bathroom."

They had spent two years digging the tunnel from the basement to the east side of the property line as a means of emergency escape. The exit at the property line was the size of a sewage access point and disguised with a plywood covering and some brush.

"We'll figure it out," Sim said. "It's only temporary. Maybe we should even consider a thirty-day quarantine while the extra brickwork is in place."

"Why is this reminding me of the story of the Three Little Pigs?" Kellogg said.

"You know what happened in that story," Shark said.

"What?" Yamil asked, shoveling the last of his seconds into his mouth.

Shark turned to Sky. "You never read them the story of the Three Little Pigs? What kind of teacher are you?"

Sky shrugged. "We did Goldilocks and the Three Bears, Three Billy Goats Gruff—"

"Why are there always three?" Leo inquired, scratching his head.

"Anyway," Shark said to Yamil, "The Three Pigs is a story where...three pigs were trying to hide from the Big Bad Wolf. First, they hid in a house of hay and the Big Bad Wolf blew it down. Then they tried a home of sticks, and he blew *that* down. Finally, they ran and hid in a house made of brick. And you want to know what happened?"

"Cuéntame, cuéntame," Yamil said, his eyes lighted up with anticipation.

"The Big Bad Wolf could not blow the brick house down, as hard as he tried, and the pigs lived happily ever after."

"Sounds promising," Kellogg said, flipping his coin and shoving it into his pocket.

"We can't take anything for granted," Sim said. "We need to prepare, and we can start today instead of waiting for the others to return."

"Okay, then," Sky said, "instead of lessons today, we are going to be hauling brick into the house."

Some children were happy to escape the library lessons with Sky, while others like Baby dreaded the thought of hauling bricks. Everyone kept their opinions to themselves, however, as they rarely complained about what was required.

As they were finishing their breakfast, a man's screams from out front captured their attention. Without hesitation, everyone scrambled from their seats. Sim, Kellogg, Big Will, and Baby rushed to the front while JZ dashed to the back. Misty, Leo, and Teddy fled to the second floor, while Sky ushered the little ones to floor three directly behind Shark who was taking stairs four at a time to get to the roof.

Kellogg moved to the west-facing windows after snatching a rifle that sat at the corner of the dining room. "Nothing on this side."

Baby and Big Will took positions at either side of the double doors of the main entrance as Gigi came barreling out from the kitchen barking madly. Big Will shushed her, but she continued to howl. Sim went to the front window on the east side in the living room and glanced out. There was a single man standing in the street, bloodied and screaming. His shirt was torn, and his face splattered with blood. He was empty-handed.

"You killed her!" he screamed. "You're gonna die! All of you! She was not supposed to die like this."

"Who is it?" Kellogg asked, peering out the front window on the west side.

"I have no idea," Sim said. "Survivor of the heights battle?"

"Why the heck is he blaming us for that?" Kellogg asked.

JZ ran from the back of the house. "It's clear back there. He must be alone."

"Then let's just shoot him and be done with it," Kellogg said. "He did want to eat me, you know."

Big Will put his hands on the doorknob, poised to open. Gigi rose from her hind legs ready to pounce.

"It could be a trap," Sim said. "JZ, take a position at the front window, floor two."

JZ ran up the stairs and the others on the first floor heard her footsteps on the ceiling as she positioned herself. Sim readied a rifle as he stood at the foyer.

"What are you doing?" Kellogg asked.

"He's unarmed," Sim said. "I'm just going to ask him what he wants. Maybe we can get a feel for where Zagan went. We need information."

Big Will opened the door on his side as Baby remained poised. Gigi squeezed in between Sim and the open space and barked madly at the bloodied intruder.

"There you are, you coward!" the man yelled, holding out his arms. "You killed my wife. You killed her stone-cold!"

Killed his wife? Murderer? "Tell me, stranger, what lies has Zagan told you about us to brainwash his army and pit you against us?"

The man fell to his knees. "She didn't have to die. This is all your fault." He pointed at Sim. "But I'll be back. We'll *all* be back, and this place will fall! You hear me! This place will fall!"

As the man cried out, a Molotov cocktail fell from the sky and shattered in front of him. The man erupted into a ball of fire and as he screamed in horror, Sim fired a shot from his rifle that entered the man's chest and sent him hurling backward. Big Will stepped out behind Sim with his Ak-47 and fired several more holes into the man's body as he collapsed into a fiery pile of skin and bones.

Big Will lowered his gun as he watched the corpse burn. "You won't be coming back."

Ace, King, Willow, Wyatt, and Jacob returned the next day and Sim filled them in on the man who they dispatched earlier in front of the fortress.

"He was nasty and bloody and said we killed his wife," Kellogg said. He arched one curious eyebrow upward. "Did we?"

"There were only a few women present at the raid yesterday and they were all killed," Willow attested.

"One thing is for sure," Sim said. "Zagan is filling his soldiers' heads with a boat load of propaganda to get them to do what he wants—which is killing me, at the very least."

"There would be no other reason why so many people would follow him blindly," Willow said, making her hair into a ponytail. "So, when do we check this steelworks out?"

"Why are *you* here?" JZ said, stepping into the living room where the older members of the house were having their conversation. She was eyeballing Willow. "The spy mission is a *man's* work."

"Well, aren't you as pretty as a peach," Wyatt said, pushing aside his greasy blond hair.

JZ regarded him with a crinkled nose. "I can see why Sim is opposed to merging our compounds."

"JZ!" Sim chided. "This is unacceptable. Go do your morning chores. Now!"

She backed away slowly, her eyes on Willow as she departed.

Sim turned to Willow awkwardly. "She's got a crush—"

"I get it," Willow said, snapping a piece of gum. "Some things never change."

"What?" Wyatt shrugged.

Jacob shook his head. "This is going to be fun. And you wanted us to stay here a month?"

King laughed.

"We'll go to the steelworks tonight," Sim said. "Perhaps today we can map out a route and you can help us brick up the doorways and windows."

"Whatcha gonna do that for, boss?" Wyatt asked. "How will we get in and out?"

Sim smiled. "We haven't spent three years here twiddling our thumbs, Wyatt."

"We have an escape tunnel that leads from the basement to the outskirts of the property."

"Hell yeah," Wyatt said with a country twang in his voice. "That's what I'm talking about. No wonder why y'all want to stay here. Even if they whoop your asses, you can still get out and they won't be none the wiser."

"That's not how we want this to go," Sim said. "The tunnel was more to initiate sneak attacks. If we wanted to run from the fight we would just go now."

"I'm just saying," Wyatt continued. "It's good to have the option in case shit goes south."

King grimaced, though he was no stranger to cursing. He knew Sim would be less accepting of people coming into the fortress and using foul language.

"We don't swear in the fortress," Sim said in passing.

Wyatt regarded him with a crooked glance.

Everyone went about a hard day's work hauling brick. They created brick walls in the recessed areas of every first-floor window and door, being sure to leave a brick out of each wall so they had viewing holes. At the kitchen door, they left a column of brick off the wall so they could pass in and out for the time being without having to use the underground tunnel.

As the sun dipped beneath the horizon, Sim, Ace, King, Wyatt, Willow, and Jacob headed off toward the steelworks. Shark scouted the immediate area with his scope and saw not a soul in any direction. He caught sight of a few animals, some debris floating with the gusts of wind, but no other signs of movement. He wanted to feel confident that the crew was not being observed as they left, but he had gone through the same motions before they left to the heights and yet Zagan followed them. His confidence was waning.

Sim did not take the same route, when pursuing Zagan to the steelworks, after Flip had been killed. He took the group off road, using yards, trees, fences, houses, cars, and whatever else would conceal them to his advantage on his slow approach. Every couple of minutes, he halted the group. He waited. He listened. He watched. Then brought them a little further.

The night was cold and breezy. Wyatt was skin and bones and shaking uncontrollably in his short sleeve T-shirt, his teeth chattering, audibly.

"Will you shush," Jacob whispered while they were all under cover at the side of a pick-up truck. "What's the matter with you coming in a skimpy T-shirt?"

Wyatt was holding himself in a tight embrace. "Well, heavens to Betsy, I didn't know. You're the one always fixin' to be on perimeter duty anyway. I don't typically hang out in the cold. Let me check this gosh darn truck for something."

Wyatt pulled open the door to the truck. It opened with a loud squeak and crunch of metal.

"What the hell..." King said.

Wyatt peered in and pulled out a pink sweatshirt with the word "Diva" written across the chest. He pulled it over his head and rubbed his arms.

King busted out laughing, as did Jacob and Willow.

"I had one just like it back in the day," Willow laughed.

"You sure are pretty, Wyatt," Ace remarked.

"Well, this is the worst situation I've been in since the fall of man," Wyatt said. "At least it's warm."

Everyone then turned to Sim, who was looking at them anxiously. "Are you all through?"

The group refocused and Sim led them to the next leg of the journey, crossing over a quiet broken street, down an alley between two houses, through a scrap yard, across a set of railroad tracks and into a spit of trees and brambles. Once there, he paused again, observing the outpost.

The steelworks facility had fallen to decay long before the new beginning. It was a large, open building made of brick, concrete, and metal, partially obscured in overgrowth.

Sim watched the building closely, but from one hundred yards away, it was difficult to see anything without light. The moon was offering some, but not enough to make out much more than the building's shadowy outline.

"I can't see shit," Wyatt said. "But it looks cattywampus to me."

"Nicely put, diva," King said. "Whatever the fuck that means."

"You guys stay here, and I'll take a closer look," Sim said.

"We didn't come to sit in the bushes," Ace said. "We should all go and that way, if we run into anyone, we'll be able to handle it."

Sim replied, "Follow me, then."

Everyone had weapons clutched in their hands as they crossed another field of tall grass in single-file formation. They stopped at the side of the brick building and peered through the vertical windows, many years broken, but detected nothing but darkness.

"Hell if I see anyone in there," Wyatt said.

"I can't imagine they wouldn't have guards or anyone carrying flashlights," Ace said. "He must have fled."

Sim did not reply. He led them around the perimeter of the building to the large entrance, which had no door, but rather looked like a black hole leading into the abyss.

"I'll tell you what, I'm not going in there," Wyatt said. "Not unless I know what's waiting."

Sim pulled a pack from around his shoulder and retrieved a large flashlight he had brought along with him. He flipped it on and pointed it into the abyss. He led the group in behind the wide ray of light that he shone in various directions. The steelworks building was vast, and empty outside of a few rats that scurried to and from.

"Are we sure they were here?" Ace said. "In *this* God-awful place holing up?"

"I wouldn't have stayed *here* for two seconds," Jacob commented.

"They were here at one point," Sim said. "Which means they either relocated or—"

"Went away altogether," Willow said.

"I wouldn't count on it," Sim said. "But who knows. I guess we'll just have to stick to the plan and see what happens," he continued. "There are certainly plenty of places he could be. The county prison isn't too far from here, but I know that is already inhabited at least by one person, if he is still alive. Or Saint Peter's church, which is quite large."

"The middle school is only about a mile or so," King said.

"Well, I'm not going to spend countless nights chasing him around," Sim said. "We're going to fortify ourselves at the fortress and be on the ready for a siege."

"It sucks that we have to live in fear of this guy," King said, kicking a nearby drink can. "Brick up our doors and windows and imprison ourselves because of this nut. He's just one guy! I still say we find him wherever the hell he is and kill his ass once and for all."

Just then, gunfire lit up the sky and bullets ricocheted off the steelwork's brick walls. One of the bullets caught Jacob in the side and he collapsed to the ground. He rebounded with a groan and shuffled to his feet. The group retreated from the gunfire into the steelworks building as gunfire erupted from all four sides of the building.

"Shit!" King said. "Fucking assholes."

Once inside the building, Sim shined a light on Jacob's wound as he leaned against the wall.

"God dammit," Jacob said, lifting his shirt to reveal a small entry wound just beneath his left side rib cage. Sim checked for an exit wound but saw nothing.

Everyone else had their guns ready as they took up positions near the steelworks entryway and the windows.

"I can't see shit," King said.

"Stay calm," Sim said. "Neither can they. The darkness will be our best chance to get out. They're firing blindly."

"Hell, if we aren't sitting ducks in here," Wyatt said. "We have to get out of here fast."

"Can you walk?" Sim asked Jacob.

"I'll have to," he said.

Willow jumped into the entryway and sprayed the area with a round of bullets from her AR-15. Their foes returned fire with what appeared to be several shotgun blasts, pistol shots, and perhaps a couple rounds from automatics.

"Go out the other side and I'll continue fire bursts to keep them away," Willow said.

"We aren't leaving while you sit here and hold them off," Ace contested. "No way."

"I'll be right behind you," she said. "I'm not dying in this shit-ass building. I'm the only one with the firepower to keep them at bay."

"I'll wait with you," Ace said. He turned to Sim, who he could only see an outline of in the darkness of the steelworks. "Go. You'll need a head start with Jacob."

Sim nodded. He helped Jacob to the backend corner of the building with King and Wyatt in the lead. King had an eye on another large hole in the building where there looked to once be a loading dock of some sort. He tripped more than once on blocks of fallen concrete and steel girders that littered the ground. As he ran, he heard Willow's sporadic fire from the front as well as the response fire on all sides.

They reached the loading dock area and the hole in the brick wall that led into tall brush. King peered out while the enemies, lurking in the dark, fired upon the building.

"Their fire seems to be concentrated on the front end," King whispered.

"Well then, let's get our asses out this hole while the getting is good," Wyatt said.

"You go with Jacob," Sim said. "He's gonna need a head start."

He passed Jacob over to Wyatt. "Hands and knees," Sim instructed. "Take it slow."

"I'm going back out front with the others," King said.

"Be safe," Sim said, his voice traveling through the darkness, more powerful than a beam of light.

Wyatt and Jacob fell to a crawling position and exited the hole in the building into the darkness. Sim watched them off while King turned to get Willow and Ace and lead them back to the exit point when gunfire blazed near the area of the hole where Sim, Jacob, and Wyatt had exited.

"Fuck," King said.

A few seconds later, Wyatt dove back through the hole. King reached around and put his arm out the exit hole and fired a few shots from his pistol.

"Jacob's dead, y'all," Wyatt said, taking in large breaths. "They have this exit covered. We're surrounded. I can't die in this damn pink sweater! What the fuck. I reckon we walked right into this."

"What are we going to do?" King asked, revealing the child within for the first time in many years.

"We're going to figure it out," Sim said, and though it was impossible to see his look of reassurance, King envisioned it because he had seen it one hundred times before.

"They have us right where they want us," Willow said. "All they need to do is wait until daylight and advance. They have the numbers. We have to figure a way out of here."

"Through the front door," Sim said. "That's how it will be."

"Hold your horses," Wyatt said. "They're all over the place, hiding in the weeds."

"Zagan doesn't want this," Sim said. "He wants to take us at the fortress. Right now, there's only one way out of this." Sim sprang to his feet. "Follow me."

He dashed to the front of the steelworks building and the others followed him, wondering what he had in mind. When he arrived back at the entrance to the steelworks, he yelled out into the night. "Zagan! I want a parley!"

Thirty seconds elapsed with no response, but no gunfire either.

"Zagan!" Sim screamed. "Do you hear me?"

Another thirty seconds passed, then Zagan's voice emerged from the depths of silence. "We have you surrounded, Sim. We can kill you all now and then go take the fortress tomorrow. Why should I agree to a parley?"

Sim swallowed hard. "Because this is not the way you want it. We both know it, or you would have killed me on the street last time when you had the chance."

Another minute went by before Zagan replied. "Fine. I except your parley, but just you. Exit slowly with your hands in the air, and if any of your people fire on me, my men will not just kill them...we will torture them and burn them alive. There are roughly fifty of us out here, and you have no chance."

"Agreed," Sim said. He turned to the others. "Don't do anything stupid."

"His men won't do shit if we take *him* out," King said. "Cutting the head off this snake is the only thing that will save us."

Sim grabbed King's sleeve. "You asked me how we were going to get out of this. *This* is how. We live. He lives. We kill him another day."

King shook off Sim's hand and turned away.

"I hope this works," Ace said.

"If it doesn't, it won't matter, because we're all dead if it fails," Willow said.

Sim put his hands in the air and exited the steelworks, his flashlight in one of his raised hands. He waited at the entrance until Zagan appeared from the dark, smiling ominously under the moonlight.

He stood there in his bloodied shirt, his wild hair caked with grime, his beard enveloping his face, his jeans falling beneath his emaciated frame, his hands on his hips, though carrying a small flashlight in his right hand.

Sim turned on his flashlight while his hands remained in the air to make sure Zagan understood it was not a weapon. Zagan turned on his own flashlight as Sim lowered his arms.

"I knew you would come back here eventually," Zagan said. "Playing defense all the time gets old."

"I'm a firm believer that the best offense is a good defense," Sim said. "Keep that in mind. I didn't come here to finish you, believe it or not. I came here to find out if you actually stayed after that mess at the heights."

Zagan stroked his beard. "Yes, it was a mess. That Charlie...for a lush, he is really one tricky son of a bitch. I like that, though. Man, he really fucked us up." Zagan started laughing maniacally.

Sim sighed. "Zagan...why can't you just go? Is it worth it?"

Zagan's laughter subsided. "Well, hell yeah it's worth it. This has been ordained. The devil has a destiny too, and the more I stay, the more my purpose is revealed. Tell me you aren't having the least bit of fun, you crazy son-of-a-bitch. You spent the last three Goddamn years fortifying your castle, and helping the heights do the same—if not to prepare for *me,* then what? I remember all those people years before this shit went down...They called them doomsday preppers. These crazy motherfuckers weren't just preparing for the end of times; they were *hoping* for the end of times so they could look around and say 'fuck you' to everyone else. You're no different. You want to win better than anyone else. You want to beat me. You say you didn't come here to kill and I believe you because you want it the way I want it. You want to say 'fuck you, Zagan...I won.'"

"If you think that's what I want, then you're crazier than I thought," Sim said. "I prepare, not so people *will* attack, but so they *won't* attack. To keep the kids safe."

Zagan inched closer to Sim. "If that's what you think, then I know you better than you know yourself."

"Whatever the case, we'll see what's what," Sim said.

"Exactly!" Zagan said, swinging his flashlight in circles. "But fuck the heights and their support. You don't need 'em. You want to face me and my men the way it was meant to be. You didn't design your fortifications around defending your fortress with the help of the heights. You trained your orphans, you built your walls, and you expected they would always do the trick." Zagan turned away, pouting. "Going to the heights is a damn cheat."

"Yet attacking us with over a hundred men and women when we have but a dozen defenders—children, at that—is fair?"

Zagan stomped his foot on the ground. "Yes! You have a fortress. How many men is that worth? I've heard the stories."

"What about the stories you told your people to villainize me so that they would have a clean conscience when they killed us all? Is that fair?"

Zagan shrugged. He leaned in to whisper so his men would not hear. "Well, they aren't going to follow me into the shit just for the fuck of it."

"You know what's not fair?" Sim said. "You are making up all the rules to what is now a childish game of cat-and-mouse. You should have just tried your best to take us down that first night. That would have been honorable. No matter which way it went. This...this is an insult."

"But accepting your parley is not an insult?" Zagan retorted. "Letting you go the other night was not an insult after you tried to blow my head off at the bridge? Giving you a chance to end this by turning over Kellogg to me was not an insult? It sounds like *you* are the one making up all the rules."

"Very well, then," Sim said. "Since you are intent on this course, maybe we should both establish rules. First one is that you leave the heights alone. You'll tell me when this attack is to take place, you let us leave here peacefully, and you don't interfere with our normal way of life between now and this dreadful day to come. In return, we'll go about our usual business, we will not try to track you, and we will not involve the heights in our defenses."

Zagan smiled as he ran a hand through his hair. "Wow. That is a hell of a lot to ask. A hell...of a lot. But most of it seems reasonable. This sounds more like how the British fought in the Revolutionary War. We are such gentlemen, aren't we?"

"One of us, anyway," Sim said.

Zagan laughed so hard he had to bend over and place his hands on his knees to recover. "You kill me, Sim. Just like you were. Little miss priss. We'll leave the heights alone for now, but you should warn them if we pass through your defenses, they'll be next, and we already know how *they* operate, which is great intel, though it cost us. Just like it did when we sicked the probing party on your...fortress. Secondly, it would be silly to tell you when I would plan my attack, but before winter, for sure, and if you leave us alone, we shall return the favor, which would be nice because right now, I must recover from this irritating gunshot wound and of course, mourn the loss of my right-hand man, Steer. It was very traumatizing to see his face end up in such a state, but he would be happy to know I returned the favor with that shot that landed right between the eyes of that bitch who took him down. Yet, I shall miss him."

"Zagan," Sim said. "You're not going to win this. This shit stops at the fortress and so many lives...people you have tricked and lied to...they're going to die for nothing."

Zagan shook his head. "You're missing the point, Sim. You always miss the point. If you got it, you could be *my* right-hand man. Hell, I would have shot Steer's ugly mug off years ago for that. War buddies. Tacticians. We could rule this place."

"I don't do the devil's work," Sim said.

"Oh, no?" Zagan answered. "If you think that, then it is you who is blind. It's all the devil's work."

Sim knew there was no winning this battle of the wills, but the resolutions adopted allowed them to escape death, except for Jacob, who would never leave that grassy field by the steelworks alive. Little did he know that King heard the negotiations as well and would have much to say about them.

Nineteen

King stayed several steps ahead of everyone else as they traveled back to the fortress, this time not ducking behind cars or in between houses, but walking the faded yellow lines of the streets under the guide of their flashlights.

"I can't believe we are just leaving him there," Willow said. "Jacob has been with the heights for two years. He deserves better."

"We can go back in the daylight and give him a proper burial," Sim said.

"He was a good man, bless his heart," Wyatt said. "He was good to me...Not everyone is."

Sim tried keeping up with King, noticing that he was apart from the group and not saying much. He called to him a few times, but King ignored him. This so bothered Sim that he did something he rarely did. He raised his voice. "King!"

King froze in his tracks, as did everyone else. He turned around slowly, a look of annoyance crossing his face—a hardened face—much older looking than that of a sixteen- year-old.

"What?"

"Say it now," Sim said. "I don't want to do it back at the fortress. Not in front of the little ones."

King eyed his surroundings as the others gathered round him in a semi-circle. "I remember this street back in the day. One of my friends was hit by a car right at that intersection down there." He pointed a short distance over Sim's shoulders and the others turned to view the intersection. "He died. I remember the article online. It was a picture of his sneaker just lying there. He had been knocked out of his sneakers. And I remember wondering why he had to die. He was a good kid. There were tons of kids at my school that weren't good, but they lived. The good ones die."

"Why are you angry?" Sim asked.

King clenched his teeth. "Because we could have shot him then and there and even if those other men swooped in and killed us, they would never have invaded the fortress without Zagan. You negotiated our safe release with terms of his attack on the fortress. That is crazy. You're just as crazy as he is. The two of you. Old war buddies, haggling over the terms of our fate. What is wrong with you?"

"It's not what you think—"

"It is!" King yelled. "He's a terrorist and you don't negotiate with terrorists!" His face reddened and the veins in his neck pulsated. "This is a personal war now. It has nothing to do with any of us. This is about your egos. The both of you!"

"First of all, we weren't war buddies; he hated me because I got men killed over my ideals...Second of all, this is about your safety and nothing else. Your life. Our lives. I don't want you to die. And I surely don't want evil to win."

King stepped forward so he was nose-to-nose with Sim. "This is a game to you."

Ace stepped beside Sim. "He has our best interest at heart, King."

"You *would* say that," King said.

"What does that mean?" Ace asked.

"I remember in junior high reading about a group of Jewish children during the holocaust that were brought to Auschwitz. They were led to the gas chambers while singing. Keep on singing Ace, and see where it gets you." King regarded the others while pointing a finger at himself. "But I want Zagan dead, and I think the best place for all of them is the heights until his head is on a pike. They have the people, they have strong defenses, and we have a better chance there. Zagan doesn't care about the fortress so long as it isn't being defended. So, the best chance *we* have to preserve what *we* built, is to leave it while we plan an attack on *him*."

"And what happens when they attack the heights?" Sim asked. "The same thing, King. We fight. Maybe we die. I'm not the problem here. Zagan is. And I'm not leading any of you to your deaths. Just because I agreed on terms to get out of there tonight doesn't mean I have any intention of honoring them. I'll do what I must in order to beat him. All I was trying to do tonight was get us out of there alive so we could live to fight another day. Like it or not, he is here to stay."

"That's why we should have killed him, then and there!"

"Maybe," Sim said. "But I called for a parley, and he didn't kill us. So, we owed him the same."

King shook his head and laughed mockingly. "Jesus Christ. You never listen to anyone but yourself."

"King," Sim said as the boy turned away. "I respect your background and where you came from, but you don't know everything. Not about this situation, or not about me and why we're even here in the first place."

"I know enough," King said as he turned and walked off into the night. "And if you don't think this past twisted relationship you had with this guy is influencing your judgment on how to handle him, you would be wrong; but since you don't care what anybody thinks because you are too much of a control freak, then so be it."

When they returned to the fortress, King gathered some things, including food and weapons.

Many of the orphans were still at the front door wondering what happened after the group returned when King came back down, a backpack slung around his shoulders.

"Where are you going?" Sky asked.

Sim stood silent at the door along with everyone else, likely wondering the same thing.

"I'm going to find him," King said. "And I'm going to kill him. I'm going to end this, to keep us all safe, because that is what needs to be done, and it can't get done here."

Sky looked to all of them with an expression of confusion. "What happened tonight?"

"Jacob died," King said. "And Sim and Zagan negotiated terms of the attack of the fortress."

"What?" Sky said, confused.

"Exactly," King said, exchanging glances with Sim.

Sky turned to Sim imploringly. Sim cocked his head back and shook his head. "Gather everyone in the living room. King, before you leave maybe you'll meet with us all."

"What's the point?" King asked.

"I don't want you to go," Sim said. "But I can't follow you this time."

King held his gaze with Sim for several seconds. "I have to go." Then he turned from Sim and walked out the front door.

Sim held his frozen expression for several seconds more as Big Will closed the doors behind King.

"Gather everyone in the living room," Sim said. "Shark included."

Fifteen minutes later, the room was full except for Miracle and Yamil, who had gone to sleep. Willow, Wyatt, Ace, JZ, Kellogg, Sky, Misty, Teddy, Leo, Big Will, Baby, and Shark. Some in chairs, some on the floor obtaining warmth from the fireplace, over which their handprint mural hung. All eyes on Sim as he stood beside the "days-gone-by" wall—a series of hashmarks revealing the days since the old world ended. Words scribbled beside it noting stories told and untold. All were transfixed, including the heights visitors.

Sim gazed upon them all with affection as he poised to reveal the intent of the meeting. There was warmth among them. Love. One could feel it all around, like an invisible shield protecting them from the new world.

"It's time, my children, for my story. Before the end. Maybe I should have told you this at the beginning...I'm sorry."

Eyes widened. The only noise was the crackling and popping of wood in the fireplace.

Sim looked around the room, but not at anyone, trying to figure out a place to begin. He raised his arms. "As you know, the fortress is my home. It was mine before it was ours."

No response.

Sim's lip quivered. "I...bought this house three months before the virus to win back my family who had left me. My wife. My daughter, Sara. Truth is, I was never there for them. I was good at many things, but I was an inattentive father and husband. But that's not the worst of it. You see...I was supposed to die back then. Amanda and Sara...we all agreed that we would go together."

The orphans looked at Sim expectantly.

Sim swallowed hard. "It's hard to say, but I...killed them both, but when I tried to kill myself after...I couldn't do it."

Sim felt the tears well in his eyes, that day raw in his mind.

"Worst yet," he continued, "Sara...wasn't even sick."

"You shot Sara?" Baby asked.

Sim nodded in shame.

"Oh, man," Ace said.

"I was meant to die after that," Sim said. "I couldn't figure out why I was still alive until Elizabeth showed up, unexpectedly. You never met her, but she was special. We all owe our lives to her." Sim offered a short, pained laugh. "Truth is, I didn't even want to let her in. I never wanted *any* of this. I just thought it was some penance that God gave me. To keep children safe to make up for what I had done. I deserved nothing else."

"You don't love us?" Teddy asked.

"I love you all," Sim said. "I guess we just can never expect what's coming. Zagan has tested me in new ways. I guess I didn't know this would be part of the plan. But make no mistake, I want him gone from this earth. I firmly believe that running is not the answer. Zagan wants the glory of a victory only he can understand, but he is not the only one we will see in these days who will challenge us. He will not be the only person that will try to kill us, that will try to take away what we built. So, we must figure out how to triumph, yet it'll be the biggest challenge to our safety we have ever known." Sim paced back and forth before them, his hands behind his back. "I will never replace your mothers or fathers, but you are as much my children now as Sara was, and I would tell her the same thing if she were with me today." He stopped to face them. "Be strong. No matter what."

"You did what you thought was best for her at the time, Sim," Sky said. "Like my uncle did for me when he led those men away. We shouldn't muddle the present with the past. It's done and over."

"You have to be right, Sky," Sim said. "Or none of this make sense. But you all have a choice to make. I can't make it for you. I was meant to die here a long time ago. So, I have to say, I *will* die here. One day. I thought my job in living was to protect all of you...but if you think you'll be better protected if you leave, then I understand."

"How safe is it to stay?" Teddy asked.

"I don't know," Sim said. "Look at Elizabeth, Tak, and now Flip. Maybe this place is more of a curse than a blessing. Maybe I was wrong about everything. About why I couldn't pull the trigger on myself after I shot my little girl. About why I didn't die three years ago. Maybe I'm just a coward."

"Are you done feeling sorry for yourself?" Sky asked. "Even if we all died today, Sim, what you have accomplished here is nothing short of a miracle. Now, let's stand up and protect our virtues. The virtues *you* instilled. You're not a ruthless or callous killer. You're a thoughtful, smart, and caring individual plagued with guilt, but it's not all guilt that motivates you. You love us like you loved your wife and child. Like you loved Elizabeth, Tak, and Flip. Don't trick yourself into believing you did all this out of penance. You're here for a reason, like you have always told us. You need to believe it yourself. You love this place and so do we. So, we must fight for it."

Sim's eyes filled with tears as he listened to Sky's wisdom. The others listened too and for an instant, Sim felt untethered from his past trauma. He nodded to Sky and she smiled back.

He cleared his throat. "In before times, it was considered a horrendous violation and crime when someone was attacked or murdered in their own home. Why? Because a home, back in those days, was the most highly regarded sanctuary. A crime against someone perpetrated in their own home, was deemed deplorable. Unforgiveable. If one is not safe in his own home, where will he ever be safe?"

"My mom and dad died at home," Leo said.

"Mine too," JZ said, a faraway look in her eyes.

"Exactly," Sim said. "Evil, including the evil of a natural or manmade virus, have been threats to mankind since the *beginning* of humanity. For that, there is no guarantee that you will always be safe in the home you make for yourself or anywhere else, for that matter. You may always run, but you can't always hide. Maybe I need to consider that message more thoughtfully myself."

"We didn't know about the virus, but we know about Zagan," Misty said. "My mother would always have our house checked by an extermination company before winter to make sure it was sealed so that critters couldn't invade us in the cold months. But one time, we did catch a couple of red squirrels and my father told me he was going to let them go in another place, but I saw from my window what he really did."

"What did he do?" Baby asked, rubbing her arms as if making them warm, though she was the closest to the fire.

"They were trapped in a cage, and he put the cage into a barrel of water and drowned them."

"Oh, no," Baby said. "Poor squirrels."

"Cool," Teddy said, blinking wildly and rubbing his hands together.

"Regardless, it is a good analogy," Sim said. "If we prepare for the pests, we won't need to exterminate them because they won't be able to get in. And won't it be grand to fight for something we love. Not just a home, but each other."

Sim was on the road for days with Ace when it was only the two of them. They scoured the lands together for resources and other children. They had gone further than they had ever gone when they spotted the country home on top of a hill in the distance. There were no other homes around it, and much like the fortress, it loomed from atop a hill sprawling with green grasses.

When they made it to the property after crossing a yellowing lawn of grass, they were met with gunfire. The initial bullet smacked the ground at Sim's feet and he and Ace took cover behind a pair of trees that were in front of the country colonial.

"Go away," a voice spoke from a window on the second floor. It was a child's voice. A girl.

"We just want to talk," Sim said from behind the sturdy oak.

"My daddy taught me how to shoot and I can hit you right between the eyes if I want, so just go."

"We are not here to harm you," Sim persisted. "I have another child with me. We only want to help."

There was silence at first, then another shot ricocheted off the tree, tearing bark from the side.

Just then, Ace took a chance and stepped out into the open with his hands raised. "Wait," Ace said. "I've been with this guy for a while now. He's good. I'm good. We just want to talk."

Ace waited in place while Sim stayed under cover. The girl did not answer for several minutes until finally she appeared at the front door, which was open behind another screen door. The girl was pale with brown, curly, shoulder-length hair. Her face was dotted with freckles and etched with apprehension. Ace could see the rifle still in her hand as she waited behind the screen door.

"How old are you?" she asked.

"Fourteen," he said. "You?"

"I only need to put four more marbles in my jar until I'm nine," she said.

"Is it only you?" Ace asked, lowering his hands.

"I have some chickens," she said. "They lay eggs for me."

"Aren't you scared being here all alone now?" Ace asked. "Especially at night?"

The girl popped open the screen door cautiously. It creaked on its hinges. She stepped out, raising the gun to eye level. "There's nothing to be scared of out here except for when a stranger comes."

She was clean and healthy looking. She had a pink shirt on underneath a pair of overall jeans.

"Not every stranger is bad," Ace noted. "The man behind the tree is good. We have been looking for other kids to join our home."

"What about *my* home?" she said. "I have a canopy bed."

Just then, Sim stepped out from behind his tree. The girl redirected her gun on him. "Others will come. Maybe next time they won't be nice.

They'll find a way to get to you even with that gun. You may feel safe now, but it won't always be that way."

She held the gun steady, contemplating. "Well, there was this one time when I heard noises while I was trying to go to sleep...I was scared, but it ended up only being a raccoon."

"You'll have peace at the fortress," Sim said.

"The fortress?" the girl said.

"Our home," Sim answered.

The girl with the freckles and overalls lowered her gun. "Sounds big."

"We have chickens," Ace smiled.

The girl smiled. Her name was Melissa and would soon be Misty. She went with them that day and brought the egg-laying chickens with her. And she told lots of stories of her former years and retold them again as more orphans were discovered.

Following up on Misty's squirrel story, Wyatt chimed in, first raising his hand to speak as if he were at school. "If y'all let me say something, I think you'll find it highly relevant."

"Of course, Wyatt," Sim said.

Wyatt cleared his throat. "Well, I once read that we shape our homes and then our homes shape us."

Everyone looked at him, as if there might be more, to which Wyatt replied. "That's it."

"That's perfect," Sim said.

"Let's fight instead of going to the heights," Kellogg said.

"Hey, that rhymes," Teddy said.

"Yes to the fight, no to the heights!" Leo smiled. He raised his arm and pumped his little bicep. "Yes to the fight, no to the heights!"

Teddy giggled and grabbed his stomach. "For Flip! Yes to the fight, no to the heights!"

Soon after, Kellogg joined in, then Misty, then Ace, then all of the others except Big Will and Sky, because Big Will was the quiet type and Sky thought it silly.

Yes to the fight, no to the heights!

Yes to the fight, no to the heights!

Yes to the fight, no to the heights!

To Sim's delight, the chant continued and most of them were united as their voices filled the firelit room. Though he couldn't help but think about King, wondering if he would ever return. Perhaps he would, with a tale that he had killed Zagan single-handedly or that he was not able to find him; to which Sim would reassure him not to worry, because Zagan had already found *them*, and he was coming.

Soon.

Twenty

Sim had hoped that King's departure was one of those pre-world-ending situations where the child "runs away from home" but hangs out in the car for an hour and then returns. By next morning, when King had not come back, Sim commissioned Ace, Shark, JZ, and Big Will to scout around for him.

"Check some houses too while you are out and pick up whatever spectacles you can scavenge," Sim noted. "Child-sized, if possible."

"Who needs glasses?" Ace asked.

"Leo," Sim noted. "According to him and Sky, anyway. We still need walkies too, if you see any stores that still have them lying around. Not the ones with rechargeable batteries, just the ones that take regular batteries."

"How far do you want us to take this?" Ace asked while the gang waited anxiously beside the kitchen door.

"Not far enough that you can't get back by dark," Sim answered.

Baby opened the door for them, and each went out one at a time through the narrow space left by the door frame and the newly minted brick wall. Gigi led the pack, panting and wagging her tail, making it clear she was in charge.

"And what if the big man attacks *today*?" Sky asked after Baby had closed the doors. "With half our amazing army away?"

Sim turned to Kellogg, who stood beside her with his hands in his pockets.

"Then we offer Zagan the original deal and toss out Kellogg for them and hope they leave." Sim smiled.

Kellogg turned his eyebrows down. "Not funny," he said.

Sim put one hand on Kellogg's shoulders. "Yes, it was, and they would have you over my dead body."

"Are you growing soft, Sim?" Sky asked.

"Maybe I'm just starting to wake up a bit," Sim said. "Perhaps we can talk more about how to get you and the other older children more involved in the decision-making process around here when this is all over...I was thinking a good start might be to form a fortress council, where we could discuss ideas, brainstorm solutions, and deploy a voting system. We can even incorporate the heights and start thinking bigger."

"A senate?" Sky said, taken aback. "How...democratic."

"What an influencer you are," Kellogg added. "Put it here, kid." He pushed out his cheek for a kiss, but Sky scoffed.

"I'll give you a kiss," Baby said sweetly, her hands folded, cheeks flushed.

"I'll take it where I can get it," Kellogg laughed. He kneeled and Baby pecked him on the cheek and ran off shouting to the others how she had kissed a boy.

"You made her day, Kellogg," Sim said. "You may never hear the end of it."

"I don't think we should waste time on lessons today," Sky said. "Whatever we are waiting for, there should not be a minute that goes by without planning for it. What do we know and what is the rest of the plan above and beyond these brick walls we've made in front of the doors and windows?"

"We're going to inventory our weapons, for starters," Sim said.

"Kellog and I will handle that," Sky said.

"We need to suit the basement up for our company from the heights," Sim said.

"I thought you agreed not to involve the heights," Sky said.

"And I will tell you what I told King: my intent was to get us out alive. But if Zagan thinks I'm honoring any kind of parley he must be crazier than we could have ever assumed."

"Then why did King leave?" Sky asked.

"King wants things his way," Sim answered. "He is not in control, and he doesn't like it. He's behaving—"

"Like a child," Sky said.

"I guess so," Sim said. "But he, like you, Ace, and Shark, isn't so little anymore."

"We've been trying to tell you," Sky said.

"I guess you all have," Sim said.

Happy and satisfied by Sim's newfound wisdom, Sky changed the subject. "And when should we expect our helpers from the heights to return?" she asked.

Willow and Wyatt had departed earlier in the day.

"A couple of days," Sim said.

"Well, then," Sky said, "let's get to it."

"Too bad we don't have time to build a moat and put alligators in it," Kellogg said.

"Yes, a shame," Sim pandered, rolling his eyes out of Kellogg's eyesight. "Zagan said he would attack before winter, so likely within the next month, or maybe tomorrow; who knows. If he has a run-in with King, he'll realize the parley concessions are dead in the water, because we also agreed to leave him alone while awaiting the attack."

"God," Kellogg said. "You really did kiss his butt at this parley. No wonder why King was so pissed."

"You should talk," Sim said. "You were ready to throw us all under the bus just so he wouldn't eat you."

"You don't know what it's like to be threatened to be eaten," Kellogg said. "I was very stressed."

"Exactly," Sim said. "Adults get stressed too, you know. Now let's stop chatting and get this show on the road."

Kellogg and Sky retreated to the basement and opened the locked door to the large storage area where they kept three years of inventory...It was a tremendous stockpile that they were able to maintain and grow over the years because they had little need to deploy their arsenal.

Kellogg had never stepped into the room before and he was mesmerized and overwhelmed. "We aren't counting all this, are we?"

"We have an inventory list, silly," Sky said. "We just have to update it. With everything that has been going on, we have used more than usual recently."

Sky led him to where the notebook was kept—a journal of their inventory, which they updated after using anything. As she went about her updates, Kellogg surveyed the lot, taking many of the weapons into his hands like any child might do. It was a toy store for a boy of his age.

"Are these loaded?" he said while holding a .357 revolver and pointing it out the supply closet door.

"Of course not," she said. "You're the last person I would have allowed in here if we had a bunch of loaded weapons sitting around."

He lowered the pistol and put it back on the shelf, in its proper place. "Why?"

"Because you've had no experience with these weapons," she said, making a notation in her book. "Most of us have spent the last three years training on all of these weapons. Cleaning them, loading them, shooting them, and learning about gun safety, which clearly you have no experience with."

Kellogg crinkled his nose. "When is he going to teach *me*, for crying out loud?"

Sky offered him downcast eyes. "I'm sure he was waiting to see if he could fully trust your silly ass. Aside from that, we've been preoccupied lately." She lowered her book. "I'm starting to forget what normal life around here was like."

"Ironic, isn't it?" Kellogg said, grabbing a grenade from a metal storage bin. "Normal life involved extensive weapons training for children." He put his finger in the circular pin of the grenade. "How much has changed."

"Stop it!" Sky yelled.

Kellogg pulled his finger from the pin. "I'm not *that* stupid. I may not have had any training, but everyone knows that pulling the pin on a grenade sets it off...Well, at least if you don't have the handle depressed."

"I guess you learned something from the movies back then," Sky said as she snatched the grenade from his hand and put it back soundly in the bucket.

"We're just about done here," Sky said as she put the notebook and pencil back on one of the shelves. "Grab some of those bottles."

Kellogg snatched up four glass bottles and tucked them into his chest while Sky grabbed several bottles of rubbing alcohol.

"We need to replenish our supplies for the upper floors," she said.

After departing the weapons supply area, she placed her bottles on the ground and shut the door. She secured the padlock and took Kellogg's bottles from him and placed them beside hers on the ground.

"Aren't we bringing these up?" he asked.

"Yes," she said. "But I wanted to show you the tunnel."

Sky led the way past the indoor garden area to the back end of the house, there lied a pair of wooden doors whose handles were bound together with a chain. Sky promptly unfastened the lock and unwrapped the chain. She pulled the doors open to reveal a dark cavernous space beyond. An invisible yet pungent and cold cloud of damp air spilled into the basement from the tunnel as she extended the doors.

"Wow," Kellogg said, cringing. "That shit's for real."

Sky switched on a flashlight that was conspicuously left beside the doors to be used as needed. She shined it into the dark tunnel that was carved beyond the foundation wall inside the smaller storage area. The tunnel was but four feet tall, so it was not a space where any of them could stand upright, save for the little ones, but it still served its purpose.

"Follow me," she said, entering the abyss.

Kellogg followed her, hunched over as she led him down the dark, damp, and earthy corridor.

"This must be what it was like being a tunnel rat in the war," Kellogg said, his voice strained from having to crook his neck.

"A tunnel rat?" Sky said trudging forward.

"Yeah, they were special soldiers trained to explore tunnels that were dug in the ground where the enemy soldiers would hide."

"Sounds like a dream job," said Sky. "This tunnel is one hundred yards long and it took us two years to dig."

"What if someone from the outside discovers it?" Kellogg asked.

"That's why we keep the doors chained," Sky said. "Anyway, it would be very difficult for anyone to discover the exit. We have it covered pretty well."

"A hundred yards?" Kellogg said. "Feels more like a hundred miles."

"We're almost there," Sky said.

When they arrived at the end Sky handed Kellogg her flashlight as she used her back to push upward on a piece of plywood that rested over the hole. Once she loosened it, she used both hands to push it aside, allowing the light to pour through. Kellogg doused the flashlight and the two pulled themselves from the awkward void and sat on the edge of the hole. The fortress stood proudly as ever in the shadow of the late morning sun beyond Usland, the fruit trees, the gardens, and the outhouse.

The two exhaled several large puffs of air.

"That was cool," Kellogg uttered.

Sky scoffed. "Only a boy would think traveling through a disgusting dirty tunnel is cool."

"No," Kellogg said. "I think *this* is cool. Sitting here. Seeing the fortress from here. Like this."

"I don't get you, sometimes," Sky said. "Foolish and joking around half the time and the other half..."

Kellogg paused before nudging her, "What?"

"Well, let's just say I find the other half much more endearing," she said.

The two sat side-by-side with their feet in the hole to the tunnel for several minutes before departing. They covered the hole back up with the wood, dirt, grass, and leaves. Then they went back to the house to retrieve their supplies from the basement and to chain lock the tunnel doors once again.

Twenty-One

In those days when Sim would scour the city for lost children, he often ran missions for this sole purpose, but sometimes, even when he wasn't looking, he would find them.

Not long after he found Ace, Yamil, Misty, and King, Sim went on a solo journey for supplies. He had just left a plaza drug store and was surprised to see a young girl entering a hair and nails salon at the other end of the compound as he exited. She was traveling indiscreetly, as if it were any other day.

Sim stowed his drug store supplies in an abandoned car close to the hair salon and peered inconspicuously through the hair salon window. There was a young girl of color sitting in one of the chairs, peering into the mirror in front of her, unmoving. Sim watched her for a few minutes before entering and when he did, she did not even turn toward him, even as the bell signaled a visitor. She remained still, one leg over the other, peering into the mirror.

"Haircut?" she finally said, though keeping her gaze forward.

"Yes," Sim said. "It's time."

"Well, then whatcha waiting for?" she said. "Get to steppin."

Sim went over and sat in the chair beside her.

The girl swiveled in her chair. "Do you really want your hair cut?"

"I probably should," he said, noting he had not had a hair cut in some time, except the ones he gave himself. "But I'm getting used to it being long."

Sim looked at himself in the mirror. He was fully bearded and his thin, light hair reached his shoulders. "I had no hair at all when I was in the military, so when I see my reflection, a stranger stares back at me."

"You were in the military?" she asked.

"Yeah," he said. "A long time ago. And I haven't looked at myself in a mirror in months."

"Why?" she asked.

It was a good question. "I guess I don't know. Maybe we give up on ourselves physically in times like these."

"Well, that's crazy," the girl said. "We can't do nothing about some things, but there are things we can do things about."

Sim smiled. "You may be right about that."

"Well, then let me cut your damn fool hair," the girl said. "They got everything we need here. My auntie used to own this place. She showed me how to cut hair, do pedicures, sweep, and welcome customers. She even gave me free stuff." She spun around on her chair and stared back into the mirror. "But now everything is free."

"I disagree," Sim said. "All of this...it came at a heavy cost."

The girl pondered. "I guess you're right."

"How about you go ahead and cut my hair," Sim said. "Then you come live with my family."

She spun around on her chair and regarded him with curiosity. "Your family?"

"I have a fortress," Sim said. "With some children. I'm looking for more. To build a life together."

"A fortress?" she said, arms crossed. "What the hell you talking 'bout?"

"A home with love and protection from the world," Sim said.

"There are kids there?" she asked.

"Yes," he said. "*They* are the fortress, in fact. And so are you."

"You talking some weird shit," she said.

"Maybe," Sim said. "But you can be part of the fortress if you come with me."

"Seems like some white bullshit to me," she said. "I've been doing just fine on my own. Haven't run across a single bastard that's going to fuck with me, or I'll put an axe between they eyes."

"An axe?" Sim inquired.

"Yeah," she said. "A motherfucking axe." She lifted her long shirt to reveal an axe tucked into her waistband.

"Wow," Sim remarked. "Impressive. If you can take care of yourself, you can help take care of the fortress. We would value that skill."

"Where is this place, anyway?" she asked.

"A few miles from here," Sim said.

"Are there any of *my* people there?" she asked.

Sim shrugged. "We have a *Spanish* kid."

She sighed. "Hell."

"Well, what do you want?"

"I want my mom, dad, and auntie!" she hissed.

Sim nodded. "I understand. If I could change my past, I would bring my wife and daughter back."

The girl laughed. "Pain is pain."

Sim pondered. "Yeah. Now, can I ask *you* something?"

"I guess," she said.

"Why didn't you throw that axe at me when I walked in?" he asked.

"Because I've been following your fool ass for a week," she said with a smile. "But I ain't never see you go to no fortress. So, let me cut that greasy looking hair of yours and we'll go see this place. But if you lying to me, I'm gonna cut your ass down quick."

Though shocked, Sim agreed. "What's your name?"

"Ja'Zara," she said proudly.

"JZ," he mumbled. "Good to meet you."

That evening, the scouting crew returned, though without King in tow, which was a disappointment to Sim and the others.

"It was a quiet journey," Ace said. "Eerily so, but we were able to find a few pair of glasses. Maybe one of them will do."

Ace fished into his deep jacket pocket and pulled out several pairs of spectacles. Some had plastic frames and others wire frames. Leo dashed into the kitchen when news broke that his spectacles had arrived.

"Did I hear that you found me some glasses?" he asked, his eyes twice the size as normal.

"I guess we don't have to worry about your ears as much as your eyes," JZ said.

Leo grabbed them one at a time, his tongue hanging from his mouth like a thirsty dog, and one at a time he tried each pair. Each time he put a new pair on, he glanced out from the kitchen in the direction of the living and dining rooms, assessing the worth of each one. JZ held a pocket mirror up so he could also see how they looked on him.

"Wooow," he said after trying on the ones with the blue frames. "It's so clear."

"Are you sure it's not just the frames you like?" Ace said.

"No, these will work," Leo said. "They really work. Everything is so clear."

"Good, then," Ace remarked. "We don't have to worry about locating an optometrist."

"What's that?" Leo asked.

"Never mind," Ace said.

"I'm out," Shark remarked as he headed up the stairs to the roof.

"We're eating in a half hour," Sim reminded. "And then having a meeting with everyone."

Their dinner was a stew composed of venison and vegetables. It was delightful and the family indulged quietly. Upon finishing and the cleaning of dishes, they gathered in the living room.

Sky took to the couch with her little ones as usual, while Ace stood, his back to the wall on the kitchen side of the room and Shark on the other near the front doors, which had been walled up with brick. Everyone else sat on the floor before him like a kindergarten classroom waiting for story time. Sim stood, hands behind his back, poised to pace and speak like a lawyer in a courtroom. The children looked upon him with soft, anticipating eyes.

"Children," he began. "We have been through a lot these past weeks. And although in our previous meeting we quite animatedly asserted our interest in staying through the thick and thin, I thought it would be important to reconvene to make sure it is truly what each of you wants, because what lies before us, is nothing like we ever faced before. We are under attack. By a man who wishes us harm for the purpose of glory in the form of violence and destruction. None of us can take that lightly. That said, I feel with all my heart that we are prepared to fight...and win."

"And if we lose?" Misty asked.

Sim answered her with a story. "Children, this fortress...in its day, was a Roman Catholic parsonage. Home to many priests. In the lot beside us was a beautiful church. It was my own church, in fact. Saint Michael's. I remember as a child watching the church burn to the ground. You could see the smoke plumes for miles." Sim raised his arms. "This place. It survived. When they relocated the church up the hill, they sold the parsonage. Over time, it switched hands, but its history remained. The cornerstone is still there from 1875. I was the last owner and was proud to be blessed with its profoundness." Sim gazed around the room. "We stand on hallowed ground, my darlings."

Sim paced, as he always did. Then he stopped and smiled at the children as he regarded the chandelier above his head that boasted several cherubim attached to the fixture, each holding a musical instrument. "Saint Michael, ironically, is the commander of the Army of God. He defends us against the world of darkness and the spirit of wickedness."

"And we should end up here," Ace said. "It is a message."

"Yes, it is. That we should live under this protection. Because we survived. And if we survived, it could not be to fall to evil."

"But Flip died," Baby said, twisting her hands together.

"Yes, he did." He looked around. "But he is still here. I feel him. Like I feel Amanda, Sara, Elizabeth, and Tak. And you. There is something about this place that the physical world, no matter what, can't take from us. In life, nor in death."

"Blessed are we," Kellogg said randomly, remembering his church days. This drew attention from Sky by way of a raised eyebrow. Certifiable he was.

"We are," Sim said. "We are. In fact, I would like to offer a prayer regarding Saint Michael the Archangel."

"Let's hear it," Ace said.

Sim nodded. "Bow your heads, my darlings."

The children complied.

Sim then read the prayer with his own head bowed.

Defend us in battle.

Be our protection

against the wickedness of the devil.

May God rebuke him we

humbly pray; and do thou, O Prince of the

Heavenly host, by the power of God, thrust

into hell Satan, and all
the evil spirits, who
prowl about the world
seeking the ruin of souls.
Amen.

After the prayer, the children all raised their heads. Leo spoke first.

"Will Saint Michael protect us if we stay?" he asked.

Sim smiled. "In one way or the other, he will."

"Are you sure about that?" Sky asked.

"There is nothing about faith that is assured," Sim answered. "So, if any of you would like to retreat to the heights, as I told you before, I understand. I am not forcing you to stay. I cannot ask you to risk your lives for a principle that I decided upon for you."

"This is our home," Shark said. "Fuck it if I'm going to let that devil take it from us without a fight. My father would turn over in his grave if I fled."

"I'm not leaving," Big Will said, unflinching. "I never was, Saint Michael or not."

"I would have been dead already if it had not been for you," Kellogg said, flipping his coin. "I'll do what I need to do. I died already anyway."

Sky rolled her eyes. "Of course I'll stay, but we can't expect the little ones to fight, so they will go to the heights until this is over."

"Agreed," Sim said.

"I stood up to a bully when I was little," Misty said. "Her name was Margaret. I called her Meanie Margaret. She picked on a girl named Winnie who had a studder. Every day while others laughed. I stepped in when I had enough and told her to stop, forever. I told her that Winnie was not alone."

"And..." Shark said.

"I slapped that girl across the face one day and Winnie and I...we became best friends."

"So, you are staying, then," Ace remarked.

"Yes," Misty said.

"Me too," Teddy said. "For Flip. Or what was it for?"

The rest of them asserted their eagerness to remain. Sim was proud. But he was scared. He could feel the day of reckoning was soon coming, and he did not want to see his children perish, but there was a higher purpose to fulfill that transcended physical life. One might not see this ideal until put to the test. But he was confident his orphans saw the truth.

A truth worth fighting for. A truth worth dying for.

Amen.

Twenty-Two

It was thirty-seven days after the battle at the heights. King had not returned, but Charlie, along with Willow and Wyatt, had returned weeks before and now worked at fitting in with the various routines as everyone went about their daily lives as normally as they could while understanding that, at any moment, they could be under attack. Yamil and Miracle had gone to the heights with an emotional farewell and there they would stay until the feud with Zagan was over.

They hoped that with so much time passed, Zagan had given up or King had found and killed him and moved on to a new life for himself, but it was impossible to let down their guard, for they knew that when they did, Zagan would be there.

The trio from the heights stayed for five days at a time and returned to the heights for two, if only to stay connected to their own homes. Especially Charlie, who was in charge and needed to make sure all was well with his people.

It was on one such weekend night that Charlie asked to speak to Sim privately before he went back. That is when he told Sim the truth of things.

"He's with me," Charlie said, anxiously so, and tossing back whiskey from his flask.

"Who?" Sim asked.

Charlie released the flask from his mouth and took in some deep breaths. "King."

Sim, after a huge sigh of relief, offered Charlie a gaze of disappointment. "For how long?"

"He arrived a few days after he left the fortress," Charlie said. "He begged me not to tell you. But he needed a change." He took another drink. "You know teens."

Sim shook his head. He reached out for Charlie's flask and Charlie handed it over. Sim took his own large sip and handed it back. "I don't think I do. It's always been my biggest struggle. Especially now as they beg for me to loosen the leash. Give me some more of that." He grabbed the flask before Charlie had a chance to hand it over and took another drink. "Anyway, I'm just glad he's not dead. So instead of going on this big mission to find Zagan and kill him, he simply ran away from home to the heights to indulge of the fruits of life."

Charlie shook his head. "I've been keeping him honest, and busy with perimeter duty and lots of chores."

"It's just so...disappointing," Sim said. "Had you not opened the damn door he would have been back here in two seconds. And there is no doubt Ace knew this whole time about this as well. I'm surprised he didn't join him. I feel like I'm at the threshold of mutiny around here. Saving children...it's not all it's cracked up to be."

"I never made any assumptions about that," Charlie laughed. "Sim, he just needed space, nothing more. Not much different than the old days. If you knew what I was like at that age you would be quite proud of him."

"I know what you were like, Charlie," Sim said. "So, he's just going to sit up there while Zagan attacks us and tries to kill his brothers and sisters?"

"I'll bring him back with me when I return," Charlie said.

"And bring more of that whisky, too," Sim said.

Charlie eyed him curiously. "Is someone starting to loosen up? You better be careful, or before you know it, it'll look like the heights down here."

"Yeah, well, if you can't beat them..." Sim placed his hands on his hips and kicked into his pace. "Don't force him to come, Charlie. Just tell him we'll handle it and that maybe we'll see him soon."

"I will tell him that you would love to see him," Charlie said.

Sim smiled.

Charlie left that evening and things continued as normal through the evening hours with dinner and bedtime routines.

Little did they know, they were being watched.

A man named Cairo, brought on by Zagan, stealthily made his way to the fortress ahead of the group of one hundred and thirty-nine marauders under the cover of night. He proceeded in and around houses and trees and crept his way across the vacant lot beside the fortress in slow deliberate moves. Once at the house, he scaled the lower wall, which was adjacent to the outhouse and climbed his way like a spider to the first level roof and continued his ascent to the second level roof using a drainpipe.

Of course, Shark was doing what he always did, though not at the pinnacle of the home. The fortress had three rooftops in total. The first was over a former garage in the back, while the second was much higher and accessible through the skylight in the attic. The third roof was above that and though the smallest of the rooftop surfaces, offered a panoramic view of their surroundings. To get to it, one had to scale the shingle siding above the skylight.

Shark spent most of his time on the second level roof that offered a view of three sides of the property, only occasionally visiting the third level roof when compelled to be thorough and to keep tabs on, not only the front of the home, but a large portion of the city.

That night, he was keeping watch on and off using his binoculars, looking for signs of life, and making sure nobody was sneaking up on the fortress from the lot, the woods, or through Restland or Usland. When Cairo was making his way across the lot, however, Shark was watching the stars, radiant as they were, never thinking that this evening would be the one much discussed over the past weeks.

Cairo had run into Zagan not too long after the group branched out from the steelworks building to the county prison, which was a more befitting sanctuary for the crew.

Cairo was a prisoner at county who had never left. In fact, he and Sim had faced off when Sim visited scavenging weapons. Instead of fighting, they agreed to split the number of weapons that the prison had and at one point, Sim was tempted to inform Cairo about the heights community but waited to check with Charlie first. As it turned out, Cairo was a former grizzie who Charlie knew and who Charlie did not want anywhere near the heights.

He's trouble, Mr. Ford. And that'll never change. You should have just put him out of his misery.

Cairo was more than willing to talk about his prison days, though, while the two reminisced on Sim's many visits to gather guns and ammo. Cairo had been awaiting trial on armed robbery and murder stemming from a holdup at a local store in the days before everything went to hell. He had killed a seventeen-year-old who was at the register when the boy instinctively tried calling for help.

It's not what I wanted to happen. I only wanted the money and I panicked.

His reasoning mattered little to Sim. Cairo's instincts to kill an unarmed child reflexively in the way of self-preservation was something Sim found unsettling, and he soon understood why Charlie did not trust him.

The man's physical scars were etched across his face and arms, as if his body was a patchwork of horrendous life experiences. His features were haggard and drawn, his facial bones angular and unforgiving.

Don't be a stranger, Sim. We could be friends.

Sim acknowledged this sentiment with a smile and a nod, but never intended that he would return to touch base, yet he decided against Charlie's recommendation to kill him. With the weapons seized, Sim had everything he needed to justify never returning to the prison.

Three years later, Cairo submitted to Zagan's authority and was now prepared to do Zagan's bidding.

As Cairo made it to the second-level rooftop, he peered over the edge and noticed a shadowy figure lying there, gazing into the night sky. The person was lying roughly ten feet away and though straddling the drainpipe was a physical burden, Cairo did not act in haste.

He decided on a slow approach, pulling himself over the edge of the roof quietly and then sliding one leg over until he was straddling the roof's edge with a tight hug. He lingered for a moment, making sure to be one with the night. While he lay there, he thought of his wife. How she left him when he was arrested. His son, who was only five when Cairo went to prison. His journey through juvenile detention and foster homes did not prepare him for a traditional life with a job, house, and white picket fence, but instead a life of crime—petty at first, until someone died.

Yet, Cairo did love his wife and child. He just didn't know how to function in a traditional family sense, always reverting to his criminal instincts to get by. Three years of solitary penance gave cause for him to reflect on many things and he resigned himself to believe that he was in purgatory. He wondered if the mission Zagan had given him could be his ticket to the next level of eternity and redemption. The culmination of his prayers to be forgiven and released from the mental torture that had engulfed him since that fateful day.

He mourned the boy he had killed. He thought about him often. And though the boy would have been likely devoured by the plague regardless, this did not give him cause to be flippant about what he had done.

But could his test to escape purgatory truly be this? He wondered this while straddling the cold prickly shingles, and as a light turned on from the attic and shone faintly through the rooftop window. Soon after, a small figure toting a large weapon squeezed through the window's opening and onto the roof. The larger person raised himself from his back.

"What's up, big man Will?" the older boy said to the other, known as Will. "You're coming up here an awful lot lately. What is that front door doing without you?"

"What front door?" Will said. "There ain't no front door ever since they blocked it up with brick."

The older boy laughed. "Don't worry, things will get back to normal soon. Right after we waste Zagan and his cronies."

Cairo listened to the exchange, upset that he hadn't acted in haste, as there were now two of them to worry about instead of one. But they sounded like children. Zagan had not given him too many details of the job. He only gave him a few short instructions.

Get onto the roof. Kill whoever is there. Then light the flare to let us know of your success. But make sure the flare goes up at 3 a.m. to ensure everyone is asleep.

As he lay straddling the side of the rooftop, he reassessed what he was doing. *This isn't right. Kids? He didn't say anything about kids. I killed a kid before and where did it get me? Purgatory. You don't go to heaven by killing kids.* He began to sweat, despite the chilly air, and the beads rolled from his left temple down into the corner of his eye. As his vision blurred, he tried blinking the sting away.

Will began to pace the roof, while the older boy lied back down.

"When is the last time you checked things out?" asked Will.

"Why?" the older boy asked. "Did Sim send you up here to spy on me to make sure I was doing my job?"

"I was just curious," the younger boy said as he peered into the vastness of night. "I can't see a thing, Shark."

Shark. Interesting.

"That's why I use the night vision binoculars, dipshit." Shark said. "It's the only way to see anything out there at night."

Cairo noticed Will was facing him only five steps away, but thankfully the boy didn't notice him and finally turned away and walked back toward Shark.

"Well, then get off your lazy ass and give me a look," Will retorted.

"If you must," Shark huffed, rising once again to a standing position. "It's actually pretty cool. If I have to shoot, I'll use the night vision scope, but for basic nighttime surveillance, the binoculars do."

Shark grabbed the binoculars from the ground and handed them to Will, who released his own weapon, letting it fall on its strap so that he could take hold of the binoculars. He peered through them curiously as Shark powered them on and observed the surrounding area.

"Wow," he said. "You never told me you had these. Teddy and the others would think these were the bomb."

"How else did you think I kept an eye on things at night?" Shark scoffed. "And don't go telling the others. I don't want Teddy or Leo up here messing about. The pair of them will probably fall off in no time. We'll be scraping pieces of them off the ground."

Will spun around on his feet in circular fashion to observe his surroundings. He saw the field beside the house and the land behind the fortress. "This is neat. But we can't see the bridge or the river."

"You have to go up to the top level for that," Shark said. "It's a bit of a pain going up and down all night."

Will lowered the binoculars and gazed upward. The topmost level was only several feet beyond the skylight.

"I'll have to try it in the daytime," Will said.

"Good," Shark said. "Maybe I can train you for the job so I can have a break from it once in a while." He then sighed. "But I do like it up here. It's peaceful, you know. My mom and dad talk to me up here."

Cairo suddenly found himself lost in thought. *I talk to my wife and son too, all the time.*

"What do they say?" Will asked, a hint of vulnerability in his voice.

"They tell me to clean my fucking room," Shark laughed. Will also laughed, full belly laughs, in fact, and the two shook their heads thinking about how crazy the world was then and now. Cairo laughed quietly along with them.

"Maybe I'll talk to my mom too up here," Will said.

"What do you think she'll say to *you*?" Shark asked.

Will pondered for several seconds before answering. "To clean my fucking room."

The boys doubled over in the sweetest laughter ever known in this day, and it was like those other days had never ended. All the smiles, love, and joy from a child's play date, birthday party, or swimming party came to life in one second of truth and made themselves known, as if to spite the wickedness of the new world.

Though they could have lived in that moment forever, a slight noise interrupted their glee, and they grew vigilant. It was a peculiar sound coming from the west side of the house that caused them both to turn. Of course, it was difficult to see what may have caused the noise, for beyond the light offered through the window from the attic, their surroundings were pitch black.

"Did you hear that?" Big Will asked.

"It's probably just a bird or a bat," Shark said. "Once you spend enough time up here you get used to all the noises."

Yes. It's just a bird. Go away, children.

Erring on the side of caution, Will ignored Shark's explanation and raised the binoculars to his eyes while facing Cairo. When he did, he saw two small glowing eyes peering back at him.

"Oh shit," Big Will said simply.

They see me. Fuck. No turning back. Cairo sprang from his position on the edge and held up his arms in surrender position. "Wait!"

"Fuck me," Shark screamed as he rushed the intruder.

Cairo defended himself. He threw two punches as Shark advanced, both landing solidly on the boy's face. Shark fell backward as Will tossed the binoculars and drew up his weapon.

"No, wait, please!" Cairo said.

Will was waiting for nothing. He prepared to fire, and Cairo knew that if he did not act accordingly, he would be dead. He lunged forward and knocked the gun away and shoved Will to the ground. From the ground, Will scurried away and repositioned his gun for another chance to shoot.

Fuck. Don't do this. Don't do this.

Post-traumatic stress triggered Cairo's next action. He withdrew a knife from its sheath, which was belted to his side and lunged forward at Will. He plunged the blade into Big Will's thigh before the boy could answer the attack with bullet spray. Big Will screamed out in pain as the knife penetrated his flesh.

Shark had gotten to his feet and attacked the intruder from behind with both fists flailing. His large hands pounded away at each side of Cairo's frail body. Cairo, adrenaline kicking, absorbed the painful body strikes while yanking the knife from Big Will's thigh. He then spun around and slashed Shark across the chest before whirling back around to make sure Will was not in position to shoot him.

Shark gave Cairo no time to advance on Big Will as the boy continued to howl, clutching his thigh. He tackled him to the ground. Cairo's knife fell from his hand as the two collapsed onto the roof, Shark's body landing squarely upon Cairo. The tangled-up pair landed across Big Will's legs and the boy screamed.

Cairo fought to reverse his position, but Shark, though only sixteen, had Cairo outsized and overpowered. As the man struggled to break free from him, Ace popped his head through the skylight from the attic, flashlight in one hand and revolver in the other.

"What the hell is going on up here?" he exclaimed as he illuminated the area with his light.

"Help!" Shark cried. "This bastard attacked us!"

I had to. I had to. You were going to kill me. You wouldn't listen.

Ace shimmied through the opening and dashed over to the crumpled pair. He leaned over and placed the barrel of his revolver against the intruder's head. "Stop struggling or I will kill you."

"Do it!" Shark said. "He stabbed Will."

"No, don't kill me!" cried Cairo. "I was only defending myself. I swear I meant nobody harm."

Ace pulled back the hammer on his gun. "Is that why you sneaked up here? To do no harm?"

"I didn't know you was all kids," he yelped. "I have information. I'll tell you everything. Just don't kill me. I've been contrite. I did my time. I'm supposed to go to heaven. I'm supposed to be restored."

"What is he babbling about?" Shark said, still working to keep the man pinned to the ground.

Ace scoffed at the man's ramblings. "If you want to live, don't make a move."

Shark released his weight from Cairo's back and stood, hovering over him, catching his breath.

"Now get up," Ace commanded. "And if you do anything stupid, I swear it's the last move you'll make."

Cairo put his hands over his head and cinched his way up onto his knees. "Please. I can help you. I was trying to complete my penance. I was trying to win back favor with God."

"Shut up!" Shark said, examining his ripped shirt and the slash wound to his chest that lie beneath. He flexed his wound in the light of the attic. "Is this how you win favor with God?"

Ace regarded Shark's slash wound and then returned his attention to Cairo. "You're going to march your way through the skylight, carefully keeping your hands over your head and doing exactly what I say."

Cairo moved from his knees to his feet and headed in the direction of the open skylight with Ace standing behind him, gun pointed squarely in his back. Shark helped Big Will to his feet.

"Yell down to someone to help Big Will," Shark said. "There could be more, so I have to go to the top. He's been stabbed through the thigh."

"There is nobody else," Cairo uttered. "It's just me. Only me. I was sent by God and—"

"I said shut up!" Ace said, hitting the man over the head with the butt of his gun.

"Ow, fuck!" Cairo wailed. "It's a mistake."

When the pair reached the skylight, Ace called through it. "I need help!"

Sim, JZ, Kellogg, and Sky answered the call to the attic.

"We have a prisoner," Ace called through. "He stabbed Big Will."

"A prisoner?" Kellogg said. "On the roof?"

"Get him here," Sim said. "Sky and Kellogg, you'll help Big Will. Shark, do a tight scan of the area to see if there are any more."

The group carefully monitored Cairo as he entered through the skylight and set foot into the attic space. When Sim and Cairo came face to face, Sim's eyes widened, as did Cairo's.

"Cairo," Sim said, not quietly enough.

"Do you know *all* the bad guys?" Kellogg asked.

Sky slapped him. "Didn't you ever hear the expression keep your friends close, but your enemies closer?"

Kellogg smiled. "I sure wish I had been here for all your library lessons."

"I don't," Sky scoffed. "You would have been...a distraction."

Kellogg raised his eyebrows up and down. "I get it."

She slapped him again as Sim pulled Cairo out of the way to allow Ace to step through. Sky and Kellogg helped Big Will through the window as Sim, Ace, and Cairo exited the enclave.

Big Will's injury was to the outer thigh. Sky examined the blood on the knife to determine the depth of the injury to be roughly two inches. The opening was roughly an inch and a half wide. He refused stiches, so Sky disinfected the wound, affixed butterfly band aids and wrapped it tightly so he could continue about his business, though with a limp. Sky suggested he use their makeshift crutches, but Big Will refused with a scowl that betrayed his soft features.

Sim directed Ace with Cairo to the living room. Ace kept his gun pointed at the frightened man as Sim pushed him into the center of the room.

Cairo gazed around the room curiously.

"What are you looking at?" Ace asked. "Do you want to die?"

Sim raised a hand to calm his next in charge.

Cairo trembled as he and Sim locked eyes. "I didn't know it was you, Sim."

"It doesn't matter," Sim said, remembering earlier conversations he had had with the man. "What the hell were you thinking? What about all that talk of asking for forgiveness and trying to be a better person? And this is your contrition?"

"It was," Cairo stated. "It was. God spoke to me. But I couldn't do it. I was going to leave but they saw me. I tried to tell them."

Sim nodded. Then he rushed Cairo, whose eyes grew twice the size with fright. Sim grabbed him by the head and forced his body around so that he was staring at the banner above the mantle which bore the painted handprints of the orphans.

"You see this?" Sim said. "Look! You know what the handprints mean?"

Cairo tried to shake his head but had little mobility under the pressure of Sim's hands.

"We have no problem getting blood on our hands," Sim growled.

As he stood there with Cairo's head in his hands, Baby, Teddy, Leo, and JZ entered.

"They're so small," Cairo said. "Those hands."

His remarks brought on several seconds of silence.

"I'm sorry," Cairo then said. "I was finishing my penance. I was supposed to be free after this."

"I know all about penance, and it doesn't look like this," Sim screamed in his ear. "Why should we not kill you?"

"I don't know, I don't know," Cairo said. "He never said they were kids. He never said nothing. I told him about Julie and Tristan and the pain...He wanted to help redeem me."

"Who?" Sim asked, releasing Cairo's head with a shove that sent his whole body forward. "Zagan? He put you up to this?"

Cairo turned to face Sim, lips quivering. "He said you killed his family. He said we could live together...in this place. And there were lots of people and we would all live in peace."

Sim's face hardened. "Well, he lied," Sim growled between clenched teeth.

"Where are they?" Ace asked. "Are they out there?"

JZ instinctively ran to the front set of windows, forgetting that they had been sealed, save for small peek holes through which she could see nothing.

"They're not coming till morning," Cairo said. "I was supposed to light a flare after you all fell asleep once I took the top, so they knew the roof was under control."

Cairo patted his right-side pant leg and attempted to reach inside. Sim grabbed him and shoved him against the wall face first. "Put your hands against the wall and spread your legs."

Cairo, remembering the day he was arrested for the convenience store robbery and murder, shook his head in anguish. He never dreamed in this world that he would be going through these motions again. Instead of finishing his journey of contrition, he had returned to the starting line.

Sim patted Cairo down and removed the flare from his pocket. He checked the rest of his body with aggressive pats, only finding the empty sheath that had earlier secured his knife.

He spun him back round. "What else?"

"I was to wait there until morning. Sunrise. To witness the glory of God."

"You mean the devil," Sim remarked. "There's only one God, and Zagan is not Him."

"How many people do they have?" Ace demanded.

Cairo shook his head. "I don't know. One hundred and fifty or so."

Ace threw up his arms. "Great, and the others aren't even back from the heights yet."

"They are expected back tomorrow, so hopefully they'll not fall into this trap while it's unfolding," Sim retorted. "We need to send this flare up. At least now we have the advantage of knowing their attack plan. Instead of taking us by surprise we'll take *them* by surprise."

"If he's telling the truth," Sky said.

The others in the room turned and saw Big Will leaning against the door jam, wincing in pain, Gigi beside him licking his hand. Kellogg pet the dog as the animal regarded Cairo with steely eyes.

"You should keep an eye on that wound," Sim said. "Without stiches, it'll need time to seal. Walking about on it is not going to help."

"So, you want me to sit and take it easy?" Big Will asked, raising his gun. "When they are on the way?"

Gigi barked.

Unexpectedly, Cairo dropped to his knees and covered his face with his bony hands. He cried into them as the others looked on, unphased. After a few minutes, he raised his head from his hands. "There's something else."

"What?" Sim asked, a hint of anger in his voice.

"One of the other men he recruited...Crazy Joe, they call him." Cairo's eyes glazed over.

"Go on," Sim said.

"He found an RPG launcher on his travels that had a single rocket with it," Cairo said. "They plan to use it to take out the front entryway. Even that wall of brick won't stop that rocket."

"Jesus," Ace muttered. "How well armed is the group aside from the launcher?"

"Rifles, shotguns, knives," Cairo said. "Some heavier stuff...They took everything you left with me, Sim. I had never used the stuff."

Sim remembered that stockpile well.

"Get up to the roof with this, Ace," Sim said, handing him the flare. "Fire it off."

As the flare changed hands, Baby stepped in between them, her eyes on Cairo, who regarded her with a crooked smile, half anguished, half enamored. Ace and Sim looked down on her as she approached the man. Then Ace dashed off.

"You scared me," Baby said softly. "You scared all of us."

A single tear ran down Cairo's cheek as Baby thrust her hands in swift, letter X fashion. Cairo did not realize what happened at first, until blood spurted out of his neck and across Baby's chest. He grabbed his neck and coughed as blood continued to squirt out. His attempts to use both hands to stop it were futile. Within seconds, he fell sideways. In silence, everyone watched him bleed out as he lay helpless on the floor until the last of his coughing faded.

"May God forgive you," Sim muttered.

Twenty-Three

Ace sent up the flare and he and Shark watched it erupt in the night sky like a splendid firework of the kind they hadn't seen in years.

"I hope that guy was telling the truth," Shark said, his face aglow in red.

"Me too," Ace conceded. "Do you think King will come with Charlie and the others tomorrow?"

"I don't know," he said. "I can't imagine he won't."

"So, this is it then," Ace said as the flare embers faded to dust.

Shark turned to Ace and smiled. "For them. Not for us."

JZ and Teddy removed the body of Cairo to the basement after loading it onto a tarp, while Baby, Leo, and Misty cleaned up the blood. Thereafter, the entire group of orphans gathered in the living room for a meeting. The group was melancholy, all realizing that the day they had hoped would never come was upon them.

"Here we are," Sim said. "I just want to say before we enter battle how proud I am of all of you. Without you, there is no purpose, because in order to restore this world, love, commitment, passion, desire, and education must prevail. You represent the best of everything that was left behind and I hope when this is over, we can all sit here again together and share a story."

Sim took in a breath as the orphans looked upon him. "Our strongest defense will come from the second and third floors as well as the roof, but do not leave yourself exposed in front of those windows." He turned to

Big Will. "I'm assigning you the tunnel and you can kill anyone you see back there; but keep your head down to the extent possible, as it will be the only part of your body exposed. If you are stealthy enough, they'll never know where your shots are coming from." He turned back to the larger group. "We have deployed the entire arsenal, so every room is equipped with plenty of firepower. JZ, you are taking the back on floor one, as usual. Shark will stay on the roof. Misty, Teddy, and Leo, you will have floor two. Sky, Kellogg, and Baby, you will have floor three. Ace and I will be on floor one. The sixteen grenades we have on hand have been divided between the second and third floors. Don't use them unless you can take out a group with them and avoid using them inside." Sim drew in a breath and closed his eyes in quiet mediation. "Children, this battle is ours. We have the advantage of knowing they are coming, we have higher ground, stronger firepower, and a hallowed fortress that will be almost impossible to penetrate. We likewise have training, skill, but most of all, passion to save our home and avenge Flip. We're going to kill everyone that tries to take what we have built, and we are going to live through this day."

"What about the RPG?" Sky asked.

"Our best advantage in that regard is Shark. Hopefully, they'll position themselves in the open to use it so he can snipe them, believing the roof has been compromised, but even if they tear down that front wall, that doesn't mean we'll allow them to enter. The game is the same."

"If one hundred men rush the front door, should it become hollow, we'll have no chance to—"

"Enough, Sky," Sim said. "We can't control how they use that weapon; only how we respond."

"Can we say that prayer?" Teddy asked.

Sim smiled. "Of course, Teddy."

Sim found Teddy while he was scouting for weapons. He was in an upscale apartment complex, cautiously going from one residence to the next. Teddy was in one of the apartments sitting at the dining room table when Sim opened the door. The boy did not look up, but continued to stare at the table, hands folded.

Sim lowered his gun, which he held at the ready in case he confronted a hostile. "What are you doing, boy?" he asked.

The boy remained unphased. "Praying."

Sim lowered his gun. "What are you praying about?"

"I don't know," the boy said. "Just saying a prayer."

"What prayer?" Sim asked.

"The Our Father," the boy said.

"Can you teach me?" Sim asked.

"Sure," the boy replied.

Sim walked over to the table and pulled out a chair opposite the small child and sat down. He was eating, apparently, as there was a plate in front of him with a pile of peas on it and a bottle of water beside the plate.

"Fold your hands," the boy said. "Like this." He held up his hands, which were clasped together.

Sim followed suit and the boy nodded his approval. Sim was aware of the traditional nuances of Christian prayer, but he allowed the boy to teach him anyway.

Our father, who art in heaven,
hallowed be thy name.
Thy kingdom come, thy will be done,
on earth as it is in heaven.
Give us this day, our daily bread,
and forgive us our trespassers,
as we forgive those who trespass against us,
and deliver us not into temptation,

but deliver us from evil.

Amen.

Sim followed along, reciting the words in his head as the boy proclaimed them. When finished, the boy unfolded his hands and prepared his fork to eat.

"Do you want any peas?" he asked. "They're cold, though. Everything is cold."

"No, thank you," Sim said.

The boy went about his business of eating his peas and drinking his water as Sim studied him from across the table.

"Is this where you live?" Sim asked.

He continued eating as he responded. "We moved here when I was in kindergarten."

"Where are your parents?" Sim asked.

The boy was about to shovel a spoonful of peas into his mouth but lowered the spoon. He locked eyes with Sim, appearing melancholy. He then quietly resumed eating. Sim got up from his chair and proceeded around the corner. To his right, there was a bedroom. The door was opened, and he could see into it. A disheveled bed, a mess of toys on the floor. He turned to his left and noticed another room at the other end of the short, carpeted corridor past the bathroom, which was centrally located between the two rooms.

There were words scrolled in black marker across the closed door. He proceeded more closely so he could read them. *My boy is Teddy. If he is still alive, please take him and protect him. He's hyper, but very loving. I'm scared for him, but I couldn't take him with me. Always remind him how much I love him. His mom.* Sim tried turning the doorknob, but the door was locked from the other side. He jiggled firmly to make sure, but it would not budge, so he returned to the dining room table.

The boy's peas were gone, and he was chugging his bottle of water. He couldn't be more than seven. His hair was overgrown, uneven, and mussed. He had his pajamas on, a one-piece Minecraft outfit that zippered from the neck down to the foot.

"How was it?" Sim asked after the boy lowered his bottle.

The boy shrugged. "It was just peas," he said. "Mom used to make chicken with them. Potatoes, too."

"I understand," Sim said. "Are your parents in the room with the locked door?"

The boy peered at him. His eyes were large and dark. Sim had never seen such dark eyes on anyone. "Just my mom. She kissed me and said she loved me, but not to come in anymore." He looked down solemnly. "I try knocking lots of times, but she never answers. She put all the food on the counter and told me to make sure I eat, drink, and wash every day until someone came."

Sim looked over the boy's shoulder and saw the countertop was flooded with empty cans of vegetables, fruits, and other assorted non-perishable cans and packages. On the floor, there were several cases of water, the top one open and half depleted. Sim leaned over the table and smiled, though he wanted to cry. For the boy, yes, but for the world gone by.

"You were smart, young man," Sim said, "to listen to your mother, but I'm here now. I've come for you. Your mother asked me to take care of you."

"She did?" The boy crooked his neck. "Where are we going?"

"To the fortress," Sim said.

"What's a fortress?" the boy asked.

"*You* are, Teddy." Sim said. "But it's also a place with other kids and we can even have chicken and potatoes."

The boy scrunched up his face, awed. "How did you know my name?"

Sim shrugged and smiled. "Your mother told me."

The two gathered up supplies and left together. When Teddy arrived at the fortress, he was still in his pajamas, and he was mesmerized by the fortress. Flip greeted him kindly and after thirty days, Sim asked Teddy his fortress name, to which the boy shrugged.

"My name is Teddy," he said.

Defend us in battle.
Be our protection
against the wickedness of the devil.
May God rebuke him we
humbly pray; and do thou, O Prince of the
Heavenly host, by the power of God, thrust
into hell Satan, and all
the evil spirits, who
prowl about the world
seeking the ruin of souls.
Amen.

When the prayer was completed, the group formed a standing circle holding hands. Together, they recited their pledge.

We, the orphans of the new world, pledge to: do our best, work together, defend our home, live and die for one another, love, lead, remember. We are the fortress, and the fortress is us.

Then Sim said, "I know it seems silly to suggest you sleep, but going into battle with no rest could stifle your reflexes and abilities, so do try to shut your eyes. There will be guards up all night, so rest assured you will not miss the fight."

"I wouldn't mind sleeping through it," Kellogg said. His joke fell on deaf ears except for Sky, who offered him a look of disapproval. "I was only kidding. I think it is important to keep our sense of humor at a time like this."

"You won't be laughing tomorrow," Sky said. "Do you know how scary it was when only ten of his men were attacking us? Now we have a hundred and fifty of them coming at us and one of them has a rocket launcher."

"With only one rocket," Kellogg said. "His men are a bunch of buffoons. They'll probably blow themselves up with it."

"We certainly can't count on that," Sky said.

Then Sky did something that Kellogg never expected. She leaned in and kissed him on the cheek. Kellogg placed a hand over his cheek, and blushed. "What was that for?"

Sky smiled. "I suppose if we could die, we shouldn't have any regrets."

"I'm happy to know one of your life's regrets would have been not kissing me on the cheek."

Sky was taken aback, feigning insult. "It wouldn't have been *my* regret. I just assumed it would have been yours."

"Oh," Kellogg said as the pair made their ascent to the third floor.

Big Will took to the couch on the first floor with Gigi in his lap. He stroked her fur as he lay with his head back and his eyes closed.

"Well, girl, you can't come in the tunnel with me tomorrow," he said to her. "I'll miss you during the fight, but I don't want your barking to give me away down there."

Gigi responded with typical dog noises, and he wondered if she sensed danger. He had heard that dogs could.

A few steps away, Sim and Ace were shaking hands.

"If anything happens to me," Sim said. "You know what to do. Keep everyone together and...survive. I'm proud of all of you and I think what you all can envision for the future of this place would far surpass anything and everything I've done."

"I don't know about that, Sim," Ace said. "But we would try. I want you to know how much I appreciate all you've done for us. This place shines for the world to see. And that is what Zagan hates the most."

Sim nodded and the two embraced.

Upstairs, JZ painted Misty's nails. She colored them red with black polka dots to resemble the lady bugs they always found on their windowsills in the spring. As they were drying, Misty told yet another tale.

"This reminds me of those days when my mother would take me to get a manicure. There was this one time when the lady next to us was getting a pedicure, and while the technician was clipping the lady's toenails, a piece of her nail flew onto the technician's lip and stuck to her lipstick. She screamed and brushed the nail off and smeared her lipstick across her face while doing so. It was the most hilarious thing I ever saw."

The girls laughed as Teddy, Leo, and Baby entered.

"Perfect timing," JZ said. "Let's all get our nails done the same exact way. A symbol of solidarity."

Misty giggled. "I don't think you'll get the older boys to paint ladybugs on their fingernails. Maybe if you were painting lightning bolts or something."

"Yeah," Leo said. "I want lightning bolts."

"I want my face painted," Teddy said.

JZ sighed as she continued with Misty's nails. "These aren't face paints, but we do have face paints and camouflage paint sticks in the library." She put Misty's nails aside as a new idea crossed her mind. "That would be a cool idea. War paint. We could all do our faces. How scary would that be?"

"Too scary," Baby said.

"This from the girl who just slaughtered a man in our living room," Misty said.

The room grew quiet, and Baby bowed her head, shamefully.

"Don't listen to dem fools, Baby," JZ said, changing the subject. "We could paint your face ghost white. That would look dope. They would get one good look at you and run the other way!"

"Or they would think they were at a circus," Teddy said with a laugh.

"OMG. Never mind, then," JZ huffed as she grabbed Misty's hand to finish her nails.

"I'll still do ladybugs on my fingers," Baby said.

"Fine," JZ said.

The night wore on and some of the orphans did get to sleep, the younger ones mostly, but the older ones stayed vigilant. They weren't sure if Cairo was telling the truth about the dawn attack, but when put together with his mission, it made sense.

Shark was on high alert, lying on his stomach on the topmost rooftop as the sun peaked over the horizon behind him. He anxiously peered through this rifle scope for any signs of Zagan and his men. He knew how important his role was at that moment because the first-floor visibility was next to nothing since they bricked up the windows and doors downstairs. Granted, the second and third floor rooms still offered views, and he was confident that the others had their eyes nestled in their binoculars, but he wasn't going to take any chances. He felt guilty that Cairo was able to sneak up on him without warning and nearly kill him and Big Will. He never saw it coming. Just like he never saw when Flip was taken. Not to mention he was the first line of defense against this so-called Crazy Joe with the RPG. He had to make sure he was in a good position to take him out before he could launch that rocket at the front door.

When the sun cleared the horizon, he saw them, and they were most likely assuming with the signal flare that the rooftop had been cleared, paving the way to their surprise attack.

The surprise is ours, you bastards.

They were weaving in and out of bushes, creeping up between houses, ducking behind cars, and coming down the wooded hill using the trees as coverage.

Shark took a moment to shout through the skylight to Sky and Baby on the third floor. "Here they come!"

The pair took that message to the second floor, who delivered it to the first floor. Shark rocketed back up to the rooftop and though he knew the men were on all sides, he decided to keep his focus on the front of the house, where the threat of the RPG lied. The fortress was separated from a row of houses across the street, which is where many of the advancing marauders seemed to be located.

He waited patiently, as did everyone else on the floors below. He wondered about their initial plan of attack. Clearly, they were expecting the element of surprise, but what would they do to take advantage of that extra time?

The answer came swiftly once the marauders on every side halted their advance all at once. Shark kept a close eye on them as they waited. His heart pounded in his chest. He double-checked to make sure the bag of ammunition was beside him.

What are you up to? In his mind, Shark heard the loud ticking of a clock as the seconds pounded away. The day had come. They were out there. Waiting to bring death to them all.

Thump, thump, thump. Tick tock, tick tock, tick tock. Well, get on with it!

Then, Cairo's truth revealed itself as a single man appeared from between two houses at the edge of the road across from the fortress. He was holding a large device in his hand and Shark knew it was time for him to act, but as the man raised the rocket launcher upon his shoulder in preparation to blow an entry hole into the fortress, something unexpected happened.

After Shark had passed the word to Sky about the advancing marauders, she went to deliver word to Kellogg, who she hadn't seen in quite some time. She called to him frantically and it was Baby who answered.

"What is it, Baby?" Sky asked. "Where the heck is Kellogg? They're about to attack us."

"He told me to give you this after the bad men showed up," she said as she handed Sky an envelope.

Sky snatched it from her. It was weighted with something. She tore into the envelope frantically. "What games is he playing now?" she mumbled.

As she opened the envelope a coin fell out. Sky saw it in slow motion as it made its descent and pinged off the floor. She stared at it there, confused, until she noticed the letter that was also inside the envelope.

Dear Sky,

I want to thank you for the kiss, and more than that, for giving me perpose. I was honered to be part of the fortress, if only as a guest. This short time gave me a perpose I have not had in three years. I now know why I lived after I died. It was for this momint. This coin turned out to be lucky for me, after all. I would like you to have it as you save the new world from the evil that lurks. For now, I shall use the one weapon that I know how to use so I can play my part in this epic batle. Don't forget me and tell Sim thank you. For me. For Flip. For you. For the fortress.

With love,

Kellogg

Sky's heart sank and adrenaline surged. "Noooooo!" She raced to the front window on the second floor and as she saw Kellogg approach the man with the rocket launcher, she bellowed painfully.

Kellogg wrote his letter carefully through the night. He had completed three drafts before settling on the fourth version of his letter. When he was done, he carefully sealed it and his coin in an envelope and woke Baby from her sleep. She rubbed her eyes and positioned herself on her elbows.

"Are the bad people here?" she asked.

"They're coming," he said. He handed Baby the envelope and smiled at her. "Give this to Sky, but only after we know the bad men are here."

"What is it?" she asked.

"A letter," Kellogg said. "But I don't want her to read it too early. It's a surprise."

"Okay," she said. She shook it. "There's something in here."

"Yes," Kellogg acknowledged. "It's for luck."

Kellog smiled at her sweetly and left her bedside.

When he heard Shark's cries at dawn, he snatched up a grenade that was designated for second floor use and proceeded swiftly downstairs to the first floor where he came across JZ, pacing, her face appearing anxious.

"What good am I here?" she asked. "The windows are bricked up, as well as the door, except for this silly little passageway, which I can hardly see a thing through."

Kellogg shrugged. "I suspect that silly little passageway is an easy way to get in if any of those men make it up to the porch."

"There's going to be nothing easy about getting past me," JZ said.

"Exactly," Kellogg retorted with a smile. "Just be patient."

"OMG, you sound like Sim. Anyway, whatcha doing down here?" she asked with a crooked stare. "Aren't you supposed to be with your girlfriend on the third floor?"

Kellogg laughed. "I'm going back. Just fetching an apple." He grabbed an apple from the bowl on the kitchen table.

"There are a hundred fifty men out there ready to attack us and you left your assignment to come get a friggin apple? Hell, no!"

"It's actually for Baby," he replied. "I thought chewing on something would help calm her nerves. Oh, and when I got down here Sim said he wanted to see you."

She huffed. "What in da hell is going on in this place today? Has everyone lost dey minds?"

As she stomped out into the living room, Kellogg sneaked out the side door, slipping stealthily between the brick barrier and the wall. He rounded the house quickly and saw a man across the street, and this was the man he had expected would be there.

Kellogg was not a master strategist, but his only thought as to why Cairo was sent to secure the rooftop was to give Zagan the element of surprise. What surprise? The RPG. Kellogg assumed this would be their first move, and predictably, it was.

Ha ha. A tactical military leader outsmarted by a thirteen-year-old. Bitch.

As the man raised the weapon upon his shoulder Kellogg dashed into the street.

"Hey," Kellogg said, as naturally as if the two were friends in normal times, bumping into each other at the coffee shop.

The man lowered the RPG. "What shit is this?" he asked.

Thereafter, a man emerged from a yard behind one of the houses. "Kellogg!"

Kellogg smiled as he locked eyes with Zagan. He then opened his palm to reveal the grenade, the pin on which had been removed. Crazy Joe's eyes widened, but before he could react a large-scale explosion enveloped the entire area.

Gone was the RPG.

Gone was Crazy Joe.

Gone was Kellogg. But he had died before and knew exactly what it was like. And at the threshold of those gates he was greeted again, embraced by love and warmth.

Twenty-Four

When Sky saw the massive explosion, her days of hiding in the annex with the little ones during a scare were over. She screamed so loudly that some would say the brick walls of the fortress shook. She grabbed a machine gun that lie beside her and open-fired through the window, unleashing a rain of bullets upon the streets below. As she discharged a furious load of multiple rounds, a war cry of fifteen dozen marauders shattered the silence of the morning and instantly, dozens of people were rushing the fortress from all sides, screaming, shooting, and unleashing a terror the inhabitants of the fortress have never known. Among the attacking men were pairs carrying battering rams, rushing for the front and side doors.

From the rooftop, Shark began firing single shots, one after the other, aiming for the men carrying the battering rams, no doubt fruits of the local prison or police stations. If one of them fell to a bullet, another in the pack would come and pick up the fallen end of the heavy tool until many of them made it to the house, where the closeness to the fortress shielded them from gunfire.

Though, it didn't shield them from the cocktails and grenades. From the second and third floors, Baby, Sky, Misty, Leo, and Teddy dispelled anyone who got close enough to the fortress with firebombs, which they let go without mercy from their respective floors. The homemade bombs landed with fiery vengeance upon the marauders who had successfully made it to the edge of the fortress.

Across the street, several of Zagan's men entered neighboring two-story homes to gain access to higher ground inside and on rooftops, a plan Sim had brainstormed to create a hellfire gauntlet, but ultimately decided against for fear of his children being outside of the fortress during the assault.

The rooftops, more so than the second-floor windows of these homes, gave the enemy clear lines into the upper floors of the fortress, but consequently left them with little place to hide, save for behind small ventilation pipes and chimney stacks.

Shark killed several threats with single shots as they advanced upon the rooftops. Misty and Sky, from their respective window assignments, also fired upon them as they took up positions. The girls were forced to take cover away from the windows, which had immediately succumbed, in shattering ferocity, to the hail of bullets from the other side of the street when the marauders returned fire. Otherwise, the brick home served its purpose.

"Baby, left to right with those firebombs!" Sky shouted as bullets whizzed through the house. "But be careful in front of the windows!"

On the first floor, Ace and Sim used the small openings in the bricked-up windows to take pot-shots at advancing enemies.

"This is a waste of time!" Ace shouted in frustration, blinded from what was going on the other side.

"Not if they breach," Sim said. "We're going to need guns on the door if they get through with those battering rams."

As he said this, the house shook as intruders from outside hammered away at the brick barrier. Ace ran to the stairs and shouted up. "We need a firebomb at the front door!"

Misty shouted back down. "They're shooting at us! I'm trying!"

"I'm going to the basement," Sim said. "I have to check on that side-door.

Ace continued from peep hole to peep hole, scurrying from the living room to the dining room and firing through those holes at anything that moved.

Fuck this. He ran to the kitchen where JZ stood at the door listening to the noise of a man outside battering the wooden door behind the brick wall, which boasted an eighteen-inch vertical entry and exit gap.

"Just fire through the damn thing," he said as he pulled open a kitchen drawer. "They're going to get through anyway."

"I'll wait," she said. "No reason to give them any help."

Ace pulled a hammer from the drawer and returned with it to the living room and started hammering out a brick beneath one of the peep holes, noting that he needed not only room to fire, but to see what he was firing at.

In the kitchen, JZ had her AR-47 ready to shoot as the wooden door leading into the kitchen showed signs of breaking. She had a basket of ammunition on the table alongside the apples that Kellogg used as a ruse to leave the building.

Defend us in battle. Be our protection against the wickedness of the devil.

JZ uttered the words to the prayer over and over in her head as the wooden door split in half. Sunlight spilled through the opening and as soon as she saw the face of one of the wicked attackers, she opened fire. The bullets from the gun annihilated what was left of the door and she heard men scream in pain and terror outside.

That's right. Come and get you some.

JZ knew it was on her alone to keep the intruders out.

Before the siege had unfolded, Big Will had taken up position at the end of the tunnel. He stood upon a milk crate and removed the plywood covering halfway so he had the mobility to go above and below ground as needed, but without fully exposing the opening in the ground. Before the men had made their warrior advance, he took a moment of silence as Gigi stood by his side panting, never taking her eyes from the boy.

Big Will shook his head. "I told you not to come down here, girl. You better keep that bark to yourself." She tilted her head and whined. "But seriously, I'm glad you're here. It's always been me and you, hasn't it?" He leaned down and patted Gigi on the head.

Then came the sound of an explosion from out front. Big Will shuddered and popped his head out of the hole and suddenly, a dozen men with weapons were screaming as they cascaded down the hillside like a human waterfall. Big Will pulled his head back down into the hole and readied his weapon.

"Here we go girl," he said. "Ten...nine...eight...seven...six...five...four...three...two...one!"

Big Will took a deep breath as Gigi rose from her haunches and started barking furiously. Like a gopher emerging from hiding, Big Will popped out of the hole and fired his weapon with ruthless precision at anyone in range. The trespassers fell haplessly to the ground. Some of them cold-stopped when they saw others fall, wondering where the bullets were coming from. One of them caught sight of Big Will spraying the surroundings with gunfire from his foxhole, but before he had time to react, Big Will had taken him out.

Big Will rotated his body three hundred and sixty degrees to make sure he was covering his bases. From his vantage point, he saw several intruders plastered to the house seeking a way in. He fired on them and others who were on the hill using the trees for cover. Those men, upon realizing they were being fired upon from the field, answered back. Bullets whizzed over

Big Will's head and a few of them smacked the ground nearby his head with ominous thwaps, kicking dirt into his face.

He came back down and took some breaths while reloading his gun. "I must have gotten ten of them, girl!" He yelled.

Gigi barked as she tried turning around in circles, nerves getting the best of her.

"I guess with all this noise, you can bark all you want," he said.

He smiled at Gigi and as he took that second to connect with her, a grenade plummeted into the hole and hit off the milk crate he was standing on. When he saw it come to rest in the dirt, he screamed.

"Run, Gigi!"

Big Will, gun in hand, jumped out of the hole just before the massive explosion collapsed the tunnel's hole.

"Gigi!" Big Will scurried to his feet as several bullets slapped the dirt around him. One of the bullets grazed his arm and Big Will answered with a thunderous round of ammunition aimed at the woods.

Still suffering the wound to his leg that Cairo had inflicted, he hobbled off as fast as he could to beat it to the tree line. As he was running, another bullet caught his right side and propelled him to the ground. He moaned but recovered quickly and pulled himself the rest of the way into the trees. Once under cover, he pulled up his shirt. The bullet had entered his body slightly above his hip in the front and had not exited.

He leaned his head back against a tree.

Gigi.

From the living room, Sim dashed down the basement steps to check on the side door of the basement that led to the lot. He heard noise on the other side, but the brick wall was intact. It was evident that nobody had gotten through the metal door behind it. He placed his ear against the basement wall and heard muffled cries, screaming, and explosions, but it didn't sound like they were at work on the door. Satisfied, he turned around to leave when he heard an explosion from the other end of the tunnel.

He ran to the tunnel entrance steadfastly. "Will!" he yelled. He ran, hunched over, several feet down the tunnel corridor, staring into the void. "Will!"

Seconds later, Gigi bolted from the darkness of the hole, her fur covered with dust and dirt. When she saw Sim, she barked frantically but came to rest, panting heavily.

Oh no.

Sim wondered about the tunnel exit. If Big Will didn't make it, was the tunnel a potential way in for Zagan and his men? He did not want to rely on the chained doors to keep them out if they made their way through the tunnel to the fortress, so he retrieved a flashlight from the supply closet and sprinted down the dirt corridor, hunched over and making his way as fast as he could to the other end. No light revealed itself as he got closer to the exit.

Gigi barked as they reached the end. Sim's flashlight revealed a grim sight. The hole had been almost completely sealed by a mound of clay, dirt, rocks, and other earthly debris. The only space left was not enough for anyone to fit through without digging. He wondered if Big Will was beneath the debris or somewhere above. The picture told him only one thing: the group, like them, had grenades to use, which he should have known.

He could not linger to consider Big Will's fate as he was needed to get back to keep up with the fortress defenses.

After the explosion that took Kellogg's life, Zagan retreated to a flank position by proceeding up the street, using the houses as cover, and ultimately coming back down through the trees, through which several of his men already had traversed. He carried with him two pistols, holstered to each side, and a knife that was in a sheath attached to his leg.

Kellogg. I should have killed that little shit when I had the chance. So much for the element of surprise.

Zagan was furious that his best chance of breaching the fortress had been thwarted by the same child who previously betrayed him. He felt the boy did not deserve a death so glorious.

And what of Cairo? The flare had gone up, but the fortress clearly knew they were coming, and the roof had not been compromised as he had hoped in order to facilitate a sneak attack. That could only mean that Cairo had been caught and provided Sim with every piece of information he needed to prepare.

He forged his way to the top of the hill and from there, realized a great vantage point. He could see the entire fortress from the roof to the ground. Several of his men had proceeded down the slope, positioning themselves behind trees. Others had vacated the tree line to the side porch in attempts to breach the door leading into the kitchen.

Zagan ventured down the hill where one of his men stood, rifle in hand, taking pot-shots at what appeared to be air.

"What the hell are you shooting at?" Zagan asked the man.

"Some little shit is in a foxhole down there with an automatic," The grizzled man offered.

Zagan peered around a few trees and saw him. "Well, I'll be damned." He turned back to the man with the rifle, noting the scope attached. "You have a scope on that thing? You should be able to easily take him out. Weren't you a hunter back in the day?"

The man peered through the scope to get a view. "Hell no. I just stole this thing from Walmart after the fall. I practiced, but I don't have the steadiest hand."

"For fuck sake," Zagan said. "Get closer to him then, you idiot. There are a half dozen trees further down the hill you could position yourself behind."

Zagan slid further down the steep hill using trees to steady himself toward another man who was firing indiscriminately at all the windows on the second and third floors. Zagan took stock of the belt the man had around his waist. He had several grenades clipped to it. Zagan grabbed one of them.

The man turned quickly. "What the f—" When he realized it was Zagan, he collected himself. "Hey, Z," he offered.

"I think I got one of them on the second floor," he said proudly, raising his rifle to eye level again.

"We can get them all much more easily if we can get inside the fucking house," he said. "You have these grenades, so go join the group on that porch and blow the fuck out of that brick barrier that's keeping them out!"

"Sure thing, boss," he said.

Zagan immediately proceeded in another direction toward the boy in the foxhole, who was taking out several men with machine gun spray. He got as close as he could to the edge of the tree line without exposing himself, removed the pin from the grenade and launched it straight at the hole.

Hole in one. Zagan smiled as the boy sprung from the hole. The explosion tossed dirt and debris into the sky, but the boy picked himself up and headed for the trees. Zagan removed one of his pistols and fired at him as he retreated. The boy collapsed but continued moving. Zagan raised his gun again to fire, but the boy made it to the trees before he could finish the job.

Zagan went left, hoping to find him.

On the second floor, Teddy firebombed the tree side of the house, while Leo fire-bombed the lot side of the house. Misty kept to the front set of windows, going back and forth from the hallway window to the bedroom window, looking for shots. After the initial run at the fortress, most of the men had taken cover or had made it close enough to the fortress where they were out of range of gunfire. The windows had all been shattered, so it was nothing but open air behind the tattered curtains, which blew in and out of the window with the breeze. She could hear the men below battering the front door, as well as sporadic gunfire from every direction as she watched the curtains dance in the wind.

"Teddy, keep an eye on the back window in case they try climbing," she said.

"I'll shoot them dead in the face!" he exclaimed with a wild laugh as he moved to the rear of the second floor. The window was still intact, as it was less exposed, and not as many intruders were concentrated on the back end of the house. He noted that the roof was clear and headed back to his side. As he entered JZ's bedroom, a bullet whizzed through the hollow window and struck him in the right leg at his inner thigh. Teddy fell to the ground gasping.

"Ahhh," he screamed. "It hurts."

He turned himself around on his stomach and dragged himself across the floor toward the front, leaving a trail of blood in his wake. By the time he made it to Misty, he was bleeding out. She screamed for Sky. Seconds later, Sky appeared on the landing, eyes wide. She froze for a few seconds but rushed to his side.

She turned Teddy over on his back and saw the wound to his leg. She called to Leo. "I need a towel!"

Leo came dashing out of Baby's room with a pillowcase. He thrust it at her. Sky pressed it against his wound, and he winced. "It'll be fine, Teddy. Stay calm."

"It hurts," he whined. "So bad."

"I know," she said. "Just stay calm."

"Am I going to die like Flip?" he asked.

Sky put her hand on his forehead. "I will not allow it. We'll create a torniquet to stop the bleeding. You should have been more careful around the window, Teddy."

Teddy grabbed the sheet and pressed it against the hole in his leg while Sky ran back up the stairs to the third floor. "Keep an eye on him, Misty," she cried in her retreat.

As she made it upstairs Baby was standing in front of the upstairs windows.

"Baby!" She cried. "What the hell are you doing?'

Baby, shocked, jumped away from the open space.

"Don't be foolish," Sky said. "Teddy was just shot through one of the windows and if you aren't careful, you'll be next. This is not a game."

"I know," she said frantically. "I'm sorry. Did he die?"

Sky rolled her eyes. "He's fine. Now go do your job and for heaven's sake, stay clear of the windows."

"I'm sorry," she said.

Sky leaned over and grabbed one of the grenades meant for her floor. She pulled the pin and placed her hand out the window and dropped it straight down. Seconds later, there was an explosion, and with it came many screams. She was hoping she had hit her targets at the front door.

She could not allow them to get through.

Twenty-Five

As Charlie, King, Willow, and Wyatt neared the fortress on their journey back from the heights, they heard the explosions and gunfire. They regarded each other and then sprinted off in unison, trying to devise a plan as they approached.

"King and Willow, you take the hill," Charlie said. "Wyatt and I will come up from behind the houses across the street. I guess this is it. I hope we're not too late."

The pairs split off in opposite directions as the gunfire raged. King and Willow veered off road and weaved between a series of houses before arriving at the top of the tree-studded hill that flowed steeply downward to the fortress. From their vantage point, they could see the fortress under siege, as well as several men taking up positions behind trees who fortunately had their attention directed at the fortress instead of behind them.

"We waited all this time for them to come and then aren't even here when shit goes down," Willow said, catching her breath.

"Maybe they waited purposefully until we were gone," King said. "Looks like a shit show. This could work in our favor, though. With Charlie and Wyatt on the other side and us coming down the hill, we have them trapped."

Willow didn't respond. She aimed her M16 downward and opened fire. A hail of bullets cut through branches, slapped at the trees, and some hit their mark, slamming into the unsuspecting attackers who had taken up behind trees to carry out their assault on the fortress. King followed suit with a SIG SG 550 and within a few minutes, at least five of Zagan's men had fallen and several others repositioned themselves and opened fire on Willow and King, who found their own trees to take up position behind.

The pair had Zagan's right flank compromised, except for those who had already made it to the porch and who were vying to get through JZ's defense.

"We are in a perfect position to annihilate everyone on this side," King said, "but we have to get down the hill."

"Just use the trees wisely," Willow said, slapping another ammunition cartridge into her weapon as if it were as natural as brushing her teeth.

"Just make sure our own people don't take us out," King said. "We have to reach them somehow and let them know we're down here."

The two made their way downhill from tree to tree, taking cover from enemy fire, and returning fire where appropriate.

Charlie and Wyatt made their way down the hill, moving from yard to yard behind the homes that lined the street across from the fortress. As they got close enough to the fortress, Charlie stopped them alongside a rotted and dilapidated woodshed. He peered out cautiously to scan the other yards downhill from them. He paused while he took a drink from his flask. At the same time, they heard gunfire on the hill across the street pick up and assumed that Willow and King had started their advance from the top.

"What do you see, Charlie boy?" Wyatt said, his back glued to the shed.

"There's a handful of people taking up in the yards a few houses up. We got a couple of guys on the rooftops. I can't see what's going on in front of the fortress. We need another vantage point."

"Let's just go shoot those sons of bitches," Wyatt said. "They damn well won't see it coming."

"The first few, perhaps," Charlie said. "But after we've given ourselves away, they'll turn on us quick. But at least it will redirect them away from the fortress."

"Let's do it, then," Wyatt said.

"Wait here for a minute," Charlie said. "I just want to see what else is going on over there."

Charlie stuffed his flask back into his pocket and bolted from the shed and headed toward the street through a tight alleyway between two houses just as an explosion rang out. *Grenade.* He wondered if that was good or bad. As he was halfway down the narrow stretch of space, one of Zagan's attackers, a giant of a man, came lumbering around the corner from the front of the house. He was holding a handgun and when he saw Charlie he doubled over and clutched his knees.

"Jesus," he huffed, not understanding that Charlie was on Team Fortress. "We can't get in. There's a hundred and fifty of us and we can't get in that damn house."

"It's a fortress," Charlie said.

The man stood up. "Yeah, right. That's what they say. And for good Goddamn reason. We must have lost fifty men at least so far. It's useless unless we can get the fuck in. Now I know why castles were made of stone."

You never knew that? "Is it worth dying for?" Charlie asked.

The man, at least six-foot-five, rugged, weathered and his eyes wild, suddenly looked confused.

"Why are we even here?" Charlie asked.

"Zagan said—"

"Fuck what Zagan said," Charlie answered. "What do you or any of us get from this?"

Charlie truly wanted to know the man's train of thought, as he could think of no reason why any logical person, part of a one-hundred-and-fifty-man army, would risk his life for what amounted to a single house full of kids. Maybe the answer was in the question. Maybe all logic went out the door after years of loneliness, isolation, and unpredictability.

The man's eyes glazed over. "It's like Zagan said: for the glory and a new beginning for us all."

"And you will consent to have him govern you in this glorious new beginning that starts with the fall of this place?" Charlie said.

The man shook free of his thoughts and eyed Charlie curiously for the first time. "Who are you?"

"He's lying to you," Charlie said, not answering the man's question. "He's lied to all of you to fulfill his own selfish petty glory and your men, so desperate for leadership in a rotted world, fell for it. Instead, fight with *me*, and I will bring you to a place you can call home when it's done."

"What is this?" he said, raising his gun and pointing it at Charlie's head. "You know what he said. He's not a liar." The man gritted his teeth as several blood vessels on his head began to surge, but before he could pull the trigger Charlie swatted the man's meaty hand aside. The gun went off. Charlie took two steps back and raised his assault weapon. He fired multiple shots into the man's chest and the man fell backward onto the ground with a thunderous thud.

At least I tried. He would have loved to be a fly on the wall for Zagan's pep rally speech. A speech so powerful that dozens of men would follow him into a meaningless battle where many of them would die, regardless of the outcome. And with victory, what would they have? What will they have gained?

As he pondered over the large man's bulky carcass, Wyatt called to him from behind. "Heavens to Betsy, what are you doing?"

Charlie had just enough room in the alley to turn to him.

"Sorry," Charlie said. "I ran into one of Zagan's men. I'll be right there."

Charlie stepped over the dead man's body and peered around the corner, down and across the street where he could see the fortress, surrounded by dozens of men, alive and fallen. Some were at the doorway attempting to force their way through it with what looked to be a battering ram. Many others were plastered to the brick like shadows on the wall, perhaps waiting for the breach. He had to assume there were men on all sides trying to get in and it at least it didn't appear as if anyone had. The groups traded gunfire with shots coming from both sides. He peered upward and noticed with a closer eye the men on the rooftops on his side firing into the second and third floor windows. He saw gunfire exchange between the men in the wooded lot and the various floors of the fortress. There were no less than ten men on the side porch looking for a way in through the back. When he had seen enough, he fell back.

"What did you see?" Wyatt asked.

"There are guys all over," Charlie said. "I'll let King and Willow take care of the ones on the west side of the house. We'll focus on the front. It looks like there are some above us on these rooftops, so if we can get up there and take control, Zagan's men will be sitting ducks.

"Sounds like a plan, man," Wyatt said, licking his teeth.

The two pulled out of the alley and headed to the next yard over. As they jumped a rusty fence, they came across some of Zagan's men. They seemed to be everywhere holing up. Some were in the alleyways, others behind the houses waiting for some unknown call to action. It made sense, as there were only so many bullets one could fire at a brick façade without calling it a waste of ammunition, a coveted resource in these days.

Charlie and Wyatt surprised them when they opened fire. The men had no idea they weren't with Zagan until it was too late. As men fell to the ground lifeless, others appeared from the alleyways to see what was going on and they too were felled. Some of the men fired back and took cover as Charlie headed into one of the houses. Wyatt followed behind him, but Charlie halted him.

"You go to the next house over," Charlie said. "That way we'll have two roofs covered. And watch for people inside these houses."

"Over and out, Charlie-boy," Wyatt said.

Charlie then proceeded forward into the house through the back door, which led into the kitchen. He bypassed a dusty, dank table and chair set and headed into the living room, the only light being the sun beaming through the shattered glass windows. He moved with caution, not knowing if any of Zagan's men were inside.

Soon he found a stairway off the living room and proceeded upward to the second floor. He made his way to the front side of the house with his gun at the ready and peered out a front window on the second floor that was covered with three years of muck and grime. He thought about making a stance from there, but it would do little to eliminate the threat of whoever was on the roof. So he turned and proceeded down a hallway past several rooms to the back of the house. At the rear end was a window that he had spotted from the ground that he hoped would be ideal enough to give him access to the roof.

He used the gun strap to secure his weapon around his shoulder and maneuvered the gun so that it was saddled on his back. He then opened the window, which took a lot of effort due to the wooden frame being warped and rotted. He would have kicked it out, but he did not want to draw unnecessary attention to himself. Once he had jimmied it open, he looked out and up. The edge of the rooftop was about three feet above the window. He backed out of the window slowly, securing one foot first on the windowsill, followed by the other, holding onto the window frame to keep from falling. Once both feet were on the windowsill, he rose to a full stand, plastered to the side of the wall like Spiderman. He extended his right arm upward and placed one hand on the edge of the roof. He then reached the left arm up and grabbed the roof with his other hand. With both hands in place, he began pulling himself up, but it was too much. His feet had come off the windowsill and he was hanging limply from both hands, struggling to find his footing. Just as he was about to fall, a man from on top grabbed his hands and helped pull him up as bullets whizzed over his crouched body.

"Pull!" he shouted frantically. "Hurry. They got clear shots at us!"

With the man's help, Charlie was able to pull his right leg over the top and from there roll over onto his back and then onto his stomach. He would have taken more recovery time, but a bullet slapped the rubber surface of the roof only one inch away from his head as he dallied. He jumped to his feet with a start, unstrapped his gun and took it into his hands.

The man who had helped him up had retreated behind a large chimney and had begun to provide cover fire for Charlie. Charlie took advantage of the man's ignorance and peppered his back with a few rounds, which tore through the man's body in a series of exploding thumps. The man toppled over lifeless.

Thanks for the help, my good man. Charlie took up behind the chimney and used his feet to push the man's dead body out of the way. At that point, he glanced over to the other neighboring rooftops. He saw two men on the rooftop to his right and one man on the rooftop to his left. He did not see any sign of Wyatt.

Charlie opened fire first on the two men to his right. His first set of shots collided with the side of the house and part of the chimney. Startled, the men looked over to find out where the shots were coming from. Thankfully, Charlie had readjusted his aim and was able to fire off another set of bursts before they had time to react. Both men collapsed in a heap.

He turned to the other side, as he was preparing to take out the lone wolf on the neighboring roof, Wyatt appeared and saved him the trouble. They gave each other a thumbs up. The rooftops were secure, and it was time to do more damage while hopefully conveying to the fortress that there were now friendlies in control of the rooftops.

The hellfire gauntlet that Sim had envisioned once before had become a reality.

Twenty-Six

Sim returned to the first floor with Gigi behind him. Gigi dashed to the kitchen while Sim paced the first floor.

"Everything okay down there?" he asked.

"The tunnel collapsed," Sim said.

Ace's eyes widened. "Big Will?"

Sim shook his head. "I don't know. I hope he's out there. He's a smart kid. I guess they have some grenades."

Ace pondered Big Will's fate, but the ongoing battering of the front door soon shook him from his trance. He continued hammering away at a couple of the holes to increase the void so he could see better. The easiest shots came when attackers, not realizing or forgetting there were some openings in the brick barriers, happened by at close range. Ace was quick to fire on them. One guy even peered in, eyes wide, and Ace landed a shot between his eyes.

"Why did you knock out more brick?" Sim asked.

"Because I can't see a damn thing," Ace said. "I am literally accomplishing nothing here."

"You're where you are supposed to be," Sim said. "And don't take out any more bricks from the barriers or you'll make us vulnerable."

"How long do you think this brick wall will stand up to those battering rams?" Ace asked.

"A freestanding brick wall...probably not long."

"I'm surprised they haven't tried to blast it down with a grenade," Ace said.

"They probably will once they are through the wooden doors," Sim said. "So, time is running out. We should be ready with the heavy artillery, because as soon as there is any kind of breach, we need to keep the bullets flying and kill anyone who tries to get through."

"I'm ready," he said.

As he said this, Sim's face contorted as he observed a hand with a grenade pop through the double-brick size opening behind Ace.

"Down!"

Sim and Ace dove to the other side of the living room as the grenade explosion tore through the living room, filling the room with smoke and debris. The force of the explosion blew the banner from the wall, and it floated through the air as freely as a feather until it came to rest over Sim and Ace's backs. Gunfire followed the explosion as one of the marauders stuck the muzzle of an automatic machine gun through the opening and fired. Bullets tore through the living room and ricocheted off the walls and tore up the couch, which sent stuffing and small bits of wood into the air.

Sim shimmied his way over to the hole with his pistol as gunfire raged and fired a round off over the top of the barrel of the marauder's gun. The marauder's gun fell limply out of the hole and the gunfire ceased. Ace and Sim choked as the smoke-filled room engulfed the interior of the home.

"Shit," Ace said. "What was I thinking making those holes bigger? There are only two areas with wider openings," he said. "You take one and I'll take the other."

Ace waved the smoke away as he made his way to the west side of the house. Before he could get there, another marauder had seized control of the other larger opening and fired off some rounds through the hole. Several bullets found their mark on Ace, and he fell to the ground in agony.

He couldn't tell where he had been hit.

"Fuck!" he screamed. "They got me!" He felt intense pain and pressure on his left leg and lower torso. The marauder continued to level the inside of the house from the west with gunfire, but abruptly stopped shooting as some unknown chaos erupted from outside.

Sim scurried over to Ace, who was on the floor wailing. Ace was shaking and his lips trembling. Sim was trying to assess where he had been shot but the smoke from the grenade and gunfire made everything hazy. He felt around on the boy and was able to locate two wounds. One on his left thigh and another in his lower right-side stomach, which caused him concern.

"Shit," Sim said as Misty yelled down from the top of the stairs.

"What the hell is going on down there?" she asked. "Are they in?"

"Not yet!" Sim yelled back, pressing on the wound in Ace's stomach. "Just stay on them up there, for Christ's sake!"

"I think Charlie made it," she said. "I think he and Wyatt got to the rooftops across the way."

Sim could not rejoice over her news.

"Okay, Ace," Sim said. "Keep pressure on the stomach. Our people have the rooftops...the attackers in the front are sitting ducks. I have to get a towel or something. Hang in there."

Ace was breathing heavily in and out as he lay on the floor. "Bring me to the stairs."

Sim helped him to his feet and the two hobbled over to the stairwell where Sim propped him on the lower part of the stairs as Ace clutched his wound and screamed in pain.

"This is where Flip died," Ace said, his face sweaty, bloody, and desperate.

"You're not going to die," Sim said, his eyes feral. "Not like this. You made this place with me." Sim shook his head as he grabbed Ace's hand. "I won't let you die."

Ace looked at Sim imploringly. His hair was matted to his face with sweat and his face was pained. "I don't think fate cares what you want, Sim," Ace said. "Can you do me a favor and bring me the banner."

Sim let go of his hand and ran to the living room and snatched up the fallen banner. He returned with it and used it to cover Ace from his chest down. He grabbed Ace's hand again.

"Fight, Ace," Sim said. "Please."

"I did," he smiled through obvious pain. "We all did." He gazed into Sim's eyes and tightened his grip. He lurched forward, wincing. "I love you. I always have. That's why I could never doubt you."

Sim, shocked, could only nod as his words lie trapped in his throat.

"Tell them…I love them all and it was worth it," Ace muttered. "If you were looking for redemption for your wife and child…you've long since found it."

"You *are* my child," Sim cried.

Sim looked down as blood soaked through the banner from Ace's stomach wound and when he looked back up, Ace was dead.

Sim pulled Ace into his body and cried fiercely. He then stood up and roared. His cries filled the house from bottom to top and some might say that even the enemy froze in place, wondering if it wasn't the tortured souls of every man, woman, and child of the apocalypse crying out from the depths.

As Big Will sat against a tree, he fired on every man he saw on the hill and surprised intruders with slow short bursts. He had gotten good at targeting. Sim had taught them all. He tried to ignore the pain that shot through his body from head to toe as he nurtured his wounds. Sim had taught them all meditative strategies to relieve stress and anxiety, but being in the middle of a battle made it hard to meditate. There were men all around, and though most of them did not see *him*, he saw them. As it turned out, his position in the trees was more strategic than being in the hole.

As he popped off more rounds, he heard Gigi barking from a distance. *Gigi?* He pulled his head out of the trees and saw Gigi leap off the side porch into the backyard. The men she passed seemed to ignore her as she bolted across the field. *Come on, Gigi.* Big Will wanted Gigi to know where he was, but he didn't want to risk exposing himself.

Gigi kept her stride across the field, as if she knew by instinct where he was hidden. He pulled himself halfway from the trees so she could see him, and their eyes connected just as a bullet from some unknown place tore through his chest. Big Will collapsed, half in and half out of the trees. Gigi made it to his side as he was spitting out blood. She bit down on his coat and started yanking him back into the trees.

Big Will dropped his gun and hacked up more blood. He lay down in the thickets staring up through the cracks in the trees. The sky was blue. Gigi laid beside him and put her head on his stomach as he stared to the heavens.

"This is how it was when Sim found us," Big Will said. "Eh, Gigi."

Gigi whined as Big Will took in a huge breath. "I see her Gigi. I see Mom."

When he released his breath, Big Will was dead.

Zagan made his way down the hill in clumsy motions, slipping on mud and clay, and traversing thorns and other prickly bushes and brambles. He was looking for the boy who had escaped the hole and who was still killing all his men. He was there somewhere, hiding and shooting.

He stepped over a large log, jumped over a narrow valley carved by water draining into the hill and slowly but surely made his way to the edge of the woods. As he crept his way closer to the boy, a dog dashed across the field from the house, and he knew it was the boy's dog. *And a dog, not a child, shall lead the way.* He waited patiently in the bushes until the dog got closer then fired off some shots at it. He knew putting the dog in danger would reveal the dog's best friend.

No sooner, the boy was there, exposing himself so the dog would know where he was. And that is when Zagan took his shot. A single shot that punched the boy's chest and sent him sprawling to the ground. *Lights out.*

He aimed at the dog as the dog pulled the boy into the trees, but disregarded the shot. As he lowered his gun, shots from behind him cut branches on his right and left. Zagan ducked instinctively and as he turned to fire back, someone tackled him. The pair crashed through bushes and out into the yard. The attacker was on top of him, and Zagan wasted no time trying to see who it was. He smacked his attacker on the side of the head with the butt of his gun and the two rolled over. Zagan had gotten on top and immediately drew his firearm to take a shot, but as he was about to fire, he saw who had attacked him.

It was King.

The boy had his arms crossed over his face as Zagan had the gun pointed to his head. Zagan's hands shook as he realized who it was and he pushed himself up and off the boy, still holding the gun on him. Slowly, Zagan backed away as he and King maintained eye contact.

When Zagan was far enough away, he lowered the gun and sprinted for the fortress.

Twenty-Seven

YES, KING DID END up at the heights, but before he arrived there, he had done exactly what he had set out to do when he left the fortress after the encounter with Zagan and his men at the steelworks building. He scoured the large venues in the city within a mile of the fortress looking for Zagan.

He caught up with Zagan's crew at the prison, the fourth location on his scouting jaunt. He saw Zagan's men out front patrolling and thought how he might reach the man. *Through the front door.* And though King wanted to go in blasting, he knew he would only make it so far and did not want to end up dead before meeting this man who had killed Flip and threatened their way of life.

So he abandoned his weapons behind a nearby residence and entered the compound with his arms above his head. The patrolling guards, astonished, raised their guns at him as they rushed forward.

"You're one of them," one of the men sneered. "We should kill you right now."

"Why?" King said.

The two men exchanged confused glances.

"I want to see Zagan," King said, arms still raised.

"Frisk him," the second in the pair said.

As the first man patted him down, he continued taunting, "What makes you think Zagan will want to see *you*? He'll probably put a bullet in your head the second you walk in."

King laughed. Just seventeen and he laughed in this man's face. The man who held a weapon to his head. The man who could kill him without thought or conscience. "You know what's funny?"

"What?" the man challenged as he backed away.

"I know Zagan better than you do," he said, baring his crooked teeth to the man.

The man responded by placing himself behind King with a huff and pushing him forward with the butt of his rifle. The two of them escorted him inside, through a series of steel doors that had been propped open with water jugs, and into a cafeteria space where they directed him to a circular table.

"Wait here," the quieter of the two said. "And pray he's in a good mood."

King waited. He glanced around. There were a couple of men walking in and out and a few seated at some of the other tables not paying him much attention. There were others pacing the elevated catwalks that were nestled between a set of railings and jail cells on the upper level.

The prison was a smart move. It was already equipped with hundreds of beds, toilets—albeit non-working—a kitchen, and infirmary. It was right on the river's edge. They could have made a deluxe fortress at the prison, and for the first time, he wondered why Sim chose what boiled down to a glorified house to shelter orphans in this new world.

As he sat there, hands folded across the table, Zagan entered with a smile, his arms outstretched as if he were welcoming a family member or an old friend.

"Look at this!" he yelled. His voice echoed through the hall. The men on the catwalks stopped walking and peered down on them, curious. "Look at fucking this! So much for the fucking parley!" Zagan immediately sat down across from King, beaming. "What fucking balls coming in here unarmed. I remember you from the other night at the steelworks. One of Sim's finest."

King stared at him, curious but not impressed. He did not immediately say anything.

"Well, you found us." Zagan broke out into a hysterical fit. He lurched forward over the table and his face stretched to its limits. His eyes bulged from their sockets and then he clapped his hands together. "Are you alone?"

"Yes," King said.

Zagan, regaining control, sat back. "Well then, to whom do we owe this honor..."

"King," he replied.

Zagan gave him a proud fatherly gaze. "A king, at that! A full-fledged fucking king. How bout that." Zagan looked up to the catwalks and screamed. "We have a king in the house!"

One of the men from above issued a cat call and King rolled his eyes.

"Enough of the bullshit," King said.

Zagan's eyes widened. "Whoa. Intense. Are you here to join us, Mr. King? Because I do have an opening and I have to say, the intel you could provide us on the fortress would be...valuable."

"I came here to kill you, actually," King said. "But that can wait."

"I could say the same," Zagan said. "Why not put off today, what can wait till tomorrow?"

"Why do you want the fortress?" King asked, staring intently into Zagan's dead eyes. "Look at this place. Isn't it enough?"

Zagan laughed again, less hysterically than the first time around. His teeth were yellow, his face pocked from bad acne scarring, and his beard was snarled and tangled from weeks, maybe months, of abandonment. "I don't want the fortress no more than I want this shithole. I don't...want...any place. I just don't want anyone to *have* a place." Zagan suddenly became more maniacal looking. His smile eroded, his eyes narrowed and the wrinkles on his forehead tightened. "Why are *you* here?"

"I want to know," King said.

"What do you want to know, dear King?" Zagan asked, exuding patience.

"Who you are," he said. "Sim always used to tell us kids that he knew who we were. Who are *you*?"

Zagan fell back, aghast. "You want to know who *I* am?"

"My father died when I was a boy," King began. "After that, I never met a man like Sim my whole life. My step-father beat me and my mother looked the other way until finally I left for good. When everyone started to die, I thought about going back to check on her, but then I realized..."

"What exactly did you realize, King?" Zagan prodded.

"That I didn't *care* if she was dead or alive," King said, tears welling in his eyes.

"Such a history...and yet you take up with a man that pretends the world is a good place," Zagan said. "You buy into it hook, line, and sinker until you realize it's all a lie. Like Santa Claus. Like the jolly fat man, everyone eventually realizes that all the best parts of life are nothing but fantasy. That trip you'll never take to the beach, the house you'll never buy, the love you'll never have...All the worst parts...that's reality. Sim...he supplies you with fantasy. Me...I'm all reality."

"What happened to you?" King asked.

Zagan laughed. "Wow. I didn't realize I was going to have a therapy session today. You don't charge do you?"

"What happened to you?" King asked.

"Why do you care?" Zagan said impatiently.

"I want to know!" King smashed the table with a closed fist. "You killed Flip and maybe you'll kill us all, so I want to know who you are and why!"

"Fuck you, King," Zagan said with clenched teeth.

King stood up. "No, fuck you!"

Zagan broke into a fit of laughter. "Holy shit, you are intense, young man. Are you sure you belong with Sim? The anger..."

King calmed himself and sat back down. "No, I'm not. I don't know exactly where I belong, but I know it's not with you. A murderer and liar."

"And how many people have you killed for Sim? For the fortress?"

"I told you enough about me, I want to know you."

"What do you want to know, King?" Zagan finally relented, his voice shrinking to a whisper as if he wanted no one else to hear. "That I too was beaten? That my father strangled my mother in front of me when I was eight years old just before he pummeled me nearly to death? That I spent years in foster care and then juvenile detention like half the people in this shit ass city before murdering my father in cold blood...and then found the military to be the only wait out. Which ended up being another violent nightmare. For my whole life, I traded one hell for another, and another, and another, and you want me to see the beauty of life outside of a fantasy?" Zagan was breathing heavily at this point, but still calm. "I've known nothing but death, hate, deceit, and horror...and so that is all I can see." Then he screamed. "That's all I want to see!" Then he calmed. "Everything else...just doesn't feel right."

"I know the temptation to give up," King said. "I just never did."

Zagan nodded. "Well, I did. But there is a difference between you and me, King."

"There are lot of differences," King corrected.

"But this is a big one," Zagan said. "You see, I did love once. My mother. I nearly died trying to save her. I attacked my father while he had his hands around her dying throat and until she drew her last breath. I was just...not strong enough." Then Zagan did shed a tear. The first maybe, in many years. "You...you only wanted to save yourself."

Then King really started to cry. Zagan was right, in some regard, and King knew it. He had lived with it since the day he left. "Maybe that's why I have to die for Sim."

"A penance," Zagan said. "Ahh. And what a penance that is. A man I know taught me that guilt holds us back, so I never ask for redemption...and neither should you, and I would never be forgiven anyway for the things I've done."

"Then I will see you soon," King said.

"Yes, King...yes," Zagan muttered. "And thank you for coming."

King stood to leave, and a man approached Zagan, gun in hand. "Shall I kill him out back?"

Zagan looked up at the man with wild eyes then jumped out of his seat. He took the knife from a sheath on his side and stabbed the man several times in his stomach. The man dropped his gun and shortly after, fell to the floor. Zagan stomped on him repeatedly while screaming wildly. The men from the catwalks looked down upon him, unmoving, as did King who slowly backed away. In short order, Zagan gathered himself and peered at two other guards who had arrived behind King. The men were speechless and waiting for directions.

"Stop staring at me and escort him out without harm!" Zagan screamed. "Now!"

And so, King left the prison under armed escort, and headed toward the heights to figure out what his next move should be.

It would be weeks later when Zagan gathered his men in that very cafeteria while he stood upon the catwalk, exalted, ready to issue a speech to the many men and handful of women who had joined him at the prison in preparation for the invasion upon the fortress. Nearly one hundred and fifty souls packed into the gathering space, silenced by his presence and waiting for his utterance.

"Dear people," he began. "We have worked together to scour the city so that we could find each other in this world. All the while with the understanding that our alliance would forge a new existence for us all. Here, at the prison and settlements all throughout this great city. This...is the beginning."

The crowd looked up at him, silent, awed.

"And though we are not conquerors, we must see the importance of seizing control to make this city safe from all who would threaten our growth!"

Men hooted and hollered, some raising their guns over their heads.

"The crown jewel...the gateway of this city and to our ultimate success is what many call the fortress. A castle-like house that overlooks the entryway to the city and whose inner workings are so complex that it is defended with heavy might and power. Whoever holds control of this location holds the key to the future. Now, we know that many of the defenders of this fortress are what some may call children, but don't you...be...fooled. Though they are young, they have been trained to hate. Trained to fight. Trained to kill. Trained to mock. By a leader who all but dares us to attack. He has exploited younger people of this new world to manipulate us, to make us weak, to make us afraid and take away our privilege to indulge in the fruits of a truly free world." Zagan shook his head. "But we mustn't bite. We must look beyond the sheep's clothing to see the wolves...for the water, dear people, is always deeper than what it reflects." Zagan lifted his arms as if in praise. "And so it is that we will devour this fortress and make it our own! For us and for our friends in the east. And a new life shall be given birth to. One filled with power, glory, and all the wonderful things this new world has to offer. This I promise. Follow me!"

The crowd whooped it up in the prison that afternoon as they prepared their assault on the fortress the next morning.

Twenty-Eight

SHARK HELD HIS POSITION even as many men had gotten too close to the fortress to be fired upon. He was keeping the men on the rooftops across the street at bay, firing on them any time he saw the smallest parts of their bodies emerge from behind the chimney stacks. He had gotten several of them thanks to there being only one place to take cover and had nearly mooted their purpose of being on the roof.

As he scanned the area across the street, he observed a lot of commotion and scrambling amidst the intruders taking cover in between and behind those houses and wondered what it could be. He kept his eye on the scope, occasionally drifting over to fire at attackers that were on the hill shooting from behind trees. The lot side of the house was clear, given there was nowhere to hide, as was the rear of the fortress for the same reason.

He wondered what was going on with the floors beneath him. He wondered how safe everyone was. It pained him to be so isolated while his brothers and sisters were in potential danger, and he could only hope that they were successfully fending off the attackers. He could hear those men battering the house, explosions that could be in their favor or against them.

One such explosion came from the rear of the house earlier on and he had observed its source was a grenade that took out the tunnel's entrance where Big Will had been stationed. He saw the boy stumble to the forest and even assisted as men tried to fire on him. He had lost track of him once he reached the trees but was thankful he had not been harmed in the blast.

Stay safe, Will.

He had heard another explosion that rocked the house. *Was that from inside?* He dared not leave his post. He knew if anything serious had happened that Sky would yell up to him.

He kept his eyes on the houses. Every now and again, someone would pop his head out from behind a chimney and fire at the fortress, probably aiming through the second and third floor windows. Shark would fire back sharply, but the targets proved too small.

He had new chance when one of the men directly across from them scurried to the edge of the roof to help another soldier on top. He fired twice but missed, as sweat poured down from his forehead into his eyes. He wiped the sweat from his brow and when he retrained himself, he took another shot at the second man who had made it on top and was lying on his back. His shot just missed the man who, in turn, scurried to his feet, frantically heading toward cover. As he ran, Shark saw more clearly who it was. *Charlie.*

Shark watched as Charlie fired upon the man who had helped him up and as he continued to fire at the other of Zagan's men who had taken up positions on the roofs. *Get em, Charlie.* No sooner did Wyatt appear on one of the other roofs and Shark smiled as he knew what doom this would spell for the men who had made it to their front door. Though he realized as the two concealed themselves behind the chimneys that they would have no idea they had been identified as friendlies. They needed to know.

He jumped to his feet and slid down over the shingles from the uppermost platform of the roof to the lower platform which led to the skylight. He yelled through it.

"Sky!" he screamed. "Sky!"

His voice carried down the stairs and it was but two minutes later when Baby appeared on the attic steps. She stared at him wide-eyed.

"Tell Sky and the others that it's Charlie and Wyatt on those roofs across the way and not to fire at them!"

Baby looked dazed and confused.

"Our people are on the roofs across the street," he clarified. "Don't shoot them!"

Baby nodded. Then retreated. Shark smiled. It wouldn't be enough. Charlie and Wyatt had to know they were safe. So, he climbed back up to the uppermost platform and stood tall. For that moment, he was the king of the mountain.

He remembered during those other days, when he was much younger, that he would play this game with his friends. One of them would sit at the top of the grassy green hill that was near his house and everyone else would climb it and attempt to overthrow him to become the new king.

He stood tall, his sniper lying on the rooftop in front of him and cupped his hands around his mouth. He then yelled.

"Charlie!"

He lowered his hands and Charlie appeared from behind the chimney. First his head. Then his body. He then stood up and waved. Shark smiled and waved back as a hail of gunfire from the woods rained down upon him. Several bullets tore into his body, and he fell backward. His body rolled down the shingled slope and came to rest on the lower platform beside the skylight.

Shark coughed as he gazed into the blue cloud-streaked sky. He remembered his father's last words to him.

You'll fight to survive. You'll live or die, but to be alive even in an uncertain world is a gift. A privilege now. Honor your life.

Shark felt he had done just that. He had been a fortress, for the fortress, and it was indeed an honor. As he drew his last breaths, he felt warm. At peace.

When Charlie saw Shark fall, he screamed, which alerted the men waiting in front of the fortress for entry, so Charlie wasted no time. He grabbed his weapon and ran to the front edge of roof and fired wildly down upon those men with precision accuracy. When Wyatt saw Charlie leave his cover, he joined him from his own roof and the two rattled off their cartridges with unforgiving intent. Though the attackers tried to scramble, they had not enough time to take cover. Twenty-five of Zagan's men must have fallen before they started to take fire from the woods, forcing them to take cover. But they had cleared the front of the house and could assure from behind the chimney that nobody else got close.

After King had been let free by Zagan he scrambled to his feet, shocked, but thankful. That's when he saw from a short distance Big Will and Gigi lying in the brush. He ran to the boy. "Will!"

Gigi did not even take her head off his chest and King stood above them both. As he saw Big Will's body bloodied and his eyes closed, he knew his friend was dead. He fell to his knees and buried his face in his hands. He sobbed and his hands filled with tears quickly. He put them to the ground and crawled to Big Will like an animal.

"What did I do?" he said. "I left you. This is all my fault."

King curled up beside Big Will, using his hands as a pillow and crying profusely. "You're safe now, buddy. You're so safe."

JZ fired round after round through the open space leading outside once the wooden door had been splintered. They attempted to fire back, but had little chance to aim before JZ fired at them.

"Come on shitheads!" she yelled. "Try to get in here."

Though she feigned confidence, she was terrified. How long would it take for them to push through? And if they got through, then what?

As she trained her eye on the door, Gigi came dashing through the kitchen from wherever she had been, and without hesitation, exited the kitchen through the opening in the door.

"Gigi!" she called, but Gigi did not respond. She simply disappeared into the outside mayhem.

It gave her pause. *Big Will.* If Gigi was that frantic, it had to have something to do with Big Will. As she pondered and continued fire through the opening, a large explosion from the living room shook the walls.

"What the hell!" she screamed as she turned to the living room. "Ace! What is going on?"

She would have gone to explore, but she was trapped in her place. If she left for even thirty seconds, five men would make their way through. She couldn't imagine how many of them were out there just waiting to get in.

She thought of her ammunition supply and though she had a few more cartridges left, what would happen if they ran out? She felt the axe in her waistline and knew how good she was at executing death with it, but fending off several attackers with an axe alone would prove unsuccessful.

She grew anxious wondering what had happened in the living room, concerned about Sim and Ace, but felt helpless to do anything about it. She heard more shots ring out in the living room as the siege raged on.

"Come on!" she yelled. "What's happening?"

As she took time to reload her gun, one of the attackers outside pressed in. Half his body was through as she slammed the cartridge into the gun. "Fuck you!" She fired off several shots and the man's body shook and rattled as he screamed. He collapsed onto his knees and remained there, pinned between the brick barrier and the wall until a man behind him kicked him through. His body fell limply onto the kitchen floor.

"That's the only way you're getting in assholes! Dead." She yelled.

Just then a grenade soared in through the space and bounced off the dead man's body and fell to the ground. JZ's eyes widened, and she thought surely her time had come. But like a fierce wind, Sim ran into the kitchen, scooped it up in one motion, and tossed it back outside with a ferocious animalistic roar. A second later, an explosion rocked the porch outside and heavy smoke poured in through the crack.

Sim plowed through the smoke and the torn down doorway and disappeared to the outside. JZ had difficulty registering what had happened. She had only heard Sim roar like that on an occasion or two over the past three years and it was always in his most desperate moments. *Ace.*

JZ panicked, thinking that Ace could be in the living room hurt or dead, and she could no longer stand the horrific uncertainty. She sprinted from the kitchen doorway to the living room and looked around until she caught site of her first crush lying against the stairwell, covered with the fortress banner. His eyes were half slits and his body ghastly white. Her jaw dropped and she covered it with one hand to keep from vomiting. She wanted to scream, but she had no voice and no time, for she heard more men coming in.

Fury took hold of her as it had Sim and she tossed down her weapon and pulled out her axe. She bolted back to the kitchen to see two men standing there in the light haze of smoke and from a distance she threw her axe. It hit the man square in the head and as the other one tried to recover from this unexpected sight, JZ had already reached the falling dead man, pulled the axe from his forehead and sank it deep into the other man's thigh. He wallowed in pain as she pulled it out and hacked him in the neck with it. The two fell to the ground as more men pushed through.

JZ went to work swinging her axe, hacking away at every body part that was accessible to her. Men screamed, but continued to push, one after the other. JZ worried about being overwhelmed so she shoved the axe back in her waistband and ran back to the stairwell to retrieve her gun. She glanced at Ace again and screamed upstairs.

"They're coming!"

As she said this, several men poured down the corridor from the kitchen and JZ opened fire on them. Bullets ricocheted off the walls, tore through bodies, and as the attackers realized they were being fired upon, they dove to their right and left into the dining and living room areas. JZ knew they would be able to flank her easily. She stepped over Ace's body to climb the stairs but was pulled back by her shirt as one attacker took hold. JZ lost her footing and stumbled backward over Ace's body. As she was on the floor, the man picked her up and hurled her into the brick barrier that protected the front doorway. JZ reached for her axe, but the man stomped on her stomach just as more marauders rounded the two corners and proceeded down the main hall.

Several men gathered around JZ as she clutched her stomach. She managed to turn herself around, however, and as she hacked up spit and mucus, she slid her way over to Ace's body with an outstretched arm. The men jeered at her as she grabbed the banner and started pulling it from Ace's body toward her own.

We are the fortress, and the fortress is us.

JZ heard a click as one of the men pulled back the hammer on his gun. She closed her eyes to embrace her fate.

"Let's finish this," one of the men said.

"Yeah, let's," Misty said from the top of the stairwell as she and Leo opened fire on them. JZ covered her head as gunfire rang out, men screamed, and bodies fell in a heaping pile at JZ's feet.

When Misty lowered her gun, she noticed Ace for the first time. "Oh no," she said.

JZ had no words to comfort her, as she too needed comforting. She could only say, "I hear more coming."

As painful as it was, she picked herself up and managed to hobble over Ace's fallen body. Clutching her stomach, she ambled up the stairs to join the others, no longer interested in defending the back door. It was too late for that. Their next goal would be to retain control of the upper floors.

"Where's Sim?" Misty asked.

"He went out," JZ said, wincing in pain.

"Outside?" Misty asked.

"Yeah," she said. "I think he went mad over Ace."

"Charlie and Wyatt have the rooftops," she said.

JZ nodded and turned to Leo. She patted his head. "Thanks Leo," she said.

Leo adjusted his glasses. "These glasses help me see them better, so I didn't shoot you on accident."

"I appreciate that," she said.

"Teddy's been shot," Misty said. "But I think he'll be okay."

As she said this, more men rounded the stairwell. One had nearly reached JZ and she pulled out her axe and jumped on him. She hacked away at his head as the two spilled down the stairwell and Misty opened fire on the attackers that were behind them.

"Come on, JZ!"

JZ recovered and pushed herself off the man who had come to rest over Ace's body. She scrambled up the stairs as a bullet struck her in the back above her right shoulder blade. She screamed and was propelled onto the second-floor hallway floor.

"Jesus Christ!" she bellowed.

"I got this," Teddy said, appearing from one of the rooms holding a grenade. He dropped the grenade over the banister and oddly enough, a man down below caught it. As he did so, he looked up and he and Teddy locked eyes just before the grenade exploded, hurling Teddy back against the wall.

Misty changed out her cartridge and remained vigilant, intent on keeping anyone from accessing the second floor.

All their thoughts turned to the progress being made outside. If the first floor remained quiet, it could only be a good sign.

Twenty-Nine

After freeing King, Zagan fled toward the fortress. *Enough of this shit. I'm getting in.* He sprinted over the grassy lot, taking long strides and grimacing with the thought of losing. Could it be possible that Sim and his minions could thwart an army that outnumbered them ten to one? The thought made him shudder.

I will not allow that to come to pass. I will win. For the devil I will destroy them, and I will take this place apart in the aftermath brick by brick.

He smiled as he thought of this, and as he did so, his nemesis appeared to him, running fiercely through the random bullets that slapped the earth all around him. He saw Sim see him, and though he did not know how Sim knew where he was, his deadly intent was clear.

As the two closed the distance, both cried out—war cries that would have struck fear into the hearts of normal men. Men without their history of war and violence. Men who cared whether they lived or died.

The two collided on the field under the fire of the sun and because Sim was bigger, the bodily collision went in his favor. Sim ended up on top of Zagan and he wasted no time in this position pummeling Zagan with closed fists full of fury and rage. They had so many encounters over the past week where Zagan had escaped injury and death, as if the devil himself cast a shield of protective evil around him. But not this time. Sim was intent on ending this.

As he hammered away at Zagan's small but hardened body, the man unsheathed his knife and drove it into Sim's side. Sim howled but managed to subdue Zagan's arm before he could stick him again. With his other hand, he punched Zagan in the face. Sim then head-butted the man, after which he shoved his teeth into Zagan's cheek and ripped a chunk of meat from the man's face. Blood squirted as Zagan shrieked and offered his own head butt to Sim who recoiled. Zagan then drove his knee into Sim's groin. Sim's grip loosened on Zagan's free hand and Zagan used it to throw a punch that sent Sim to his back.

Sim rolled over quickly and ambled to his feet, the stab wound in his side gushing blood. Zagan got to his feet as well and backed away, the right side of his face covered in blood from his cheek. The two circled like wild animals as Sim revealed his own knife.

"I was meant to get into that fortress, and so help me, I will," Zagan growled through clenched teeth. "Over your lifeless corpse. And I will pile on top of you every last one of your children in a bloody heap that I will burn to ashes!"

Sim roared and charged at Zagan, his knife wielding forward. Zagan raised his own knife and Sim caught his arm as Zagan thrusted forward. Sim landed his knife into Zagan's side just over his hip, a wound to match his own. As he pulled it out, Zagan jumped on him and the two crashed to the ground, this time with Zagan on top.

Zagan held Sim's weaponized hand at bay while he tried to drive his own knife into Sim's throat. It was only Sim's weakened arm that kept Zagan's knife at bay, and the blade nearly pierced Sim's throat when Willow arrived from behind and hit Zagan on the back of his head with the butt of her gun.

Zagan toppled over and fell to the ground, moaning.

Willow smiled at Sim. "He's lucky I'm out of ammo," she said.

Her pause was her undoing. Zagan jumped up from the ground and plunged the knife into Willow's stomach. Not once, but twice. She moaned as he twisted the knife in her body.

"That's for the heights, you bitch," Zagan said. "I'll be sure to visit again when I'm done here, and this time I won't leave until everyone is dead."

Willow's body slid off his knife and she fell to the ground.

Sim wasted no time in taking advantage of Willow's intervention. He sprang to his feet, driven by pure adrenaline, and stuck Zagan in the back with his knife. Zagan whirled around and slashed Sim across the stomach. Sim's knife remained in Zagan's back, leaving Sim weaponless.

Zagan, weakened, threw his arm around wildly, slashing at the air to keep Sim at bay. Zagan was breathing heavily, and his face was covered in blood. Sim had him right where he wanted, that is until King called to him from the brush.

"Sim!"

Sim looked over Zagan's shoulder and his heart sank.

The brief distraction was all the time Zagan needed though. He lunged forward and plunged his knife into Sim's belly, just above his belly button. Sim's head fell on Zagan's shoulder and Zagan pushed the man away and let gravity take Sim to the ground.

Sim clutched at his stomach as he coughed up blood.

"You can die slowly," Zagan said. "Knowing that everyone else will join you. But I want to thank you, old friend. It's been epic. As I knew it would be."

Zagan turned and gimped away while contorting his right arm to remove the knife Sim had plunged into his back.

Sim came face to face with Willow as she lay there dying on the ground. Both had been seriously wounded, perhaps facing the same fate.

"How will Ace take this?" she asked.

Sim's eyes teared up. "You'll see him soon," he said. "And you'll be together forever."

The last look Willow gave Sim was one of shock as the life drained from her body. As Sim lay there, King came upon him and grabbed his bloodied hand.

"I'm sorry, Sim," King said. "I'm so sorry."

"King," Sim smiled. "People always...need to find themselves. It's only natural. I always knew...you would come home. Where you belong. You are the future. You are...the fortress."

King nodded. He might have cried, but he had given all his tears moments ago to Big Will.

"Now go kill that bastard and return it to us," Sim said.

King regarded Willow's body and performed the sign of the cross. He turned back to Sim. "I'll end this."

"You were always meant to," Sim said as he reached up and caressed King's cheek. "My King."

As carnage littered the grounds throughout the fortress land, the gunfire ceased, and all grew quiet. Zagan stumbled upon the porch. He had passed dozens of corpses that had been shot, stabbed, hacked, and exploded, yet the fortress remained. Zagan squeaked his head into the open space leading into the kitchen. With no opposition in sight, he stepped over the bodies in the kitchen and into the fortress.

Blood spattered the walls. Smoke filled the room.

"So, this is the mighty fortress...and it is no God," Zagan uttered.

Zagan slowly made his way from the kitchen to the threshold of the hallway, which led forward or to the right into the living room, or the left into the dining room. He chose right and stepped into the living room, surprised that nobody was there. *Are they all dead? Did we win?* He saw the days gone by wall with all the hashmarks and chortled.

Then there came a creaking sound from behind him. He turned around and from his left and right there appeared the residents of the fortress. JZ, Misty, Teddy, Leo, Baby, and then Sky. They stared at the bloodied man, and he returned their gaze.

"I just wanted to see what all the hype was about," Zagan said. He smiled awkwardly as the children advanced.

Baby with her knives, JZ with her axe, Sky and the others with hammers, spears, and other blunted objects, descended into madness as they attacked Zagan with the brutality of the most undisciplined kind. Zagan quickly fell and as each delivered repeated blows to his body with their choice weapon, he simply gave in to his fate. The pummeling continued not until Zagan took his last breath, but until King yelled to them from the hall.

"Stop!"

The orphans, covered with blood splatter, turned to King as he stepped forward, creating a path to the mortally wounded enemy. When Zagan saw King, his eyes opened fully from half slits, using his last bit of energy.

King hovered above him as he raised his revolver and pointed it at Zagan's head. "Speaking of mothers," he said, "if I know one thing about mothers, it's that they are less interested in themselves being saved, and more interested in seeing their children saved. But you...did not save yourself as she would have wanted. With Sim and the fortress...I did."

With that, King emptied his revolver into Zagan's head as the others looked on. Shortly thereafter, it was Sky who leaned over his body with JZ's axe and hacked Zagan's head off his shoulders.

Then it was finally over.

As the remaining attackers fled in defeat, Charlie and Wyatt joined the remaining orphans in the back where Sim lay, still alive and beside Willow's deceased body.

They gathered around Sim, and it was Sky who carried Zagan's head and showed it to Sim. He, in turn, nodded. "We did it, children," he said. "*You* did it. And those not here to celebrate will join me in yet a new world. And we will build a fortress there as well and wait for you."

"We will miss you, my friend," Charlie said. "But we will rebuild, and all will know who we are."

"That's good," Sim said. "That's good."

"And what will they say about you?" Sky asked Sim.

"What my mother said about me," Sim uttered. "That I was simple. Sim. Never fussed. Always pleased."

"If I have learned anything about you, Sim," Sky said. "It's that you are anything *but* simple."

"Well...we change," he said. "We must..."

"We love you, Sim," Sky said. "You will always be our savior. Now go see your wife and Sara. They're waiting. Tell them you saved us."

"No," he said, as he drew his last breath. "I'll tell them you saved *me*."

Then he died.

Thirty

SEVEN MONTHS LATER, AFTER much repair of the fortress and the burial of their many friends to the grounds of Usland, a woman approached the grounds of the fortress from the street. She had a child and was begging for entry.

Sky, alerted by Teddy, who had taken up Shark's position on the roof, was ready for her at the front door. She was joined at either side by Yamil and Miracle, who had grown a bit since the war with Zagan. The sun was shining and the air warm.

"Can I help you ma'am?" Sky asked.

The woman pulled the child, plump, with a head full of bright red curls, to her side. "We came from Altamont. We heard about this city. That this was the place to come first. We've been on our own, barely surviving, and need help."

"My name is Sky," Sky said. "This is the fortress. Your first stop. We process individuals here and move them to a settlement not far from here. It's a great place run by a good man."

"Yes," she said. "I've heard."

Taking no chances with visitors, Sky frisked her and the child. Observing no threat, she invited them in. They were in awe of the place, as its beauty and wholesomeness transcended brick and mortar and radiated love and hope. On the wall was a banner full of handprints, perhaps several dozen.

As they stood in the living room waiting for direction, Baby entered with a can of paint and some paintbrushes.

"Do you mind green?" Baby asked.

The woman smiled through yellow teeth. "Green?"

"Yes," Baby said. "Every person that comes here must have their hand painted and put on the banner. To show all the people that have come and whom we have helped."

"Why, yes," the woman smiled. "Green paint will be fine."

Leo then entered, Gigi at his side, and handed the woman a leaflet. "You also have to memorize our city's pledge," he said. Gigi barked.

The woman read the pledge to the girl.

We, the people of the new world, pledge to: do our best, work together, defend our city, live and die for one another, love, lead, remember. We are the fortress, and the fortress is us.

After reading it, the woman smiled.

Misty then entered, beaming. "There is a fireworks celebration tomorrow at the heights," she said. "Perhaps you can join us and see your new place and meet Charlie."

"Why, sure, that would be amazing."

King then entered and stood beside Sky. "You don't think Sim would mind the changes we have made?"

"Sim trusted us," she reassured. "How are the plans coming with the wall?"

"We have a great blueprint and Charlie, Wyatt, and I are going to start looking for materials. It's going to take a long time, but having a wall around this place is a good move. Ace would have approved."

"Then it will be," Sky said just as Misty entered.

"More people?" she said. "They're coming from all over now." She turned to the little girls with the red curly hair. "Do you want me to paint your nails?"

The girl nodded, her chin tucked into her chest. "

"I'll introduce you to JZ," Misty said, taking the girl by the hand. "She's the real artist."

Sky and King regarded the interaction with smiles.

"Sim would be proud of us," Sky said as she felt for Kellogg's coin in her pocket. She latched on to it and rubbed it.

"*I'm* proud of us," King said.

Sky nodded. "Let's have a gathering tonight while we have visitors and before the fireworks. We will share days gone by stories and remember good times."

"Everyone will love that," King said.

And so they did. They gathered as a family and remembered Sim, Ace, Big Will, Shark, Flip, Willow, and Kellogg. They had found peace and happiness from sorrow and loss. And life went on.

Because that's what life does.

Always.

THE END OF THE FORTRESS, BOOK 1

The fight for survival continues in BOOK 2, REVENANT.

About the Author

T.A. Styles earned his B.S. in Elementary Education and Mathematics and his M.S. in Developmental Reading. He taught in elementary and junior high schools for twelve years before launching his own childcare enterprise, TSL Kids Crew, which he has operated since 2009. He has had a passion for writing stories since he was a teenager, as it was a hobby and skill for which he realized at a young age he had a knack for and loved. He has two grown children and has traveled extensively including to Iceland, Australia, Greece, Italy, South America, and many other places nationally and internationally.

Connect with him at www.tastyles.com.

Made in the USA
Middletown, DE
30 November 2023

44128188R00182